City with Houses

City with Houses

Ernst-Wilhelm Händler

Translated from the German
and with an afterword by Martin Klebes

Northwestern University Press
Evanston, Illinois

Hydra Books
Northwestern University Press
Evanston, Illinois 60208-4210

Originally published in German under the title *Stadt mit Häusern*.
Copyright © 1995 by Frankfurter Verlagsanstalt. English
translation copyright © 2002 by Martin Klebes. Published 2002
by Hydra Books/Northwestern University Press. All rights reserved.

Printed in the United States of America

10 9 8 7 6 5 4 3 2 1

ISBN 0-8101-1818-1 (cloth)
ISBN 0-8101-1912-9 (paper)

Library of Congress Cataloging-in-Publication Data

Händler, Ernst-Wilhelm, 1953–
    [Stadt mit Häusern. English]
    City with houses / Ernst-Wilhelm Händler ; translated from the German
and with an afterword by Martin Klebes.
        p. cm.
    ISBN 0-8101-1818-1 (alk. paper) — ISBN 0-8101-1912-9 (pbk. : alk. paper)
    I. Klebes, Martin. II. Title
    PT2668.A27569 S713 2001
    833'.914—dc21

                                                              2001004687

People always make the mistake of taking too many clothes on a trip and nearly lugging themselves to death, only to end up—if they are somewhat reasonable—always wearing the same things when they get there.

Thomas Bernhard, Beton

Contents

City with Houses

CITY WITH HOUSES

Will they get impertinent or will they grovel? Although it's usually Hunger who handles the clients decently, while Lack treats them as though they were the competition: I can imagine Hunger shouting and Lack whimpering. To me Lack was always friendly as hell, to me he never boasted about being professor or party secretary. If Hunger gets abusive and Lack swears in the name of the Lord that he'll never do it again—then I may perhaps have no choice but to try it with Lack all over again. I act as though I believe him, I give him another chance. If only I didn't loathe him so much. I've always liked Hunger far better. But Lack has the connections. The only decent one is Hunger, the brother. He warned me about his sister-in-law, that bitch, I took it as a compliment. Hunger, the brother, was really against it. He was the director of product development at a combine, a company that got cooling units from them absolutely wanted him to be there for their tests, I tried everything to get him an exit permit, there was just no way in the world it would happen. These days I only accept cases that have to do with real estate. Real estate, that's where the money is. Not in consulting someone on dilapidated buildings. Hunger's bungalow was America. Or rather, what they thought it to be. He had even planned a swimming pool, he didn't dare go through with it because it was common knowledge that he was against it. Everybody would have thought he was a spy. On the outside Hunger's bungalow was quite something. But on the inside. Different tiles on every wall in the bathroom. A different floor covering in every room. Plastic, hardwood, carpet, natural stone. And those drapes. Yellow, brown, orange-colored drapes. Just thinking about it makes me dizzy. I don't recall the furniture at all. Maybe that was the reason for choosing those colors. I won't complain, it was very entertaining at Hunger's place. I had obtained a permanent visa for Karin. Something immensely rare in those days. The others flew to Paris or to Mauritius, we went behind the Iron Curtain to the German Democratic Republic. First we listened to Hunger's stories. About the time when he and a friend went to a restaurant and weren't served, and how they complained in a Bavarian accent. The people there actually bought it. The beer was cold and the salads fresh, the waiters fell over themselves to be helpful. We laughed a lot, I didn't ask him—I'm not always that sensitive—for a sample of his Bavarian accent. I can imagine how it sounds when he speaks Bavarian. I can't imagine for the life of me that anyone would fall for it. Even if he's never heard a Bavarian in his entire life. But then, the whole scene was set among the clueless. After that Karin and I hopped into the chilly beds. The beds were even brighter than the drapes, it had a certain appeal, Karin couldn't complain, neither could I. Hunger was actually an aviation engineer. But there no longer was any aviation industry. If there had still been an aviation industry, the ones who were done building a plane would have taken off with it every time. It would have taken time for the ones left behind to learn how to build planes, but they would have learned it, and once they had, they would have taken off again as soon as the next plane was ready, and so on. Hunger would have given everything to join Interflug, he wasn't even allowed to be near an airfield. There was a friend, he had an old plane in a shed, the friend was a party member but not an expert, they wanted out, Hunger took care of the mechanics, they weren't ready yet, they ended up getting busted instead of getting out, he got a note saying that he couldn't leave the country under any circumstances. To this day they haven't figured out their mechanics. I've never seen anything like what just happened. The gangway is being moved toward the opened exit door of the airplane. The ground crew wants to adjust the gangway, but they can't operate the levers with the big black balls, and the gangway doesn't move. What do the members of the ground crew do. They take a hammer and pound the levers until pieces of plastic go flying. Such cowering, hurt people. As if that weren't enough, I had to listen to a lecture by an older passenger because I'd shoved my way to the exit of the plane. Which was totally unnecessary, they took forever to find a gangway that worked. I let loose at the old guy who had lectured me. He responded by being friendly and asking whether I was married. You bet, a lot of people could tell you a thing or two about that. This surprised him. His father had taught him that only composure leads to strength. I said that my father had taught me different theories. Nothing good comes out of idleness. He said he always considered carefully whether or not to be idle. After all, he was a civil servant. The laughs were on me, while he had a chauffeur who carried his coat and briefcase for him, the chauffeur wore the same cheap ties as his boss and for all appearances could have been his brother. After that I moved on to the car rental counter, for once moving with measured steps. Only to find that there were three fellow passengers in front of me, I had to wait almost twenty minutes and they ended up giving me a car without a phone. Without a phone you are lost here. Quickly I became insolent again, very insolent even, and all of a sudden a car with a phone was available after all. You won't get anywhere without shoving or complaining. When I have company, I don't shove or complain. Except when my wife is that company. My wife enjoys the privilege of experiencing me the way I really am. Which I tell her all the time. The others get to hear that I tell the truth only to them and not to my wife. Every one of them gets her own privileges. I've been standing on the Autobahn for an hour now and have barely moved an inch. The usual road construction and the usual accident. If only I had taken the back road. The phone doesn't work either, all channels are busy. I can't even cancel the viewing. I've got all the time in the world to think about what I'm going to do with Hunger and Lack. I have to do something, I gave my word. When Lack told me that a new lawyer moved in around the corner, he couldn't have known that this was a friend of mine from my university days. Obviously he hasn't been that successful, otherwise he wouldn't have ended up around the corner here. I need someone I can trust. I am a lawyer and a businessman. I have less and less time to play the lawyer. My real estate management company manages more than ten thousand apartments. Only cheap housing projects unfortunately, the old buildings are left to the local real estate management companies so they can get back on their feet. Which brings me back to Lack. I have always loathed him. But he has excellent connections to the Department of Property Claims. He knows which house is being returned to whom and when, and then I either manage it or sell it. Or I buy it myself and sell it for a profit. Management, real estate, trading—one of my companies is always there to strike. In the beginning it was easy, the recycled owners were afraid that a whole lot of houses would be dumped on the market. Everybody wanted to sell quickly, before the big rush set in. But that never happened. There's almost nothing on the market. Ninety-five percent of what's being offered is junk, in disastrous condition, in disastrous locations. You can put your arm into the walls up to your elbow, and in the evening they deal used cars down the street. At the same time it's amazing how much money they want for this junk—I've never seen more greed than I have here. The people would rather have a leg cut off than sell their property below value. Many don't sell even though they're starving, because they're convinced that the prices will keep rising and they'll get even much more for their dump. Incredible, how much effort they invest in haggling over every mark, how impertinent these people become if the purchase price isn't wired immediately, they hurry to their attorney because of three days worth of overdraft interest—exemplary. Where did they get this. They can't have learned it in school. Lack or no Lack, that is the question. What if he doesn't bow. Actually I would prefer it if he got impertinent. And they're stupid, too. It was evident from the start that they would try to slip a few properties by me. Can't be avoided. They have the audacity to intercept my mail—my wife warned me. She thinks Lack is capable of anything. I don't listen to my wife as a matter of principle. Dear Dr. ———, I have inherited three million from my dear aunt and would like to invest it in tax-deductible real estate. I sent that certified letter, Lack, and you wrote back: Dear Madam, on behalf of Dr. ——— I am able to offer you the following properties. Enclosed are descriptions of houses that I've never seen or heard of. You are going to pay for that, Lack. How long has this been going on. What insolence. If they take my mail, they have to reckon with friends contacting me in person. He'll try to tell me that he was writing for me, it was just that he hadn't yet had the chance to tell me. My real estate company doesn't list houses that I've never seen or heard of. Of course, if I kick him out, there will be no more tips from the Department of Property Claims. But to make up for it I've gotten to know the assistant mayor. Not only can that guy pass on tips, he can also give orders. I don't necessarily need Lack. Lack needs me. What is he going to do without my name, without my clients. I know the people who want houses. He doesn't know anybody. He can't sell. I don't know what they think they are going to do without me. They just think that I won't find out about them. Still, I'm not so sure just how particular I can get with the assistant mayor. Hunger was on the list. Hunger was with the company, and Lack was not with the company. It's impossible, Lack must have been with the company, too. Somehow he managed to cover his tracks. To think of how he lives. His mansion in the Waldstraße neighborhood. He would never divulge to whom that mansion actually belonged. Given that he lives there already, he'll see to it that it belongs to him. On the outside, the usual condition, the same on the inside, but very arty. A library and a music room with a grand piano. He always has an art student or a music student as a subletter. Other than that, the rooms, unpainted for twenty years, a bowl under every other sink to catch the dripping water—if the mansion doesn't belong to him yet, imagine what that poor guy has invested in terms of materials and work just to preserve it. Otherwise, he has all the latest equipment: big-screen TV, VCR, camcorder, microwave, BMW, and a riding lawnmower. His wife has loads of diamonds. I really wouldn't have thought that Hunger was with the company. He hung his brother out to dry. Or he helped his brother after they had caught him with the plane. Hard to tell which. So far, I've only caught Lack red-handed and not Hunger, or rather: not his wife, who used to be with the Division of Building Management. Maybe Hunger's wife would have better tips. I keep Hunger and kick Lack out. Then I'll see what happens. Anyway, you can't keep trading forever. Another two years, maybe three, after all, the prices can't go up forever. After that the business will be all about splitting things up. I know why I want to get rid of Lack. Because of that thing with Christine. No, it was Uschi. I hadn't eaten anything all day, and in the evening I had one beer after another. Lack was no longer sober either. Anyway, I started hugging and kissing Uschi, right in front of Lack. I even reached under her skirt. All I can say in my defense is that I had just been to the Canary Islands for a week with my wife and children and hadn't had a chance to talk to Uschi alone. My wife knows me. But one shouldn't do a thing like that, in public. Would be really embarrassing if anyone told her about it. I have to pay for it. I have to discuss literature with Birgit. Never would have thought that I'd end up with a literature student, given that I usually go for students of business or law. Why else would anyone accept a position as a lecturer at a university. I give lectures at a university, too. Her father is a big shot on the insurance board, and she wanted to do him a favor and take a class in the law school. Because he had given her three condos, she decided on tenancy law. A good choice, blessed be thy father. Discussing literature is strenuous, but it's much better than discussing my wife. Birgit is the first one who's not constantly complaining about the fact that I'm married. I'm really in love with Birgit. I've never seen her father, her mother doesn't say anything, and her sister plays Chopin for me. Ever since I met her, I've gotten serious about losing weight. I don't eat anything in the evening anymore, nor do I drink any beer. I've already lost more than fifteen pounds, I feel much better. I was genuinely surprised that a literature student would want anything from me. Even though I'm also a writer. My books even sell. Still, my guides to tenancy and divorce law were hardly the reason why. She probably doesn't like the haggard literature students. She's really got something going on in bed. She never gives me the old line: I'm so in love with you, I want to live with you, I want to have your child, I want to marry you. I'm already married. I can't stand it when you're with your wife. Just forget about it then. She complains so little about my wife it almost makes you suspicious. Maybe she's seeing some sort of haggard literature student on the side, after all. A sign of jealousy. On my part, no less. It seems that nothing is impossible. Last time I had to discuss a text with her: whoever comes to this city does so either for onetime transactions, which means arriving, counting one's money, and taking off again, or else as a voyeur who gets his kicks by walking through streets of deterioration, with their appearances of deterioration and their figures of deterioration and their apocalyptic scenarios and their perspectives of disorientation and their cracked walls and crumbling facades. Desperation and poetry, grand prize. A stipend and publication in *Spiegel*. Maybe that student of hers told her to discuss the text with me. Clever comeback. The prizewinner has never owned a house, let alone sold one. If it were that easy, I wouldn't have to come here every week. To go. Only to have to deal with Lack and Hunger. Who count my money, and it doesn't belong to me. Hunger's wife is behind all of this. That fat bitch. Always clad in black, because it matches the beard on her upper lip—you can't really call that just a shadow—always decked out with big golden necklaces. She knows everything about Lack. And not only about him. I can't prove it, I'm still convinced that she constantly dealt houses behind my back. Maybe Lack became careless because he realized how many. Hunger, the engineer, lived in a comfortable bungalow, Hunger, the IM, in a housing project. There are only two possible ways of confronting power. Either one is always against everything and everyone, or one is mostly in favor and only against it if given the chance. As long as things don't come to a head, the first group does not effect any changes, while the second helps to make life bearable. If anyone brings about changes, it's not those who are against everything, if only because they aren't against everything for very long, they were very quickly by themselves in Bautzen, and if they weren't in Bautzen, they weren't against everything. When things come to a head, it's those who were always against everything and everyone who become really important people all of a sudden. Like Hunger, the brother. He's the manager of a trust company now. Those who were only against it if given the possibility are those who played along. Those who were against everything and everyone couldn't help anyone before the big turnaround. If you were one of those who didn't live to see the big turnaround, if you had to exit early, what good did those do you who were against everything and everyone. Hunger the engineer and Hunger the IM, an excellent fit. It was the perfect division of labor in case there would be an afterward, and there was an afterward. Ever since I've been seeing Birgit, I can see myself becoming a thinker. I keep Lack and kick Hunger out. Because it's already in the papers that Hunger was with the company, I can no longer expect my clients to tolerate him. I'm rid of that disgusting bitch and also of the smell of booze in the office after four. The brother is already out of the picture, and I get to keep Lack and his connections to the Department of Property Claims. Hunger is going to throw a fit, that list was in the paper three months ago and nobody said a thing. It's actually true, nobody said a thing, until last week. When Hunger and his wife realize that I'm serious about kicking them out, they'll start dragging Lack through the mud. They'll tell me everything I've always wanted to know but was afraid to ask. Will I be able to keep Lack after that. It would be easiest if I just kicked the whole clan out. Which I've actually already agreed to. But that was only because of my initial rage over Lack's response to my certified letter. I should talk with Birgit about whom to kick out. Not about the text. A depiction in a literary manner. Of course the houses are deteriorating, and so will be the apartments eventually, but not before the people are finally gone, so that the owners, each of them remaining invisible, can build something new for others on top of the ashes—does it look like I am invisible. When everybody's gone there's no more money to be made. Not for anybody, not even for someone from the Spessart. Money is made with human quantities. If there are fewer and fewer people, everybody keeps getting poorer. That trend is reversed only if you are completely alone in the world. Then you are really rich, much richer than you could ever be with other people around. Only then there's nobody there anymore to show your farmhouse with the conference room to. Then it doesn't make much difference whether you are rich or poor. If human beings have been disposed of, nobody's going to buy Coca-Cola and Levi's and Marlboro. You can't dispose of people, and when everybody's gone, you start all over again. You have to nourish people, no matter how hard it is. I keep going and even commend Hunger and Lack for having screwed me over. The houses have been deteriorating for fifty years, and they've been renovating them for two and a half years. If you get your hands dirty in your own apartment, and if vermin have gotten a foothold in the corners, cracks, and nooks: you just happen to be a filthy pig, my friend. How could it be the owner's fault, no matter who it is, if the tenants never clean up. The Germans and their cleanliness. I see a lot of apartments. Always the same. Wall unit, TV, beer can, and their feet propped up. At ten o' clock in the morning. All that dirt. Black walls, can't tell the carpet from the cleaning rag anymore, everything full of dirt. All the while, feet propped up in front of the TV. In Italy the public squares are run down and the bathrooms in bars and restaurants are filthy, in people's homes, no matter how poor they are, you can eat off the floors. The German thinker, on the contrary, sits in his Space of Substantial Dirt— *Space of Substantial Dirt* in italics, you can almost hear how the prizewinner's brain waves are sweetly resonating while thinking up such a nice word—and holds other people on the outside responsible for the fact that he's got it so filthy inside. The houses are deteriorating, the apartments inside the houses are deteriorating, the people inside the apartments are deteriorating, the streets between the houses—are not deteriorating but are all too narrow and have become too wrecked because of the lines of vehicles moving along them. Whence all that traffic. If everybody's taking off, traffic should only be a onetime affair. At the same time, grass is growing between the cobblestones on the side streets. It's as though you were stepping out of a time machine. Where can you still find this, you look around, and all you see is old houses. The streets may be bumpy and full of potholes, but something has to be done about the old houses, some of them just have to be demolished, but at least there are no houses being renovated to death with aluminum windows. The communists deserve an award for architectural preservation. Of course, large segments of downtown are completely ruined. Because the communists didn't have any money, they left everything standing that didn't collapse all by itself. Here you can get a sense of how much they demolished in the West after the war. Even Stalinist architecture has a certain appeal, at least everything matches. Unfortunately, they used materials of such lousy quality. If you left people sitting in their houses of mourning and their deteriorating apartments and were to wait until they keeled over and lay flat on the floor boards, then everything would indeed deteriorate in the meantime. Nobody waits around here, unless he's one hundred percent certain that waiting will pay off in a big way. This is boomtown. There's construction going on at every Autobahn exit. Shopping malls, industrial parks, logistics centers, and so on. Many people from the Spessart will lose their money, as a punishment for showing up only once where the action is. This isn't my line of work. I'm not the one to go to for bonds and residential developments out in the country. If it weren't for idealists like me, everything would really deteriorate. If I made a list of all the people I've talked into buying houses here, of all the investors I've brought here, and then I'm also buying myself. Only the very best properties, of course. After all, where do the architects live who build all these ugly new buildings. In old houses. Where do they have their offices. In old houses. Where do the self-employed pursue their work so as to appear presentable. In old houses. Why then tear down the old houses. The new buildings will be torn down in twenty-five years. The old houses will remain. The new buildings will only be worth the price of the site. The old houses represent a lasting value. Many people haven't gotten the point yet, unfortunately. Or maybe they don't want to get the point, because an inane new building project is much easier to plan and to execute than a halfway decent renovation. You have to give the text for that, at least it doesn't go on about the rent situation. People want to live in a quiet environment, spacious and with the latest amenities, but they don't want to pay anything for it. If the drainpipe gets clogged and the landlord doesn't fix it right away, they demand rent reduction because they can't shower normally. If the landlord does fix the drainpipe right away and is perhaps forced to tear up the pavement in front of the building, they demand rent reduction because of disruptions caused by the construction. If the landlord replaces the drainpipe before it gets clogged, they still demand rent reduction. And they complain about speculators. Nobody wants to face the fact that even the highest rent doesn't yield a return. You invest your money in a house because you hope that one day someone else will be willing to put even more money on the table for that house. Without appreciation in value it just wouldn't work. Without appreciation in value all tax breaks would also be useless. Old tenants move out, not to let the vermin roam freely but to let new people move in, people who will make a contribution toward the preservation of the house by paying the new rent. If it weren't for people like me, the whole city would really fall into a state of putrefaction that even a host of perfume corporations couldn't combat—a perfumery is a shop where perfume is sold. There are chains of perfumeries that are, however, not large enough to be called corporations. Perhaps the prizewinner means the companies that manufacture perfume. Those are called cosmetics corporations. Cosmetics is the doctrine of the feminine cosmos. Karl Kraus. No publicist would get that past anyone these days, *Spiegel* and *Zeit* would give him the boot immediately. Today you can only get an audience by writing about the Space of Substantial Dirt inside the Berlin Avenue apartment in the Berlinerstraße neighborhood, the Berlinerstraße neighborhood must surely be the most dreadful area around here. I have to be careful, I'm getting too polemical. Birgit is not one of those women who first have to get mad at you in order to work themselves up to an especially good performance in bed. If she gets annoyed discussing literature, she may even start talking about my wife, after all. Why is she defending the text. When I say that all of this isn't true, she replies that it doesn't matter if the details are not accurate. Truth is no criterion for good literature. Even if the details are not accurate, the author describes how people feel. People project their inner states outwardly. I mustn't get so polemical. Maybe he should look to another city. The Bronx, for example. There it's really the case that all the rotten smells known to man are leaking from open sewer pipes. They have far fewer lawyers and realtors. No landlord can terminate a lease. The tenant is turned out onto the streets by the people who actually have control over the building. The details don't matter. Our city is nothing but an organism of metastases anyway. Because the communists built so much—I mustn't get polemical. One should only project something outwardly, first of all, if it's valid—given some perspective or other, any perspective but that of one's own cluelessness—and, second of all, if it corresponds to something on the outside. Birgit will say, in that case the details are accurate after all and that's exactly what doesn't matter. Some details have to be accurate. Nothing fits. The words don't fit one another, the text doesn't fit reality, the images don't fit one another. Birgit will say, who gets to decide what counts as fitting. Not me, that's for sure. And not Birgit either. Hopefully, neither do those who awarded the author the prize. Some kind of compensation directed at the wrong party. A literary prize as an equalization of burdens. Who gets to decide what counts as fitting and what doesn't. Actually, it's really simple. Certain things you can remember easily, regardless of whether they are true or not, or important or not. Some things are difficult to remember, and some you can't remember at all. Even if they are really important or really true. All that remains is what fits into memory. Whatever wins out in collective memory. The truth is often so difficult to remember, especially if you can make yourself look considerably better by remembering things a little differently. Why should collective memory be any more reliable. Birgit will say, given your theory, one should look to people with a bad memory to find criteria for good literature. What they can remember, how they remember it, and if you therefore write in such and such a way, then you will remain present in collective memory. I mustn't be polemical, Birgit may. I'm the one who's married. Sometimes I really feel like ending the discussion. À la Stumpfegle. People are talking about some S&M

arrangement which this colleague of mine is supposed to have had with a female client. The retarded brother is supposed to have killed her because of it. I don't like this kind of thing, it's just that sometimes I would appreciate a little peace and quiet. I don't like pornography either. I can take the naked women. But the naked men. I can do without those films in the hotels, I'm my own program director. Afterward she's joking around with that pale literature student about how she cornered me during the discussion. The development program is no waste disposal business. Sounds like Mr. Prizewinner has never been to Saale-Park. No more indecisiveness. No more indirection. The people dart back and forth between the apparel store and the furniture store like water splashing from one stainless steel grill onto another. It doesn't matter what the stores are selling. The important thing is, they are so many, and all are new. The believers are flocking to worship. The new gods are being applied all the way, their laws heeded strictly. If there's something that would have to be disposed of, it's the furniture sold by the furniture store. Before it's set up. This white designer furniture with its triangular glass insets just as soon as the period wall units made from German oak, the old and the new walls of furniture. The furniture store presents a mockery for the decades of oppression. True, Saale-Park does put me on farmer August's grounds. New construction is not my specialty, but I do deal with properties. August is constantly hammered and never listens to me. Only Hunger can tell him that the tunnel passing underneath the Autobahn will not be approved and that the property will not be connected to Saale-Park. The Green Party may be against it, but the assistant mayor has assured me that the underpass will be built. I'll pay him the money straight away, cash on the barrelhead. The others want nothing but a handshake. If you want to develop that property, you are going to need a utilization proposal and project planning, and very quickly. He doesn't have the money. Down the road there will be no more permits for commercial developments, there are too many of them already. He has to sell to me now, even though I can't pay him the amount originally mentioned. Hunger will booze all night with him, and will take him to the notary public in the morning. Young August wants to marry and move into a condo, the wife wants something new to wear, and old August could use a brand of booze less hazardous to his health, they can have all that. But I have to keep Hunger. If I kick Hunger out, the property will be gone. Both of them are becoming impertinent, Hunger and Lack. They are always becoming impertinent when there's something they don't like. Yet they should be turning white with fear. Their own offices, just the two of them, what a joke, what are they going to do without my clients. Birgit will be curious when I tell her about the changes. A discussion about literature, followed by a discussion about ethics. I wouldn't have been part of the resistance movement. Maybe I would have tried to turn the others around. That's what everybody tried to do, according to their own statements. Even if I had been successful in doing it, it wouldn't be in the files. What sort of code name would I have had. IM Wolfi would be unimaginative. To allude to my surname, that of an aircraft engineer—I'm not at all related to that aircraft engineer, but the name aroused Hunger's affection—IM Fork-Sharpener. Well. IM Contract. Certainly there were enough lawyers with the company. IM Don Juan. Not very original. Could it be ironical, perhaps. IM Real Estate. Sounds silly somehow. What would I have done under the circumstances back then. A career like Lack's. A lawyer's job really wasn't very attractive. That's what you get for brooding. If I kick Lack out, I'm kicking myself out. My heart says yes, but my head says no. Birgit will be delighted with me for gaining so much self-knowledge. What would I do if I were in Lack's position. Would I become impertinent, or would I grovel. I would certainly not have been so obvious about my treachery. On the other hand, fifty years on the leash, now left to run free all of a sudden, makes it difficult to be patient. What if both of them grovel. Both Hunger and Lack assure me by all they hold sacred, it was a misunderstanding, it'll never happen again. They'll keep slipping houses by me like they did before. Just more carefully. They don't have a choice. I do have a choice. If only I really did have a choice. I remember exactly the first time I was here with Karin. There were so many middle-aged men in unobtrusive clothes running around in the corridor outside our room without company or baggage, they couldn't be guests of the hotel. We imagined that on our floor next to every room occupied by guests there was a company room, next to it another room with guests, and so on. Because we had to cover up our secret mission, we carried on emphatically uncommitted conversations. We were so delighted by the nice toothbrushes laid out for us in the bathroom. I remember waking up in the morning and hearing this noise humming quietly which seemed to be coming from all directions at once and which we couldn't account for. Finally Karin opened a window. Outside, there was no fresh air but a sickly sweet smell—now we knew where the noise was coming from. An endless line of Trabbis making its way to work from one end of the horizon to the other. Infinitely many vehicles, each of them much too small, much too quiet, much too far down for us to make out exactly from above, but massed together, this humming and that sickly sweet smell. I know, the whole affair ended up being much ado about nothing, absolutely nothing. I entered the country with the belief that there would be a different attitude to the things in life here. While profiteers like us are only chasing superficial values, people here would have the desire and the time to devote themselves to more important things. What did they do. They built American bungalows for themselves, if they could, and they spent forever getting ahold of their bathroom tiles. They did exactly what we did, only under aggravated circumstances, and the objects they were after were bad copies of the ones we strove for. I do have a choice. I am for the houses. With people you can do whatever you want, nothing ever turns out the way you want it to. Houses you can renovate any way you want. That doesn't mean, house without inhabitants.

TRANSLATOR'S NOTES

page 4
Interflug
The state-owned airline of the German Democratic Republic.

page 6
Department of Property Claims
Agency of the Federal Republic of Germany in charge of negotiating the claims of owners whose property, most often real estate, was expropriated by the NSDAP (1933–45), the Soviets (1945–49), or the GDR government (1949–89).

page 7
company
Common nickname for the Ministerium für Staatssicherheit (MfS), the secret service of the GDR.

page 8
Division of Building Management
GDR government agency, in charge of managing the state-owned housing units in a given municipality.

page 10
IM
Short for Inoffizieller Mitarbeiter, an unofficial, sideline informer of the Ministerium für Staatssicherheit. The MfS employed an estimated 170,000 IMs to spy on East German citizens as well as on West Germans and foreigners.

page 10
Bautzen
Bautzen II was East Germany's most infamous prison, under organizational

management by the MfS. Despite denials by the GDR government, many political prisoners were locked up here.

page 18
Trabbis

Nickname for the Trabant 601, a subcompact car with a plastic body and an engine running on a mixture of gas and oil, produced in the GDR with few modifications from 1964 to 1990.

MORGENTHAU

I don't want to go back.

The boy and the girl had reached an iron garden gate of medium height. He held her by her right arm, which he had twisted behind her back.

You are so mean.

The girl had put up a fight the entire way, she had scratched, beaten, bitten. The boy and the girl were breathing heavily. The massive gate had once been painted white but was now completely rusted out, with only a few flakes of paint remaining. They had to climb it to get inside the property. The boy would loosen his grip on the girl, he would lift her up and throw her over the gate, and then quickly jump over himself. He didn't know whether there were any other spots where the wall could be surmounted easily so that she could escape.

I don't want to.

The boy let go of the girl's arm and grasped her by the hip. When he realized that she no longer resisted, he held her a bit more loosely. Facing the gate, she seemed to resign herself to her fate.

But you have it good with her.

There was no reply.

Nobody is dressed like you are.

She wore plaid wool pants, a clean white blouse, and dark-blue ankle-high boots. Her clothes were only a bit ruffled from fighting. She had just washed her slightly curly medium-length brown hair. The boy was walking barefoot and had long hair, his baggy gray pants and faded dark-blue shirt were patched all over.

The boy and girl were about ten years old.

What do you get for bringing me back.

Food.

I'll get you food, too, if you let me go.

I don't believe you.

Once again the boy grasped the girl tighter.

I'll get you something.

I don't believe you. You won't come back.

The girl protested weakly as he pushed her up on the gate so that she had to jump down on the other side. She waited until he had made it over the gate, and then led the way.

I don't want to be dressed like this. I want to be with other children. Not always just with her. I don't want to read. I don't want to do math. Can you read. Can you do math.

It had been a neighborhood of single-family homes. All the houses were burned down and destroyed, the fences torn down. Vegetation was growing evenly over the streets, the foundations, and the ruins. The wall surrounding the property was lined by bushes and trees, bricks were missing in a number of places, but it wasn't damaged in such a way that it would have been easy to surmount anywhere. The walls of the first floor of the house behind the wall were for the most part still standing, the property was the only one in the neighborhood free of scattered debris.

The boy made his way toward the entrance, but the girl led him behind the house. A slender woman of about fifty years was lying in the sun on a faded lounger held up by a wire frame. She was wearing nothing but her gray underwear.

The woman heard the girl and the boy, but nevertheless remained in the sun, motionless and with her eyes closed.

Here I am again. Carlo brought me back. Give him what he has earned for himself.

The woman didn't open her eyes until the girl stepped to the other side of the lounger and her shadow fell on the woman's face.

She asked the boy where he had found the girl, he answered, at the station.

At the station. Don't you know that there are no longer any trains running. The woman straightened up and sat on the edge of the lounger. The boy explained that whoever came into town or left it would go to the station because people were waiting there who were looking for a ride and would pay for it.

The woman gave the boy two cans of food out of a box at the head of the lounger that he immediately stuffed into the pockets of his pants.

How did you want to pay.

The woman laughed, the girl was silent.

Answer my question.

The girl had discovered a second boy who was just about to climb the wall.

Koby, where have you been?

The second boy apparently didn't appreciate the fact that the girl had directed the woman's attention toward him. He would rather have disappeared to the other side of the wall. The girl called for him to come over. The second boy, who was dressed similarly to the first, then jumped down off the wall and slowly walked over to the group.

Koby, why weren't you at the station?

The woman rose from the lounger. The girl defiantly turned to the woman.

He knows someone who would have taken me along. I will go again, next time he will be there, and there will be someone to take me along.

You will not go to the station again.

The woman slapped the girl in the face.

Say that you will not go to the station again.

The woman slapped the girl a second time.

The girl cried.

If you go to the station again, Carlo will bring you back.

She bent down to the box and gave the first boy two more cans of food that he took with hesitation and his head bowed down.

But you will not go to the station again. Say that you will not go to the station again.

The girl cried out but didn't say anything. The woman hit the girl with the handle of an old spade.

The girl cried that she would use the next opportunity to go right to the station. The woman flew more and more into a rage and hit the girl so hard that she fell to the ground. The two boys looked on in embarrassment.

The girl was on her knees, the woman stopped for a moment.

I am teaching you that which all the others will never know, and you thank me by running away!

But I don't want to read and write!

The woman wanted to hit the girl again, but the girl grabbed the handle of the spade. The woman was taken by surprise. Meanwhile the girl was back on her feet. The woman demanded the spade back. The girl didn't heed the order, the woman slapped her once again. Then the girl hit the woman with the handle of the spade. The woman, in turn, tried to wrestle the spade away from the girl but stumbled over the lounger. She hurt her knee in the process. Even though she could barely get up, she went on screaming at the girl. The girl cried. She now held the spade upside down. When the woman continued to scream at her, the girl raised both of her hands and thrust the spade in her neck.

The woman let out a piercing cry and fell on her side.

The second boy ran to the wall, climbed it, and jumped onto the street with a long leap. The woman was lying in the grass with a bleeding wound. She was unconscious, her limbs were twitching. The girl squatted down next to her, now no longer crying.

The first boy remarked that they would have to bandage her, the girl shook her head. The boy said, but she is still alive. The girl said, not much longer. What should they tell the fathers. That they had found her like that when they came. With the spade right next to her. That they hadn't seen anyone.

Koby, where were you. Koby, why weren't you at the station? Koby, you had promised to help me. We had prepared everything. It was a deal, remember. The spankings that I got because things kept on going missing. How mother screamed when I came back without a jacket. Where is the suitcase. Koby, you knew I couldn't take it anymore. Nothing but books. Never anything else. I had to read so that people would later want the books from me. I couldn't take it anymore. I had to read all the time. I was never allowed to do anything else. I know the books. Nobody needs books. Koby, don't you remember how we thought it would be? Koby, why did you leave me hanging. Why weren't you there, Koby. Why was Carlo there. And not you. Why not.

He was sitting in the middle of the last row of the bus. He had fought hard for the only seat where he could stretch his legs out. This way he didn't have to interrupt his sleep on the bus. In the meantime he was twelve or thirteen years old, he wasn't exactly sure, but he believed that it would be a long time yet before his voice would break.

Their fathers hadn't told them the name of the city by the river that they were now approaching. They were on a wide road in good repair, to their right on the hills the charred skeletons—not completely collapsed quite yet—of what had once been high rises, before them the valley with the remains of the low rises, which were hard to make out because they were covered by vegetation, at the foot of the hills toward the river the cathedral, still standing in the midst of streets that had likewise been preserved, on the other side of the river nothing but ruins. He knew the city and its name.

It was a warm evening, and yet, light autumnal fog was already rising from the river. The bus had to stop at a barrier. Their fathers seemed not to have expected an obstacle at this point. They got off the bus with heavy limbs to negotiate with the guards at the barrier.

Koby got up and walked between the seats to the front of the bus. Ahead of them the road passed under two bridges that had completely collapsed by now, the road, even though narrowed by the debris at both points, was nevertheless passable. The exit before the second bridge, likewise passable, led to the house in which Welka had lived with her mother, a few hundred yards down the road. To get to the house you had to enter through a gap in the wall, at a spot where there had probably once been a patio door, and walk through piles of brick, pieces of concrete, and rusted steel girders to a basement stairs made of concrete. The basement was set low and was constantly flooded. Nobody would have guessed that anyone was down there. The place was filled with books. Wet, soaked books stacked on pallets, the water nothing but a pool of pulp. You had to wade to the other end of the room and move one of the pallets to get to a metal door two feet above the ground that was also accessible via concrete stairs. Welka and the mother lived behind this door. Never before or since had he seen such living quarters. One room for Welka, one room for the mother, one large room on both sides of which large ventilation pipes went up that lead into the outer wall of the house, and a bathroom. The walls and the floor were covered with white tiles, the shiny fixtures mounted above gleaming white sinks yielded as much fresh water as desired. Welka and the mother owned cabinets, beds, tables and chairs, and even couches. In the large room and in the room in which Welka's mother slept there were also books. The books were dry and undamaged, they were not stacked on the floor but lined up on shelves.

He had lived under the impression that the bus was driving on forever, that it was getting farther and farther away from the city from which Welka had wanted to escape. He never would have thought that he would return to this city. Would Welka still be there. Or had she long since gone away, as she had always wanted. Wherever they sang, everybody came. If Welka was still there, she would see him, he would see her.

The negotiations between their fathers and the guardians of the barrier were dragging on.

He noticed that the fathers at the barrier were younger than their fathers. A few still had streaks of black or blond hair between their gray streaks, some had clean-shaven faces with only a few wrinkles. They weren't older than the mother had been. The haggling was about the pay for the singing. Their fathers and the fathers at the barrier could not come to an agreement. There were many fields surrounding the city, the closest ones started not far from the house where Welka had lived. Such a powerful city with so many and such big buildings couldn't possibly suffer from a shortage of goods.

When it got dark, he returned to his seat. He didn't wake up until the bus started up. They took a road from which the ruins of the house with the basement were visible by day. They were assigned a large room in the hostel next to the cathedral where they slept on the things they brought. Beforehand they were served soup and bread. Their fathers explained to them that they would sing in the cathedral. The cathedral was much larger than he remembered it.

They weren't allowed to be absent from the group. Nobody saw him when he snuck outside through a window. The cathedral was dark, its huge windows were covered with black cloth. Now and then he went on excursions. His absence had been noticed twice. The fathers had only reprimanded and not punished him. They knew he would come back. The danger, however, was that other fathers would lock him up. He was the soloist. The cathedral didn't seem to be guarded, but in front of the entrance a few torches were burning. He deliberated whether to go to the station or to the river, he decided on the river. The houses along the streets around the cathedral and the hostel, as well as those along the narrow street leading down to the river, were entirely intact. Of all the cities he had seen, none had had as many intact buildings, and so many towers among them. Down by the landing he looked at the brightly lit Bridge of Stone spanning the river and its tributaries with its massive arches. He kept at a distance from the bridge, the bridge was always guarded, everybody who wanted to cross the river had to pay the toll.

It was a balmy night, he sat down at the edge of the pier. When his eyes had adjusted to the darkness, he noticed a bundle of clothes on a step below the edge of the pier, folded neatly and sitting on top of a pair of shoes. It looked as though someone had gone for a swim in the river. The current, however, was so strong that it was impossible to swim without immediately being carried off course, and dangerous whirlpools were swirling around the bridge. He scanned the river and was indeed unable to spot anyone. He got up to take a closer look at the bundle of clothes. When he came closer, he thought he heard a soft splash, as though a body were turning in the water. He stopped in his tracks and stood motionless for a while. Maybe he had been mistaken and it was nothing but the breaking of the waves against the wall. He walked on. From a distance he hadn't been able to make out that the pier wall had caved in where the bundle of clothes lay. A girl was swimming there, protected from the current. When the girl saw him, she seemed to briefly consider whether to swim out into the river. He called out to her not to do it. She should get out of the water. She hesitated at first, but eventually heeded his plea. She was shivering, she had noticed him a while ago and had therefore remained longer in the water than she had intended. Climbing out of the water, she covered her nakedness with her hands. She slipped into her clothes without drying herself off first.

He asked her what her name was but she didn't answer. A torn shirt was clinging to a slender body. He took her shoes so that he would get an answer.

What's your name?

Patrizia.

How old are you?

I'm twelve.

You look older.

But I'm not older.

Are you sure about that.

Yes.

The girl made a move to leave without her shoes on. The boy held the shoes out to her. She took the shoes, sat down on the ground, put the shoes on, and remained sitting in front of him, clutching her knees with her arms.

What's your name?

Koby.

What kind of name is that.

The expression on her face was now more relaxed.

That's what I'm called.

I think it's a funny name.

He sat down beside her.

How old are you?

Twelve or thirteen. I'm not sure.

You're not from around here. I've never seen you.

He didn't tell her that he was from around here. He told her that he came from far away, to sing. The two of them looked out onto the river. He asked her where she lived, but she didn't answer. She asked him what the singing was like. He told her that they were nowhere at home but were always received kindly and treated well. Tomorrow he would be singing in the cathedral. At that moment she said that she was cold because her clothes were so wet, couldn't he move closer and keep her warm. He did so, even though he got wet by doing so.

Are you going to die?

He startled and moved away from her. She did not lean over toward him again.

I don't know.

She continued matter-of-factly: Around here everyone dies at fifteen, at the latest.

Absolutely everyone?

Everyone.

But you people have enough to eat.

She shrugged her shoulders.

What happened to the ones whose voices broke. He had often asked himself that question but had never spoken about it with another boy or with one of the fathers. The boys whose voices were breaking tried to sing along, they acted as though they were singing, but they could never fool the fathers for more than a short time. They were allowed to ride along for a while after that, they were fed, they no longer sang, and all of a sudden they were no longer around. He had never seen a dead boy. He thought that some of them had died, but not all of them. The others, he thought, had turned into fathers.

If everyone dies here, where are the fathers and mothers coming from?

The fathers and mothers are coming from elsewhere.

The girl asked him where he slept. When he mentioned the hostel next to the cathedral, she wanted to visit the cathedral with him to see where he would be singing tomorrow. She should come tomorrow, when he would be singing. She shook her head sadly, she wouldn't be allowed to, she had to work. He asked what kind of work she had to do. Instead of replying she asked him to accompany her to where she lived.

They passed several towers on the ground floors of which fires were burning. Nobody was out on the streets except them. As they were walking side by side, she seemed thin and tall to him. Her arms and legs appeared to be growing continually in the pale light. Surely she was older than twelve.

She led him to a particularly large tower. They went to the back to take a look inside through a vent. Several torches illuminated about a dozen wicker baskets filled with books. He wanted to ask her something, but she covered his mouth with her hand because at that moment another child was coming down the wooden steps inside the tower. She touched Koby by the shoulder and then ran to the entrance, which she reached before the other child stepped out onto the street.

Koby could not catch a glimpse of the entrance area. There was a short exchange of words, then he heard somebody slapping someone. Finally he saw how a boy pulled the girl by the hair and slapped her once again. The boy pushed the girl under the stairs where she had her bed. He himself sat down on the stairs and made sure that the girl wrapped herself in her blankets. Koby hadn't been able to see the boy's face, or to understand what he had said to the girl. He had recognized the boy's voice. It was Carlo's voice.

Would you like a cup of tea.

They had to say yes.

The father took a bow and moved across the straw mats on his knees to prepare the beverage. The boys and their fathers were likewise kneeling. The ancient father unfolded a clean white sheet, cleaned the wooden bowls and spoons with it, put powder into the bowls, and slowly added hot water from a kettle. The father whipped the powder with a delicate whisk made of willow wood until it turned into a creamy mush that Koby could just about drink.

They were in the lobby of city hall and were waiting to be received by the mayor. The boys were excited. They had been told that the mayor wasn't a mother. They had never seen anybody who wasn't a girl and not a mother. She had to have smooth skin, she wouldn't have gray hair, she would be taller and stronger than they were, and she would be moving quickly and without effort. Her voice had to be lower than a child's voice, but it wouldn't be cracked. The boys imagined that the mayor would be very beautiful.

When the mayor, despite the promises of the city fathers, hadn't arrived at city hall after they'd had several cups of tea, the boys got the afternoon off. They visited the market in front of the cathedral, where food from the surrounding region was being offered. On the market there was also a stall where books were being sold out of baskets. Koby asked one of the fathers whether he was allowed to talk to the girl selling the books. The father allowed him to.

The baskets were standing on a large board placed over two wooden stands. The books in the baskets were not damaged but were dirty at the edges. Patrizia was squatting on the ground before them, Koby joined her.

They remained next to one another in silence for a while. The stalls were set up in rows, everything was business as usual, everybody was being a law-abiding citizen. The houses surrounding the cathedral square seemed to be inhabited. In none of the other cities had there been anyplace from which no ruins were visible. Standing on the cathedral square one got the impression that the city continued just like that beyond the houses. That's what it must have looked like once. That's what all the cities must have looked like from all the squares.

Take me along.

Patrizia didn't look at him, even when she talked to him.

I want to go away.

But you people have everything.

I want to go with you.

Do you have to work a lot?

Patrizia didn't answer.

Or do you just have to sit by the books.

She turned to him.

Can you read?

No.

She was disappointed.

He told her that he had seen how she had been beaten the night before. She was always being beaten. She wanted to be clean. Cleaner than necessary. So that she would always be ready. They knew that she wanted to get out. Every time she came back from swimming they were reminded of the fact. Then she would be beaten. Who beat her. He would find out in a minute. He came every hour to check on her. Even though there was nothing to check. She never sold anything, there was no money to be embezzled, nobody stole any books, and she wasn't taking any for herself.

Koby!

Carlo!

It really was him. Koby jumped up.

I never thought that I would see you again.

Carlo was wearing jeans, a clean shirt with blue and white stripes, and shiny, elegant leather shoes. He tried to appear friendly, but he wasn't. He laughed, but his eyes weren't laughing. He shook Koby's hand, the other hand pressed to his hip.

What are you doing here? Are you by yourself?

I sing.

You sing.

Carlo motioned for them to sit down on the ground.

And what have you been doing all this time?

I've been singing.

Both vividly remembered the scene when they had last seen each other.

Patrizia had jumped up when she saw Carlo approaching and had retreated behind the baskets in fear of being reprimanded for having talked to a stranger. Seeing how Carlo had tensed up as he caught sight of Koby and that the two of them seemed to know each other well, she was relieved at first. She felt that there was something which gave Koby power over Carlo. Soon, however, she had a foreboding that Koby's presence was a threat to Carlo, who would have to defend himself, and therefore Koby, too, was in danger. The rash sense of relief gave way to a profound concern.

Koby and Carlo remembered, as though it had been yesterday, how Welka took a swing and thrust the spade in the mother's neck.

Do you want a cup of tea.

Koby declined, he had already had a cup of tea. He had to have tea with Carlo anyway. Patrizia brought two bowls, two spoons, a tea pot, a small kettle with fire wood, as well as a mat.

Having tea was a ceremony. If they weren't already friends, people would become friends by having tea. Which they didn't have to, since they were friends already.

Patrizia heated up the water, Carlo and Koby knelt down on the mat, and Carlo went through the same motions as the father in the morning. The girl was not allowed to partake in the ceremony.

Back then we never had tea.

A lot was different back then.

Carlo tried hard to sound friendly.

But now we have the new mayor.

Koby asked Carlo to tell him about the mayor.

All that Carlo said was that he would see her. She would be there when he sang.

The cathedral was illuminated by so many candles that it was almost as bright as daylight. Koby was looking for Welka but he couldn't see her anywhere.

Carlo had left soon after the tea ceremony. Koby had stayed on the market with Patrizia until noon. Nobody was buying books. Koby had never been interested in reading and didn't know whether anybody in the other cities they had visited could read or write, and if so, how many could and how many couldn't. Koby asked why nobody was even looking at the books, since some had pictures in them. Patrizia answered that people were afraid. He asked for whom she was selling the books. For the mayor.

The girl began telling him something, she spoke fluently for the first time, he didn't interrupt her with questions, he felt paralyzed. Judging by her description, the mayor had to be Welka. Welka, who had killed the mother with the spade right before his eyes. Among the mothers and fathers of the city, there had only been a few left who could read, they were old and had bad eyesight, they died, and there was nobody around who knew a lot about numbers. She could read quickly, and she knew about numbers. She owned a lot of books where she lived. It sounded as though nobody had taught Welka reading and writing, as though she was self-taught, as though she had always lived by herself. She also knew where there were more books: in the destroyed buildings on the hills. The city's children had retrieved many books from the ruins under her orders. She, Patrizia, had been among them. Welka had put the books in order, and fathers and mothers came to the city from far away, they sat in a reading room and read the books under the supervision of the fathers and mothers of the city. They were not allowed to take the books with them. The fathers and mothers of the city had elected Welka mayor because she knew the contents of the books. She, Patrizia, sold the books Welka had said were not so important. In return, she lived in the home of the mayor who lived together with Carlo.

Koby asked whether Welka taught other children reading and writing. That wasn't necessary. The children would all die at fifteen at the latest anyway. She taught reading to select fathers and mothers, but they were only able to do it very hesitantly. Nowhere nearly as good as Welka, who read a dozen books in an hour. Welka said that she was the only one who wouldn't die. It was written in the books. The fathers and the mothers believed her. If she, Patrizia, wanted to be mayor, she too would say that she wouldn't die, even if it weren't true. Otherwise the fathers and mothers wouldn't elect her mayor. She didn't believe that it was true. Welka would die just like everybody else. It had been Welka, by the way, who had introduced the tea ceremony. Before that nobody had been drinking tea. Welka had learned from the books how to plant and harvest tea. She claimed that she had always been drinking tea. Koby knew that it wasn't true. Because she had always had so much tea, she wouldn't die. If the fathers and mothers drank tea, they would grow older. If the small children drank tea, perhaps they wouldn't have to die either.

When they had already been singing for a while, the entrance door at the portal opened once more. Even from a distance he recognized her immediately. He had thought about her so often. He hadn't spoken to anyone about the scene he and Carlo had witnessed. Neither to fathers and mothers nor to other children. From all that the fathers had taught him, he knew it hadn't been right for her to kill the mother, even though she had screamed at her the way she had. She went down the center aisle while he was singing, she looked at him, he looked at her. He was singing, but he wasn't thinking about what he was singing, he was no longer thinking about the others surrounding the two of them, he even forgot Carlo, who was walking behind her. She walked toward him between the benches—filled to the brim—of the brightly illuminated cathedral, there were flowers everywhere, and it was as though the cathedral and everything it contained at that moment had been created just for them. She no longer walked with an unwilling stumble, turning her head to the side, she no longer made brusque movements, she walked erect and with measured steps, she wore her blue and green plaid pants, her frilled blouse, and her patent leather shoes with pride. He knew she wasn't acting like this simply because she was walking toward him inside the high cathedral, by the light of the candles, in full view of the whole city. Now he could make out her face better than before. The mother had approached them with the same look in her eyes when he and Welka had wandered back and forth hesitantly along the overgrown road in front of the garden gate, with the same look in her eyes the mother had ordered Carlo to bring her back when she ran away, Carlo had done it, and Koby knew that she ordered Carlo and Carlo did what he was ordered to do. She was the mother now. He also understood the fathers and mothers of the city who had elected her mayor and who believed her when she said that she wouldn't die. You had to believe her when you saw her walking like that, even if you didn't believe her.

It took forever until she had reached the first row in front of the main altar in the large church. He had never thought it possible that Welka's deed would simply remain in the world, that afterward the world could run its course as it had before. He had always believed that something had to happen that would change either the survivors who had been involved, Welka, Carlo, himself, or the world in such a way that they would once again fit into the world. It seemed as though the world would first have to reconcile itself with Welka, and with Carlo and him who hadn't prevented what Welka had done, before they could go on living. Welka no longer wanted to go away because there was no longer anyone who kept her from going away. She was not allowed to enter the city. The other children were not allowed to play with her. She had to go away, this time against her will. Carlo was the only one in the city who knew that Welka had done it. The fathers and mothers of the city didn't know a thing. Welka was all alone with what she had done, she tried to forget, but she couldn't forget. She went to the river, the weather was the same as back then, clear but not too hot, and she kept thinking about it, she stayed at home and kept thinking about it, she went into town but couldn't forget it there either, she would go away because now she actually couldn't bear it any longer, because she had to keep thinking about what she had done, and she would go away even though she no longer wanted to go away at all, but it wouldn't help, she wouldn't forget. Even if there was no penalty for what she had done, falling out with Carlo would have been unwise at the very least, because then everyone would have found out. She couldn't send him away. As long as Carlo was around, she was always being reminded of it all. Carlo was the penalty. Carlo was too compliant to be a penalty. He now did everything for her which he had previously done for the mother. He himself would never try to appropriate the power she had. Just as he had never tried to protest against the mother. He had never teamed up with her against the mother. Carlo was no penalty.

It had been so easy. So natural. It couldn't have been wrong. If she had felt a big relief afterward—but there had been no relief. No remorse either. She hadn't felt sorry. She had expected Carlo to reproach her. Carlo didn't reproach her. She had gone to the city together with him, and they had said that they had found the mother like that, they hadn't touched anything, it had to have been strangers. She believed that Carlo kept thinking about it much more frequently than she did. She didn't ask him. She let him live at her place, she fed him, and he not only did what she told him, he even did it before she told him. When the mother lay dead before her, she knew that she no longer wanted to go away. When the mother lay dead before her, she was proud that she could do something that the others could not: read and write. The fathers and mothers of the city saw that she knew what was recorded in the books, they were astounded by the fact that she knew where still more books could be found and how many there were, they admired how she could answer the questions of those who wanted to know which book treated which subjects, the fathers and mothers of the city saw that she could also give orders, they believed her when she said that she wouldn't die, and everybody followed her orders. She no longer thought about Koby at all. Koby had run away, she no longer wanted to run away, had she ever wanted to run away? Carlo had stayed, just like she had stayed. Why shouldn't she stay, since she could leave anytime. She had achieved everything there was to achieve, nobody could achieve more than her, and still she started thinking once again about how it would be to go away. How it would be if she weren't mayor anymore. That was when she thought about Koby. She read a lot faster since the mother was dead, she read a lot more since the mother was dead, at first she had read scientific books almost exclusively, in response to the travelers' questions, now she read more and more novels. About the time when the city had still been bigger, about other countries and other people. Did the next city look like this one. Or was it altogether different. Did more people live there, or less. Did they have books, too. Could many people there read, or only a few. She didn't want to ask the travelers. She never asked questions because, after all, she knew everything. She had therefore instructed Carlo to ask the kinds of questions which she herself would have liked to ask on those occasions. But it didn't work. It was the only thing Carlo did only reluctantly. He asked the questions in such a way that the travelers never saw a point in answering them at length. She didn't want to reprimand Carlo for it, however. Carlo understood why these questions were so important to her. Carlo knew that he would never go with her if she ended up turning her back on the city. He would be the first one she would leave behind. In spite of all her reading, her imagination faltered when she tried to picture how it would be to go away. Of course the world surrounding her was no longer the same as the one described in the books. She was hurt beyond words, being so helpless with respect to anything other than the books, other than the city she knew. Koby hadn't been able to read. Nevertheless he had known what was waiting for him beyond the city. All she knew was letters and sentences. She had descriptions inside her, Koby had had living images inside himself. If even she was that helpless, then Carlo was—words failed her. Patrizia had had to answer to her about why she had come back so late. She hated the fact that Patrizia was always bathing. Even during the winter. She knew why, she knew all too well. Patrizia wanted to get out, just like she herself had once wanted to, she was waiting for a break, and she was preparing well, better than she herself had done, she hadn't even thought of the possibility that Koby might not be there, Patrizia was going about it in a smarter way, she would find someone to go with her, and maybe now that someone was here. She had immediately thought of Koby when Patrizia told her about the boy she had met. It was unlikely to be Koby, but she imagined that it was Koby. Her first thought was not to let Patrizia out of the house. Maybe Patrizia hadn't even left an impression on him. She could always lock Patrizia in later. Would it be like it had been back then, the feeling of having to go away, the feeling of wanting to go away only with him—then he wasn't there. Carlo brought her back, Koby wasn't there, later on Koby was there after all, as a spectator, then Koby ran away, she had stayed, with Carlo—it was a mixture of longing and anger, longing because she remembered how they had pictured where they would go together, how they would never come back, anger as though it had been yesterday that they had agreed to meet at the station and Koby hadn't come, if he had come, and if they had gone away together as planned, nothing would have happened to the mother, even if what had happened to the mother was all right by her and was right, anyway. She considered blaming Koby for having killed the mother. She didn't want to say anything back then because he was no longer there and nobody would have believed her. He wouldn't be punished. Nobody was being punished any longer. As opposed to back then, in the books he would be punished. That which was written in the books had happened so long ago and so far away. She wondered why there were still so many travelers coming to read the books. It seemed that they, too, had to be aware of how long past and how far out of reach the things were that were written in the books. She would force Koby to stay here. She would keep him like she kept Carlo and Patrizia. She no longer needed Carlo. She would punish Koby. She would send him to the market instead of Patrizia. She would hit him and scream at him when he hadn't sold any books. He deserved it. He had deceived her. He had killed the mother. It was not at all wrong for her to claim that he had killed her. If the boy whom Patrizia had met were Koby. She knew the boy was Koby when Carlo came up the stairs, before he even said a word. Carlo told her about his encounter with him, she then asked him how many books Patrizia had sold, none, why none, hadn't there been any people, there had been plenty of people, why then hadn't she sold any books, but she never sold any books, that wasn't true, last week she had sold a book, she wasn't remembering correctly, she hadn't sold a single book last week, how could he dare claim that she wasn't remembering correctly, she remembered everything, she was thinking of everyone and everything, where would he be without her, it was his fault that Patrizia wasn't selling enough books, maybe it wasn't true at all, maybe she sold plenty of books, maybe he was cheating her. Maybe he and Patrizia knew where there were still more books, he and Patrizia only left the house with her, Welka's, book baskets, they had other book baskets, and they were selling the other books on the market, and he and Patrizia saved the money, and Patrizia who had been so dirty that it was impossible to tell whether she was a boy or a girl was bathing every night and was only waiting to go away with him, Carlo, and to leave her, Welka, behind—he and Patrizia were cheating her for making it possible for him and Patrizia to lead the lives they were leading. She was even more enraged about the fact that Carlo hadn't even contradicted her, even though she knew that none of what she accused him of was true. She had been on the verge of hitting him because he did everything she wanted, because he did everything anybody powerful told him to do. She wouldn't swear at Koby the way she did at Carlo. She wouldn't hit Koby like she hit Carlo sometimes. Koby wouldn't let himself be kept like Carlo and Patrizia. Koby couldn't have been walking around the market all morning without the permission of the fathers. Koby had special privileges. Like her. His looks had changed as little as hers. He sang clearly and powerfully. Patrizia had had the audacity to mingle with the fathers and mothers of the city, she sat directly behind her usual seat, how could Carlo have let that happen. Even though she had intended to acknowledge neither Patrizia's nor Koby's presence, she flashed a devastating glance at Patrizia. Her anger increased even further because in full view of the whole city she had not done what she had intended to do, and once again it was Koby's fault. Everything was Koby's fault.

I will be at the station.
　　Are you really going to be there?
　　I promise.
　　Are you definitely going to be there? Back then—
　　Back then I hadn't promised.
　　But you said you would be there.
　　I just said that.
　　They were having dinner together in the hostel. The singing had earned big ovations. All anger had passed, the tension was gone. Koby was telling Welka about the cities and places where he had been singing, and once again he didn't think about Patrizia, even though he had explicitly intended to ask why Patrizia wasn't allowed to eat with them.
　　Are you serious.
　　I'm always serious.
　　Everybody could overhear what they were saying.
　　Why weren't you there back then.
　　We often agreed to meet at the station. We often said we would run away. Then we ended up not running away.
　　I always wanted to get out.
　　He asked because he was embarrassed, not because he doubted

that she was being serious. At first she was kidding. Or at least she thought that she was kidding. Now she was serious.

I want to get out. Out. Out.

When she had gotten the fathers and mothers of the city to grant the singers a whole week's stay for free, she hadn't known why she had done it. Now she knew why.

Do you want to know a secret.

He knew her secret. She knew that he knew it. She was serious, but in a way that precluded any thought of admitting her guilt.

Why did we have so many books.

Who we.

The mother and I.

Many people had books back then.

Not that many books. Why did we live in the basement.

Others lived in basements, too.

Not in basements like ours. — It was a sham.

The two of them walked through the city, which was illuminated by torches. She wrote a book. Then she had a hundred thousand copies of the book printed. It was a novel.

What is a novel.

A novel is a book that tells a story.

Aren't all books novels.

There are scientific books, too. A novel is about people. They live, they do something, they say something, they die. Or they don't die. Scientific books don't tell stories, they are about the sun and the moon, for example. What the sun and the moon are made of. How the earth is connected to the sun and the moon.

But if they talk about people and about how everything is connected, they, too, have to tell stories.

She had the book printed at her own expense.

What does that mean, at her own expense.

She paid for it herself.

Doesn't everyone who writes books pay for the printing themselves.

The ones who wrote books didn't have any money. Others who had money paid for the printing and then sold the books for a profit. If they could sell them. If not, they lost their money.

Why didn't people buy the books, if they were being printed for them.

The bad books always sold well, the good ones not necessarily.

Why wasn't it the good books that sold well?

Because people didn't understand the good books.

If people didn't understand the good books, why were they being printed.

Sometimes people would understand them later on.

You always know which is a good book, and which is a bad one.

Anyway, the mother had one hundred thousand copies printed.

Was it a good book, or a bad one?

It wasn't a good book.

Then it must have been right to print so many books.

It wasn't the right kind of bad book. You wouldn't understand. She had it printed, and she stored the copies in the garage. Then she had a new water pipe put in, going through the garage to the garden. Which leaked to heavily that all the books were soaked. The insurance company paid for the damages.

What is an insurance company.

These are people who reimburse you for your damages. You always have to pay them. Everybody pays, but only a few have damages that are reimbursed. — She had caused the damage herself. The insurance company didn't realize that. The books were worthless, no one would have bought them. The insurance company didn't realize that either. She built the secure basement with what she got for the books.

Why didn't she build the basement right away without writing the book.

She got a lot more for the books than they had cost. She got what she would have gotten if she had sold the books, but the point is that she would never have sold them, you see.

Welka never spoke with other children and only rarely with fathers and mothers who weren't able to read. She was used to being approached with respect. Maybe those who didn't read books would ask and contradict her just like Koby, but they didn't dare, like Carlo. She had tried to teach Carlo how to read. So that he would be more interesting to talk to. He had learned how to read, the way he did everything she told him to do. She gave him a book, he read it, she checked and saw that he had understood it. But he didn't read anything voluntarily. She had given up trying to force him to read.

Koby didn't understand why the past about which Welka spoke was supposed to be important. Welka wanted to master the world of books so she could be like the mother she grew up with. She tried to share that world with him. He couldn't read, he couldn't take things he saw from that other world for himself, the way he did in the real world, how could he share the other world with her if nothing but exactly those things that Welka selected were ever accessible to him. Welka was the girl who stood at the station with him, and at the same time the mother who prohibited her from going there. How could he overcome the split between himself and the mother in Welka. He had to learn how to read. He had to change his whole life. He had to stay here with her. Or else go away with her. In any case, he would no longer sing. No matter how quickly he progressed, she would always be ahead of him. He would die in two or three years at the latest. Koby didn't understand that it was the symmetry of the fact that Welka was oriented in the world of books just like he was oriented in the real world like no other person which made him more than her equal in her eyes, and which made her forget that he didn't read, which kept her from expecting him ever to read.

Sing something for us.

There were three of them.

Are you deaf. We told you to sing something.

The first boy took a swing to hit him in the face. Koby lifted his fists for cover but his opponent eased off in time. Koby lowered his fists again. At that moment the second boy kicked him to the ground from behind.

Are you deaf.

What do you want from me.

Koby tried to get up but the third boy kicked him to the ground from behind once again. This time he couldn't support himself, his head hit the pavement, and he was unconscious for a moment.

You guys want him to sing, too, right.

The one standing before Koby addressed himself to the two who had kicked him to the ground from behind. They nodded.

You really need to start singing. Or else we'll get impatient.

The leader kicked him in the stomach so that he was writhing in pain. Blood began dripping from the head wound Koby had suffered from the second kick.

Maybe he has to focus first.

The one who had inflicted the head wound kept the other two from kicking him again.

He should get up. You can't sing lying down.

Addressing Koby: It would be better for you to get up.

Koby squatted on his heels, supported himself with his arms and looked around. Those three weren't here by chance. When they had blocked his and Patrizia's way, his first thought had been that Patrizia had tricked him. She had snuck over to him into the hostel, she had walked with him on a dark street along the river to drive him into the arms of those three.

At a distance Patrizia was standing motionless in a doorway.

She didn't respond.

The leader barked at her to get lost, she didn't obey, he stopped bothering with her.

Start singing!

Koby got up.

Sing!

Koby was reeling.

You are here to sing. That's what you're getting room and board for. If you don't want to sing—we don't appreciate people who eat all our food.

The leader hit him in the face with his fist, another kicked him off balance, his head hit the pavement again, and once again he lost consciousness.

When he woke up, he found himself in Patrizia's lap. He could barely speak but immediately asked her again why she had done that. She answered that she'd had to do it. Carlo didn't want him to stay in the city. If she hadn't done it, they would have thrown him into the river on another occasion. She, Patrizia, didn't know whether he could swim. He could swim, but the rapids were extremely dangerous even for a good swimmer. They had promised her that they would only box him a little.

She supported him on the way to the hostel, she all but carried him. Nobody noticed his injury by the dim candlelight. She tore her shirt into strips, carefully parted his hair next to the wound, used the strips of cloth dipped into clean water to clean the wound at the edges, and then tried to stop the bleeding. Afterward she came along to his bed and lay down next to him as a matter of course.

He lay there with his eyes open and looked at her, she lay there with her eyes open and looked at him. He was amazed at himself for being so tranquil now, after having been so angry. Carlo saw that Welka had decided to make him, Koby, into a tool that would render him superfluous. Carlo had enticed Patrizia to betray him so that he would leave the city. As quickly as possible. So that everything would once again be as before. But he couldn't be angry at Carlo. Carlo had demonstrated his weakness so clearly, he felt rather sorry for Carlo. He had to be angry at Welka. Of course Welka would have done everything to spare him this experience. Nevertheless it was Welka who forced Carlo to do what he did. How should he, Koby, leave the city immediately if Welka had agreed with the fathers that they would stay a whole week. He wouldn't leave the city without the others. He could recover in a week, Welka would make a show of how sorry she was about it all, and for a week Carlo would have to put up with her most vicious wrath. Or maybe Carlo wanted to make sure that he would never be coming back. He would never be coming back because they would move on along the river. None of the boys on the bus had ever performed twice in the same place. He alone had returned to a city he knew because this was where he came from. He would die in two or three years and wouldn't be coming back before then. If Carlo was afraid that he would stay for good and would take his place at Welka's side, what made him think that he, Koby, could be prevented from doing so by his, Carlo's, pranks. These weren't the first beatings he'd had to suffer. If he intended to take Carlo's place at Welka's side, wouldn't he actually have to feel encouraged by Carlo's ruse, it was proof that his plan was going to work, would Carlo otherwise have resorted to such means. Did he really want to stay and take Carlo's place at Welka's side. He looked at Patrizia, and Patrizia looked at him. What could make Carlo think that he, Koby, would let himself be intimidated. Maybe Welka had never spoken to Carlo about him, and for Carlo he was only the one who had looked on passively and had eventually run away. Carlo was afraid that Welka would actually go away with him, Koby, as she had suggested to him. Carlo would be left behind on his own, he would be a nobody because he owed everything to Welka, he was nothing without her. Welka had said that she wanted to go away because back then they had always dreamed of going away together. She wanted to tie him, Koby, to her, by any means. Wasn't he, too, mad at somebody. The only person whose thoughts he knew for certain was Patrizia. She was being used and abused, she saw no chance to escape from her humiliating position, she wanted to go away with him even if she had betrayed him, in the end she had protected him, she would go anywhere he went if only away from here, he shouldn't be mad at her, if there was anyone he should be mad at, it was himself because he should have expected an attack and because he hadn't put up a fight against the three of them right away, he would have had a chance if he had hit them first, they would have been surprised, he would have gained time to get away.

Koby, I'm infinitely sorry. Koby, Carlo will pay for this. Koby, Carlo doesn't understand. He is ungrateful. You are not ungrateful. I'm not fooling you, I mean it. Koby, take me with you. Koby, I want to do everything for you. Koby, go away with me and I'll show you a different country. Koby, there are other countries that are completely different. Koby, in the books there are countries that are different altogether. I taught Carlo how to read, he doesn't want the other countries. Koby, the world in the books is still there. Carlo is too ignorant. Carlo is content with what he has here. I knew right away that something wasn't right. He was afraid that somebody would find out, somebody had to find out. Who else would do you harm. Patrizia told me everything. I came to you right away, Koby. Koby, I'm so sorry. Carlo is so ignorant. I know that the world in the books exists. He says it doesn't exist. All that Carlo wants is for things to keep going as before. You are different, Koby. We can go to another country. A country that's described in the books, the country in which the books were made, the country in which books are still being made. Koby, it is an altogether different country. The books aren't being sold out of baskets. The people who make the books work in towers higher than the cathedral. The towers aren't wide at the base and narrow at the top as they are here, they go straight up. They are not irregular and made of stone but smooth, made of steel and concrete. When the weather is bad and the clouds are hanging low, you can't even see the top stories from below. From the top stories you can't see the lower ones, or the street. Inside the towers there are cabins, people step into these, the cabins are then pulled to the top floor with incredible speed. You don't have to go to the top floor, you can choose, you can also just go up halfway. If the boss of all those who make books in one of the towers gets in, then the cabin is always pulled up to the top floor, regardless of where the others want to go, they first have to be pulled up as well, then they are lowered down to where they want to go. The people who make books are very powerful, but because they make books they are also very helpless because they belong to other people. Those other people own factories, they produce things in them, for example the towers and all that's in them, or they own markets. There are halls made of glass, you can look in from all sides, and goods are for sale everywhere, food, clothes, and books, too, not outdoors like here, everything is protected, the books are on shelves, pristine books, never opened, never read, if you open them, the pages still stick together, everything is brightly lit, you can read everywhere you like, the books that sell the most copies are there in stacks, and none of them have been read. The people who make books have to read day and night. They have to decide which books are going to be printed, whether they will be big or small books. The people who write the books are really poor. They can become very rich if their manuscript is turned into a heavy book and if stacks of copies are in the markets and if everyone buys the book. Once a year there's a market only for those people who own markets. Those who actually buy the books are not allowed in there. The people who make books show their new books, and they do everything for the people who own markets to put their books in the markets so that they may be bought. Because if a book is not in the market, it cannot be bought. Those who usually write the books make music, actors are hired to convince those who own markets to take the book, women are everywhere, no children, but no mothers either, and they are dressed particularly well. The people who make books also have to try all year long to have their books placed in the markets. That's why they try to meet the important people of the city. The important people always want to be the first to know everything, and they don't want to read about things but experience them themselves. The unimportant people then do what the important people tell them to do, or they imitate what the important people do because they think that this way they will become important themselves. Koby, I read about a man who was the boss of many people who were making books. He had dark skin, it was only light on the insides of his palms and under his feet, and he always pushed his glasses up into his hair. He often spent all night in bars and at parties, but still he was at his desk on the top floor every morning. When he introduced a new book, he would throw a party in his apartment. There was food and drink, actually the apartment was much too small for so many guests, but if he had rented a room, it would have been like any other party, he had decided to invite everyone as though they were his friends, they could see how he lived, which books were on his shelves, which books were on his desk, what he was working on at home. Those who write books are the most helpless people. They have to wait until their book is made, and they don't have the slightest influence on how it is made. If it isn't made, they have written in vain, if it isn't made, many kill themselves. Even if someone has written many books that have all been bought, it can always happen that he can no longer write such books, and everybody already knows, before he has even started on the next book, that none of his books will be made anymore, or he writes a book that's like the preceding ones, still everybody thinks that the book will no longer be bought, then the book will not be made either, even if it's just like the preceding ones. There are only very few who can always write books that everybody wants to make. Oftentimes they are very quickly forgotten, however, their books are only sold as long as they live, while others whose books were never made, or who only had small books, die, and once they are dead, all of a sudden many big books are made about their small books. The most powerful people, however, are not those who make books, or those who own the towers, the factories, and the markets. The most powerful ones are the agents. They are the ones who know exactly which people will make which books, they are the ones who know exactly which people will turn which manuscript into a heavy book and which manuscript into a light book. They are the ones who know which markets will take which books when, and how many of them. If someone who writes books wants to become rich, he goes to see an agent. If the agent thinks that the manuscript can be turned into a book, he'll say that the book is not yet written, even if it is already written, but that he knows for certain that it will be an unprecedented book, the people who make books will be particularly curious, they pay in advance for being allowed to make the book, the agent tells one of them that another has bid a certain amount for the book, it's not true at all, but because the first one wants to make the book at all cost, he believes it and raises the bid, the agent then goes to the second one who bids still more because he, too, wants to make the book at all cost, the agent goes back to the first one, or, if he no longer bids more than the second one, to a third one, until he can't find anybody to bid any higher. The agents also know which books will never be made, and which ones, of those whose books will never be made, kill themselves. Koby, in the country where the books are made there are not just children and mothers and fathers. The children don't die there. The people who make books, the people who write books, the people who own the towers, the factories, and the markets, they are often neither children nor mothers nor fathers. Koby, we'll go away from here together. Koby, we'll find the country. Koby, they have streets as wide as the river, without any curves. There are no cracks and no barriers, on those streets you can go anywhere. Koby, not all people there have dark skin, I read about an agent who had very fair skin and hair, even though he wasn't a father, only his eyes were red, and he was the most powerful of all agents. Koby, take me with you, go away with me. Koby, we'll leave everything behind, the city and Carlo, he will be nothing without me, they will vent their anger on him when I'm gone, but he doesn't deserve better after what he did to you. Koby, you have to take me along. Koby, all of this wouldn't have happened if you had been at the station back then, we would have already left then, but you weren't there, that's why I had to go back, you followed me, but then you left without me, you left me alone, only Carlo was there, I would have liked to go with you so much more, Koby, but you were gone, I was there, with Carlo, with the dead mother, we can start all over, Koby, if we go away together now, the world in the books exists, we'll go to the country where books are made, Koby, with the towers that are sometimes made of nothing but glass so that the other towers are mirrored in it, as well as the sky and the people.

Because the wounds hurt considerably whenever he moved, and the bruises even more so, he spent the first half of the week in the hostel. When he went out to go on his first walks again, the clear blue sky behind the pointed towers of the cathedral yielded to a dense cover of gray clouds. The weather had turned humid and foggy, but it wasn't raining. The river, wide and of the same opaque color as always, didn't seem to be flowing, only the whirlpools were in motion, slowly but all the more relentlessly. The river bred clouds that hovered low above the city so that the view of the foothills and their ruins was blocked for the inhabitants, surrounded by clouds of fog the river crept between the old houses and tried to withdraw the towers of the cathedral from their beholders. With the sunshine coming into the hostel, it had seemed to Koby as though the house in which Welka had lived with the mother could be reached in a few minutes. After the river had smothered the sun, the house was much farther away all of a sudden. He didn't want to go back to that place. Anything to avoid admitting it, he was prepared to push the events completely into the background because he wanted to go away with Welka. Where the streets never ended and the houses were like giant mirrors and mirrored each other. Where nothing would remind them of her and his past. To the windows in the high towers where the new books were presented. He had traveled far. The fathers and mothers didn't travel much. The children didn't travel at all. Only those who sang, like him. Of all the cities that Koby had seen, this one had been the biggest, the most powerful, the wealthiest. The city in which he had grown up, which he had left, and to which he had now returned. He hadn't met any people with dark skin who made new books, or people with fair skin and red eyes who knew which books would be made and which ones wouldn't. Only Welka, who collected and put old books in order. And Patrizia, who sold really old books out of baskets on the market, surrounded by fruits and animals. Could they reach the country with the mirroring houses. Welka had time, she wouldn't die. Or was it all made up. Was it just the world in the books, which didn't really exist. What if this country didn't exist, and if Welka knew that this country didn't exist. This country couldn't exist. Otherwise he, Koby, would have known about it, even without books. Otherwise he would have met someone who knew this country. Otherwise he, Koby, would have made it to this country by himself. He had known back then, too, that she was serious about it. Although she didn't lack anything even then, although she had no reason to leave even then.

He hadn't been at the station because he had to allow for the possibility that she would indeed run away at the first opportunity she got. Back then she ordered him to do something, he didn't obey. Now she no longer ordered him to do anything. She asked him because she knew she could no longer give him orders. She knew now that she had never been in a position to give him orders. He was the only one whom she couldn't give orders. If Carlo really did everything she wanted, why had he dared to instigate the assault against him. He had to be aware that she would punish him for it. Or maybe Carlo knew that she would go away with him, Koby, regardless, he would lose his position no matter what, and it didn't matter, was that why he had set the trap. It didn't matter. He, Koby, wanted to go away with her. He realized that he didn't mind the thought that they might perhaps never get to where the houses were mirrors and the streets as wide as the river. It didn't matter so much whether they would really manage to get there. Whether this country existed. Still existed. Not only did she ask him, she put his hand into hers. She had never done that before. He had always believed she would never touch him. The touch had been different from all others. Completely different from the way Patrizia, always freshly bathed, had snuggled up against him, before the three had beaten him, after they had beaten him. When Welka touched him, he didn't need to close his eyes. Everything was like it had been back then. The plaid pants, the white blouse, the dark shoes, the white stockings.

Behind the facade of his submissive demeanor Carlo was nothing if not desperate. Welka had never talked to him about Koby. Hence, Koby was for Carlo indeed only that Koby who hadn't been at the station even though he had promised to be there, and who had run away when action was called for. Why had Welka led the fathers and mothers of the city to offer the singers to stay longer than they had asked for. Even now, after he had turned up again, she didn't say a word about Koby to him. Like Koby, he didn't believe in the cities with houses in which other houses are mirrored. Welka had everything anybody could wish for, still she wanted to go away. Like back then. With Koby. Like back then. If Welka were to go away, he would have to move out of the tower, then he would once again be the kid on the street that he had been before he guarded Welka under the mother's orders. He had to prevent it, he couldn't just stand by and let Welka go away with Koby. He had let Patrizia in on it. She didn't even need to tell him that she wanted to go away with Koby. That she had only been waiting for Koby. That's why she had taken a bath in the river every night, even during the winter, she had even risked catching pneumonia, and then she had indeed met Koby while she was bathing, he had been able to see how clean she was, everybody wanted to go away with Koby, not just her, every girl in the city, Welka, too, of course, Welka, like she had always wanted, Koby had run away, he, Carlo, had stayed to help her, he had always helped her, and now she wanted to go away and leave him behind, she, Patrizia, wouldn't stand a chance, even if Koby had said that he wanted to go away with her, Patrizia, maybe he really meant it at that moment, but one look into Welka's eyes and Koby would do what Welka wanted, that was all she, Patrizia, could expect from him, it would happen just like that, Koby and Welka would go away together and leave him, Carlo, and her, Patrizia, behind, but he would prevent it, he would put up a fight, he wouldn't let it happen, he would do something that neither of them were expecting, to which Patrizia replied that Welka might as well go, she hated Welka like Welka had hated the mother, she knew everything, Welka had told her, she, Patrizia, could read as well, she could sort the books like Welka, and she knew, like Welka, what was written in the books, it wasn't true, and Carlo knew that it wasn't true, Patrizia had read only a few books, but Welka wouldn't go away, Welka would never go away by herself, Koby would run away, Koby was always looking on and then running away, without Welka, without her, Patrizia, maybe he, Carlo, would go away like Koby, whom everybody admired because he was always running away, and everybody wanted to be with him, perhaps they would all admire him, Carlo, too, if he were to run away, like Koby.

We're going away.

Who's going away.

The two of us.

Carlo had never even considered the possibility that Welka might be going away with him.

We're only taking the most important books along. There aren't many. One half of the money is mine, the other half is yours. You can do what you want with it.

This was impossible.

Move.

Carlo was standing with folded arms before the low wooden door behind which there were the books and the money. Welka tried to push him aside.

Let me go in.

He didn't move from the door.

You're not going away.

Have you lost it.

She smacked him.

It had only been a pretext. Welka would never go away with him. She had nevertheless been serious about the offer to share the money. She made no effort to convince Carlo of that, however. They both knew that he was lost without her telling him what to do, the money wouldn't help him any.

Koby, do something.

This time everything had been planned more carefully. She had told Koby that she would go away no matter what. She had no longer put any pressure on him to go with her. All he had to do was to help her get out of the city. From there she would move on by herself. Koby could not refuse to walk her out of the city. Koby had come, this time.

Koby, he won't let me.

Welka walked over to Koby and put her arm through his.

Koby, you're stronger than he is.

Koby could no longer run away. Not this time.

Koby, he has to let me go.

Carlo continued to stand motionless.

They were high above ground, right underneath the platform of the tower. The floor could be secured by a large iron trapdoor opposite the stairs that was now open, supported by an iron bar. Welka let go of Koby, walked over to the stairs, and yanked the iron rod from its foundation so that the trapdoor fell shut with a bang.

Koby, I can't leave, without any books and without any money. Everything belongs to me, Koby. Carlo can have half of it. Koby, we need the books and the money.

She slipped the iron bar into Koby's hands. Koby grew pale as a sheet.

Koby, do it!

You must be out of your mind!

This was the first sentence Koby had uttered.

Carlo laughed: He's running away again! He's always running away!

Koby held the iron bar in his hands.

Koby, do it! Do it, do it, do it!

Welka screamed at Carlo and was crying at the same time. Carlo laughed loudly.

At that moment Welka grabbed the iron bar, walked up to Carlo, and took a swing. Carlo was still laughing and did not get out of the way. The strike brushed the side of his head, almost ripped off his ear, and crushed his right shoulder. Carlo staggered out onto the little balcony underneath the platform of the tower. Blood started gushing from the wound on his head immediately. Koby tried to hold Welka back, who wanted to follow Carlo out onto the balcony.

Coward! Coward! Coward!

Welka screamed at Koby, she wrenched herself from his grasp, she dragged the iron bar out onto the balcony where Carlo was leaning against the railing, bleeding, slumped over, she took another swing, Koby no longer tried to stop her, she hit Carlo in the head, she didn't let go of the iron bar, her momentum carried her over the dilapidated railing, she fell together with the iron bar, first the iron bar, then she herself, down onto the pavement.

Everything was like it had been back then, after Welka had killed the mother. Basically, it didn't matter that Welka herself had been killed at the same time. It had been the same rage to which nobody could put up any resistance. She had told Carlo to move, and he hadn't moved. If she had still been alive, it would still have been her conviction that Carlo had gotten what he deserved. Koby reproached himself for the same reasons as he had back then. He had held her back before she had attacked Carlo again. He was stronger than she was. Why had he let go of her. Because she had called him a coward. So that they were free to go away over Carlo's dead body, just like she had been free to stay over the mother's dead body. She had to realize, after all, how Carlo would react when she announced her intention to leave. She had to realize, after all, that the servile Carlo would resist only one thing: the end of his servitude. Perhaps it had even been Welka who had given Carlo the idea to stage the attack on him so that he wouldn't try holding her back when it came down to it—and he, Koby, had been a tool, used to get rid of another tool. But what if it hadn't been a plan, what if she just wanted to go away with him, of course he was aware that it wasn't just about getting her out of the city, what if she hadn't reckoned with Carlo opposing her, them, so forcefully, what if she had attacked him in a sudden fit of anger, what if she had asked him, Koby, to strike Carlo dead in the rage of the moment—after all, he knew that she was evil, he and Carlo, they had always known it, no one had known it better than he and Carlo. How could he have forgotten. How could he have forgotten Patrizia, who wanted to leave, without money or books, just with him, Koby, who had nursed his wounds and who'd had to witness how Welka had bewitched him. He flushed with shame when he thought of how Welka had touched him and of what injustice he had done to Patrizia. But all was not yet lost. Not for him and not for Patrizia. Now they would go away together. He wouldn't sing anymore. They would go away without Welka's money and without the books. They would finally be free. Patrizia would be free from her oppression, he from his past. At the moment when he let go of Welka, was it perhaps then that he'd had the hope that all that which eventually happened would indeed happen, both of them, Welka and Carlo, would suffer their downfall, or they would at least fill their hell so completely by what they did to each other that no third party could be wrapped up in any kind of relation to one of them. Maybe it hadn't been wrong of him to let go of Welka. Maybe it hadn't been wrong of him either not to have intervened when Welka killed the mother. Everything would be all right if he went away with Patrizia now.

He ran to the market, but Patrizia wasn't there, the stall was empty, he ran back to Welka's tower where from a distance he already became aware of the crowd of people that had formed around Welka's corpse. Completely disregarding the fact that nobody knew he was a witness, he was concerned to be questioned in detail about what had happened and to be called to account for his failure to intervene. Now he really wanted to go away, as quickly as possible. They would never let him leave. They wouldn't let Patrizia leave either, who had been in closest contact with the two who were now dead. He wandered through the city all day, and he thought of the wide streets that Welka had described for him, he looked up at the towers of the city, which were higher than all other houses in all of the other cities he knew, they were built from irregular and rough stones, they weren't made of iron and glass, he saw the inhabitants of the city, they weren't dark, but neither were they altogether fair, he returned to the market again, hoping to meet Patrizia at her stall after all, but the market was almost completely deserted, the inhabitants of the city had gone to the tower in front of which Welka lay dead on the pavement, and the goods were being offered on boards placed over wooden stands, and the market was outside, and they weren't the halls made of glass that Welka had described for him.

In the meantime night had fallen, by now the fathers and the boys at the hostel must have heard about what happened to Welka and Carlo. They knew what importance the mayor had attached to his presence in the city, now the mayor was dead, Carlo was dead, and he, Koby, had not returned to the hostel. He still hadn't found Patrizia.

By the river. If she wasn't anywhere, then she was by the river.

She was swimming on her back. The water was cold, but she moved as though she was bathing in a warm lake.

He sat down on the edge of the pier wall.

It's over.

It couldn't have remained a secret to her what Welka was planning and that Carlo would stop at nothing to prevent exactly that from happening.

What did the fathers say.

Oh, there must have been a fight.

Why a fight.

That's hard to tell. But it's not important.

She must have known that things would come to a head and that according to Welka's plans he, Koby, would play an important role in all of this. Why didn't she question him about how exactly it all happened.

We are free.

Patrizia flipped over on her belly, held on to the wall with her hands, and continued to make swimming strokes with her legs.

Was Welka still alive when she was lying on the pavement? No. But Carlo was still alive for a long time. He could no longer speak, however.

Patrizia had all the time in the world. She would no longer be beaten by anybody where she came from, no matter how late she returned.

There were a few fathers and mothers on the street who saw how Welka attacked Carlo with the iron bar and how she fell over the railing.

We can go away now.

Everything about Patrizia told him that she wouldn't go away with him. None of what he had imagined was right. If she had wanted to go away with him, she would have waited for him at her market stall in the afternoon, if she wanted to go away with him, she would have looked for him at the hostel in the evening, if she wanted to go away with him, she wouldn't now turn her face toward the Bridge of Stone, if she wanted to go away with him, she would say something now, but in fact she didn't say anything.

What's keeping us here?

She remained silent.

Don't you want to go away with me anymore?

Wait, I'll get out of the water.

She hadn't asked him for it, but he still turned around until she had dried herself off and had gotten dressed.

Why don't you want to go anymore? Now that no one can keep us from going?

She buttoned her shirt.

If you want, I'll go away with you.

She put on her shoes.

But it was you who wanted to leave! You!

He screamed at her.

I can always leave.

She remained totally calm.

I can read, too. Welka taught me how.

The fathers and mothers have offered you—

Koby didn't finish his sentence.

I don't know as much about the books as Welka. But they won't find out. If they find out, they won't care.

You want to stay here.

You can stay here, too.

Like Carlo.

Not like Carlo.

Her reply, nothing but a compulsory exercise.

She was now fully dressed.

The cities with the mirroring houses and the streets as wide as the river, they don't exist.

This—she pointed to the Bridge of Stone and to the skyline of the cathedral—is the biggest city anywhere. Everybody who comes says so. Nobody has seen a bigger church, nobody has seen a more massive bridge.

It wasn't because of the towers and the streets.

Why else?

We wanted to go away together.

Where to?

THE NEW GUYS

He drives a black Golf, the base model. What kind of car he has at home I don't know. He's always coming in by plane, the Golf is parked at the airport, he drives it to the company and back. You think he's already up in years? He must be between sixty-five and seventy, and he's hard of hearing, but that's got nothing to do with his age, he was an antiaircraft auxiliary during the war. He's very robust. He's from the consulting firm that's conducting the search for the new CEO. How often he is around? Not all week. He's getting paid on a per diem basis. They wrote to the customers that he would be acting as an interim consultant to the present management until the CEO was appointed. Actually, he has the authority to instruct the other managers. The advisory board wants him to end the bickering. I would have ended the bickering, too. If only they'd let me. Ending the quarreling is very simple. All you have to do is kick out the family. Send Heini to Lugano, his son Fritz to St. Moritz, and Georg back to his books, then everything will run all by itself! The company meeting is tomorrow, I'm writing his speech just now. What you mustn't do to anyone—He has many years of experience working on critical situations of industrial corporations . . . his job is to redevelop the existing structures of the company with respect to technology and the organization of sales and administration. . . . He doesn't even know the company. I didn't even have my own chair when I started working for the company as an apprentice, I was sitting on a roll of corrugated cardboard, I've gone through all the stages up to being manager, I could redevelop the company, if they would let me, even though there's nothing to redevelop, all you have to do is kick out the family and take care of the customers, everything else will organize itself. He will coordinate the basic measures and decisions found to be necessary with the advisory board. . . . With the duds who kicked me out. A hunchbacked lawyer, an international consultant who doesn't even know how to sell a used car and who betrays his best friend, the only reasonable one is the fat tax consultant. They'll ruin the company for good. The shareholders waive the formal and deadline requirements in advance—he'll see what the father does about forms and deadlines once he seizes the son's reins. Each of them thinks that first they give him the power, and then they can get him on their side. When Heini was in Lugano and Fritz in St. Moritz, I went out to the customers with Georg Sr., and we picked up the orders. When Georg Sr. couldn't do it anymore, and his son, the one with the doctorate, was pouring over his books, I went out to the customers by myself, and I picked up the orders myself. The only reason why the company remained in business after Georg Sr. died was that I kept bringing in the orders. They thanked me by kicking me out. Because they believed Fritz. Everybody in the company knows that he's lying like a trooper, only the advisory board doesn't know. That dimwit, that born loser, he pokes his nose into everything and never finishes anything! These are the wish lists for the new guy. Lowering of unproductive costs by cutting maintenance management and assigning it to an outside provider—the castle on the hill is already built, they won't have to manage that anymore. Quantitative reduction in preproduction, qualitative increase in construction. What a bunch of morons. Degreed engineers and business administrators are what they need! The new guy is an engineer, too, he'll sure like the part about construction. Assessment of environmental impact—he's the one responsible for that. Improvement of the distribution plan, because during the first quarter there's never enough business, while orders are lost in the second quarter because the delivery periods are too long. It's always been that way. It's never been any different. That's why Georg Sr. would always have the facilities expanded in the last and first quarters, during the second and third quarters we would work overtime, and that way we made good money for years. You have to reeducate the customers. The customers should kindly conform to his production schedule. And what would he like to see? In Section I: a campaign to win back the trust of those customers who have been ordering less since my departure—can't argue with that. In Section II the sales department is supposed to be split off and regional sales centers are to be set up. He's not even in charge of this section! He's writing about all of the sections. Section III: securing production capacity to meet adequate delivery periods . . . Section IV: determining the respective responsibilities of construction and shop, product development should be more methodical—why didn't he take care of that himself? Section VI: determining a clear strategic focus, providing the necessary capacity for construction. What's that all about? We've been seeing a lot of that lately. Our experiences as of late are unfortunately incompatible with the expectations we had formed on the basis of your guarantees. This is reflected in unsatisfactory compliance with deadlines, nonstandard delivery periods, lack of flexibility in the project business as well as in demands for an unreasonable price level that the market doesn't bear out in any way . . . we are therefore led to assume that the volume of our business with your company exceeds your capacities. We haven't gotten letters like that in thirty years. In the old days, if we had a complaint, we wouldn't even take the stairs but would jump right out the window into the car, and we were with the customer before any memos or letters. The lunatic inherited this section from me, and that's the result. The new guy has to kick him out! He tries his best to ice him. That's not enough. And it wouldn't even be a punishment if he were to kick him out. He'll always be provided for, even if there is absolutely no money left. Idleness must be rewarded. There has to be some justice, after all. I worked for the company for thirty-five years, and they kicked me out. I remember exactly when I became manager, how Heini gave me a pat on the back and said, Peter, I'm glad you're here, you have to watch what the young people are doing, my son and the doctor. What a hypocrite, what a scoundrel. Even though things might still have worked out with him. In the end, Heini always did what Georg told him. He would turn red, blow up, and shout everyone down, then his brother would come along, he wouldn't even raise his voice, and he would collapse straight away. Georg Jr. also knew how to deal with Heini. I remember when the lunatic was building his house. Peter, see to it that my son doesn't spend so much money. I should have prevented the golden faucets and the pool slide, can you imagine, he lets himself drop from the bed into the pipe, he slides down, and then he lets himself drop again into the pool, and the dumb waiter, just so food could be served on every floor without having to suffer the stairs. I know how to punish him. I build a house on the slope, looking out on the river. On the lot in front of his own. My house isn't tall. But it has a tower. He has put all his money into his house, all the money he has and all the money he doesn't have, thirty-five-thousand hours of company time, only to find a tower in front of him. Whenever he sits on his back porch, he has to decide whether to look past the tower on the left-hand or the right-hand side. My lot is as big as his, I could have put the house with the tower somewhere else, why did I have to build the tower right there. He tried everything to prevent the building of the tower, he didn't give his signature as my neighbor, but I know the authorities, he filed a lawsuit against the building permit, but he lost, even though it's a modern tower, there are historical precedents in the city, after all. He sneaked onto the construction site at night to attempt sabotage, but he didn't dare go through with it. Now the tower is there. He regrets not having attempted sabotage during construction, not having taken a load of dynamite and blown up the tower, of course he knows that I would have rebuilt the tower immediately, it would have been useless, but he just likes to imagine that it would have been good for something anyway. Everybody pities him because of the tower, and they ask why he didn't prevent the building of the tower, he tried to retaliate, he built an ugly concrete wall on the border of the lots, I never look up, I only look down, onto the river and the city, I have a wonderful view, he has blocked his own view even further with the wall, I don't mind the wall, the only time I notice it is when I'm on the john, I didn't even plant a hedge in front of it, when I'm on the john I always read the paper anyway. He imagines that things are coming to a head, that I call him names, or that I damage his wall, he doesn't want to restrain himself any longer, he buys a few hand grenades and blows up the tower after all. He pictures it, the police, the neighbors, the court, the papers, everybody understands, he couldn't stand looking at the tower cutting his view in two, and if the one who built the tower then goes on to insult him—everybody congratulates him on the tower lying in ruins, and he can even prevent the tower from being rebuilt. Maybe he goes so far as to actually stockpile dynamite and hand grenades. I won't insult him. The company will go bankrupt, or else will be sold for peanuts, his house is all he's ever owned and will ever own, he cannot leave, and he won't leave. He will grow old, I will grow even older, he will hate me more and more, I will hate him less and less, his hate will absorb mine, I know he hates me, so I don't need to hate him, it's enough if one person hates to such an extent. When he can no longer go skiing, when I can no longer play tennis, when he can barely go for walks anymore, when he's reduced to looking out the window, he'll always be reminded of the fact that I worked for him in his company—although it never did belong to him, it was always his uncle's and his father's company—for thirty-five years, that I earned money for him for thirty-five years, that I built up the company with Georg Sr., that he then gave me the boot, and that it's his own fault if all he has left is his house and nothing else. I will call him. He won't recognize my voice because he hasn't heard my voice in years, and because he has grown deaf, of course, he will say that he doesn't believe that it's me, still he won't hang up, he won't admit that he believes that it's me, he will be so agitated that he will be afraid of having a heart attack. I will say that I want to talk to him, he should come over, no tricks, he will say that I must be crazy and will wish that I had shouted at him, that I had insulted him, anything but that I had asked him to come over. He will think about the dynamite and the hand grenades in his basement, he will consult his family, and he will come. He will call me from the street, I will call for him to come in through the open front door and to keep walking straight, he will bring a gun, against our understanding, and he will bring his son along, also carrying a gun, they will see me sitting by myself in the living room, in front of the glass wall, in front of the unobstructed view onto the river and the city. I will tell him that I no longer think about the past. I am sorry about the tower. I have been unable to walk for years, and therefore I don't want to live any longer. He can help me. He has always hated me, after all. Me and the tower. I point to the open door, he should go get his dynamite and his hand grenades. To blow up everything. The tower and me. I will say it such that he will know that I mean it. He will leave without saying a word. His wife, who has been waiting for him, will ask him what it was that I wanted from him. He will shout at her that all I want to do is to trick him. I will leave all doors open at all times. He will hate me even more. He will tell himself he won't do it because I'm an old man. Or because one cannot do such a thing, blow up a house and an old man, even if that's what he wants. Or he won't do it simply because I want it. Maybe he will even try to tell himself that he no longer hates me and that the tower no longer bothers him that much. He knows why he won't do it. He's been wanting to do it all these years, he didn't have the opportunity, now he has the opportunity, he's too much of a coward. He knows he won't do it because he's too much of a coward. He has always been too much of a coward! Projects are assigned to him. He's supposed to work out a plan for Plant III. He wants to relocate Sections II, V, and VI to Plant III. Phase one is rebuilding the paint shop, phase two moving of all the machines, phase three reviewing which administrative functions can be moved to Plant III: preproduction, buying, cost system accounting. . . . Of course he wants to move all of the functions for these sections to Plant III. That would leave nothing over here! The new guy is just now having the turnover volume calculated that would be lacking in the end. This project doesn't stand a chance, nevertheless, he has been asked to quantify all three phases. The new guy will concentrate everything over here and is more likely to close Plant III rather than to develop it. It's nothing but occupational therapy. By the way, he wants to go to the Seychelles with his wife, for three weeks. If you ask me, nothing will be the same here after those three weeks that he'll be gone. Today the two guys who did the analysis started their jobs. The new guy is explicitly authorized to employ more interim managers. How are these two? The business administrator has a wooden leg, and the technician has high blood pressure. As of yet there is no organizational diagram, but everybody has been instructed orally to go only to those two from now on. They will run the show. Fritz hasn't even realized it yet because he is so busy with his project. And Georg Jr.? He gets along fine with the new guy. He lets him do his thing.

He was riding through the woods at a gallop, his wife following behind at a trot. Because his wife was falling ever farther behind, he stopped at a large, sun-drenched clearing and waited for her.

When she finally came, she was all out of breath.

You never used to dare to gallop in the woods.

The horse knows when to get out of the way.

They slackened their hold on the reins.

What a gorgeous day! Why are we riding so far?

I wanted to be alone with you. To tell you something.

She had no idea what this could be about.

They have given me Sections III and IV as well.

Now this, after all the trouble? How can that be? — You haven't told me anything. — I was so afraid, I thought they were going to kick you out, Fritz and Heini.

The doctor will devote himself to his scientific career. He says that his father would have wanted me to take over his former sections.

Fritz and Heini went along with it?

They realized that I'm the only one who can sell. They didn't admit it, but they did go along with it.

His wife looked up into the sun, she acted as though it was the sun that brought tears to her eyes, she didn't want him to notice that she was crying.

He led his horse up to her to put her hand into his.

If Georg Jr. quits the active business, then it looks like Fritz has won. Heini's lawyer has indicated that Fritz will also quit after a grace period. Then I will be the only manager.

Of the whole company?

She could hardly believe it. After all that had happened.

You'll see.

I'm proud of you.

They rode back at a leisurely trot.

I have something concerning you, as well. Me? Your testimonial. My lawyer has contacted you umpteen times about it. Who's writing it? The new guy. But he doesn't even know me. Qualified testimonial. Mr. Peter Simon, born on, worked as comanager for our company from until. He was responsible for sales of. We were always and without reservations satisfied with Mr. Simon's efforts. Mr. Simon consistently devoted himself eagerly and with interest to the tasks assigned to him. His knowledge of the market and his considerable commitment to the customers made Mr. Simon a valuable associate. Mr. Simon's employment was terminated in mutual agreement, effective. That's supposed to be a testimonial for somebody who was with the company for thirty-five years? Who built up the company! The formulations were suggested by the advisory council. I worked day and night. I drove out there and picked up orders. I wasn't paid on a per diem basis. The new guys are getting in three days what I got in a whole month. I know that, and not from them. What do they do for their money. Sell the machines and then lease them back because otherwise they cannot stay below the credit line. We didn't need any credit. The banks were saying to Georg Sr.: you can have any credit you like. Any. We didn't need a penny! The credit line was raised, too. Georg Jr. and the advisory council were in favor of it, Heini was opposed to it, but they talked him into it. The galvanizing shop will be closed because the parts are fifty percent more expensive than they would be if they were to order them from outside. They shouldn't only consider the galvanizing department. They should consider the whole company. If we were only fifty percent more expensive than the competition, we would be good. The organization of the internal transport will be modified. The night porters will be cut. The cafeteria costs are to be calculated exactly, the subsidy is supposed to be raised. The customers are what they should worry about! Not the cafeteria. Do you know how they strike me. The new manager, the one with the wooden leg, and the one who has high blood pressure, they wear garments that look like nightgowns, and they come into the office barefoot, the new guy recites, with a deep voice, you write down what he recites, he goes to get the one with the wooden leg and the one who has high blood pressure, they recite together, again you write down what they recite, then the three of them go over to production, barefoot, the new manager has the brightest garment, the others follow behind him, the new manager recites without interruption, once in a while the other two recite as well, they walk by all machines and all assembly points, sometimes all three of them recite simultaneously and loudly, so that they can be heard throughout the shop, and everything turns out for the best. The machines are running faster. The workers work harder. The constructions become simpler. Developing becomes cheaper. The products become better and cheaper at the same time. The customers order continuously. Nobody needs to meet anymore with the little buyer from the big company in a cheap café with dirty curtains who talks about how he has just sold four combat helicopters to the Near East, great deal, huge commission, on his own account, his company doesn't know about it, fantastically rich Arabs and Jews, and this was only the beginning, but he doesn't have enough money to pay for the tune-up for his car, which is in the shop right now. The company no longer needs the little buyer from the big company who is actually not little at all but weighs two hundred pounds and has only one lung, who still drinks between five and ten liters of beer every day, and who tells my wife to kindly wear a dirndl so that one may see her rack. No need to flirt with Ms. S. anymore who is already forty-five, who keeps wanting to invite you on a hiking trip for the weekend, to the Juifen or the Denkalm, but unfortunately you cannot oblige, you would have to bring the wife who doesn't have a body as well trained as Ms. S., even though Ms. S. is twice as large as she is. Also, the company no longer needs anyone to inquire downtown whether new ladies are available every time Mr. O. is in town, if they are the same, the order volume is zero, if they are new ones, there is an urgent project, and if it's a black woman, a major project is in the works!

Everything turned out the way he had described it to his wife when they were out riding. Soon after he had taken over Sections III and IV, he was able to register a huge increase in turnover in Section IV. Because he no longer had to waste his time with useless bickering, turnover shot up in his old sections as well. At long last he was in control of production. The head of production answered to him, he determined the priorities for the production, he no longer had to take extended walks through the plant and do the jobs of the foremen and the people in preproduction in addition to everything else. He was therefore able to set much quicker delivery dates, which increased the turnover even more. The company generated big profits again, which finally prompted the family shareholders to do what they should have done long ago: they stopped interfering with the business. Georg Jr. became professor at a university in Switzerland, his cousin Friedrich quit the management one year after Georg Jr., as he had predicted to his wife. The family turned over the management to him alone, with the explicit approval of the advisory council. Around this time Section III was the last one to finally show progress. Things had taken longer because the product line had to be completely revamped first. Now that he no longer had to fear that important information would be used against him, he supported young people in all the sections who had both technical know-how and people skills, relieving him of having to be in direct contact with everyone. The company became so profitable that shareholder meetings and advisory council meetings turned into mere formalities. The shareholders were able to make large withdrawals, nevertheless, all investments were financed from company resources. Consequently, the members of the advisory council received generous compensations. He was left to act as he saw fit. Which prompted him, among other things, to build up a new section. Section VIII had no relation whatsoever to the traditional sections of the company and wasn't conceived to change in that respect. He wouldn't stay with the company forever. The company where he had been working for forty years, but which didn't belong to him. Without him the company wouldn't exist anymore, nobody could fault him if he were to take care of himself now, if he were to found his own company. He would leave the company in a position that would make it easy for his successor to continue business successfully. Maybe they would give him the product

from Section VIII as a recognition of his efforts, the turnover it gener-
ated wasn't large yet, and the production sites weren't yet large either.
If they didn't, it would be easy for him to develop the product from
scratch and to build new production sites.

Organizational instruction no. 5. New mail distribution, effective.
One: any mail received is to be presorted by the secretary into: bills
received, accounting mail, buying mail, finance mail, human
resources mail, sales mail, management mail, general mail, personal mail. Two: the incoming bills are to be forwarded directly to
the phone desk. They are to be registered, sorted, and to be forwarded to accounting. Human resources mail and management
mail are to be distributed immediately. All other mail is to be
deposited in the management conference room for the mail conference. During the mail conference even they will perhaps realize
that the number of orders is steadily declining. The guy with the
wooden leg is taking care of sales as well, by the way. The business
management draws up all the plans, including the sales plans. For
how long are you under the restraint clause? Two years. You can't
get around it? If it were that simple, with my wife or abroad, but
that's not it. I would risk my compensation if I violated the clause.
The new guy listens to Georg Jr. when it comes to customer contacts. After you're gone, he will be the only one who still knows
any of the customers. Maybe he will retain the upper hand in the
end. If Heini and Fritz need too much money for their lawyers and
are forced to sell to Georg, maybe we'll have you back here. They
want a new head of production and a new head of construction
below the technical manager. More interim managers are supposed
to be hired because they can't find permanent ones. They're also
looking for a head of quality control. We'll see a lot more bills for
consulting around here in the near future. I worked for the company for thirty-five years, I made millions for them, and they
kicked me out. Because I said the same thing that the new man-

ager says, that the lunatic turns a deaf ear. That he doesn't belong in a company. That he doesn't have the slightest idea about technology. That he doesn't have a clue about anything. They're all in it together. The only one who wasn't part of it was Georg Sr. Heini, who was only made a partner of the company because he had to feed his children, turns into the lunatic who spends the money Heini didn't dare spend even after his brother's death, and who keeps on shouting whenever Heini wouldn't have kept on shouting, they turn into Georg Sr.'s son who never shouts, so that Heini, impersonated by the lunatic, can shout even more, Georg Jr. is the biggest moron of them all, the only question is whether he doesn't want to, or whether he's incapable. The advisory council, that's also Heini or the lunatic or Georg Jr. as a hunchbacked shyster who will do anything Heini says because Heini is an old, overburdened man, and who falls for every one of his and his son's lies, as a whiz consultant, Georg Jr. thought he was doing what he wanted, but he always does the opposite of what he wants because he doesn't own a company himself, when Krapp, the only one who was against my suspension, but Krapp, too, is Georg Jr. is the lunatic is Heini, he always lets himself be outvoted—it must be a bad dream, or else my imagination is doing overtime since they kicked me out—it's just one person, and he wants to run the company over the cliff, wants to destroy everything until nothing is left, why?

The withdrawal from the old company turns out to be more difficult than he expected. They don't want to give him Section VIII. He spoiled the family and the advisory council with success to such a degree that they take it for granted and do not let him go. Instead, they reproach him for being ungrateful. Georg Jr. alone pleads for him to be given Section VIII, but he doesn't prevail. He doesn't even go on vacation after quitting the old company. He buys a piece of property and immediately begins the construction of the facility. One year after leaving the old company he is already employing 50 people and can hardly fill his orders. The desks, including his own, are right next to the machines because he doesn't begin the construction of the office building until the production facility is completed. Section VIII of the old company has already shrunk to the size of irrelevance, he hires all employees from this section who apply to him. His successor at the old company soon decides to close down Section VIII altogether. He buys all the patents and machines, as well as the facility, and takes over the remaining employees. Even though he has doubled his capacities with one fell swoop, he still cannot master the flood of orders. Three years after leaving the old company he is already employing 500 people and his company continues to grow at double-digit rates. Meanwhile, the old company is stagnating. The successor does the best he can, but the old family feuds are raging once again. Heini has died by now, his son has gotten the better of the sisters and brought all company shares on his side, he's pushing to get back into management, which prompts his cousin to suspend his professorship and to move back into an office in the company. He still has contact with the advisory council, he pleads with them, disinterestedly, to prevent the two family shareholders from getting involved in day-to-day business once again. Still, the advisory council lets it happen. The advisory council figures that all that work will dampen their enthusiasm and that they will withdraw again. But that turns out to be a miscalculation. Neither of them keeps to the tasks they were assigned, Instead, they both meddle in everything. With the result that many good employees quit their jobs and come to him instead. Five years after leaving the old company he is employing more than a thousand people and his company still continues to grow. The old company is in decline in all the sections and turns losses in almost all of them. Meanwhile, he is generating a return of twenty percent on his turnover. The two family shareholders cannot be driven out of the company because they have to approve the resources to cover the loss. The CEO leaves, and the largest part of the remaining management along with him. The advisory council dissolves likewise. Total *chaos is reigning within the old company. In this hour of need, Krapp, the longtime tax consultant of the old company, asks him whether he wouldn't be interested in buying the company. He is both interested and in a position to do so. Georg Jr. agrees to sell right away, his cousin has to be talked into it over the course of a virtually endless number of meetings. At the time of sale his own new company and the old company are approximately the same size. He pays only a low price. Thanks to his old contacts, he is able to set his old company, which now belongs to him officially, back on track toward growth and profit.*

Here's your personal file. Someone brought it over to the business office and then left it here. Nobody knows that I have your personal file. It's better for you to take it with you. Who knows what they may end pinning on you. You have to promise me that you won't speak to anyone about this. OK?

He will use the production facilities of the old company to manufacture his product even more economically. Thus, he will be in a position to export for the first time. He will become the leader of the domestic market. He will dominate the European market. He will become leader of the world market.

BY THE SENGSEN MOUNTAINS,
BY THE DEAD MOUNTAINS

It's as though all the raindrops were coming down right in front of the house, as though it weren't raining at all on the stable with the dunghill, or on the path leading up to the house where the idiot and his mother live. Nor on the ravine, hidden from view beyond the house with the Teichl River, or on the highway, likewise hidden from view beyond the ravine.

She tries hard to listen for the highway noises. The falling rain is hardly audible next to the drumming sound with which the water is pouring from the gutter into the gravel pit next to the stairs. Now there's a truck. Trucks make more noise when it's raining, cars don't. Maybe cars, too, make more noise when it's raining. The drumming is even noisier. Then there's a train. The train always makes the same kind of noise, it drowns out everything. It'll drown out the Autobahn, too, which will be next to the highway.

She's paying close attention. She compares the raindrops in front of the mountains on the other side of the valley and in front of mother's black windbreaker that father used to wear. The same amount of raindrops. Not any more dense in front of the mountain than in front of mother's windbreaker. Maybe that's because the mountain forest is of a lighter color than the windbreaker.

The hallway on the second floor is clean. She's the only one still using the children's room on the second floor. When her three sisters and her two brothers were living in the house, the children's room was always too small. One of the sisters slept in the living room. Of course they weren't allowed to use Madam's rooms. Mother cleans Madam's rooms once a week. The daughter has to clean the hallway.

Now she hears a truck and several cars on the highway. Engines accelerating one after the other, the cars are passing the truck. Once the Autobahn is here, you'll hear a lot more. Then all cars can go as fast as the ones now passing. Father, who is around every other weekend, says that you won't see anything from the house. She wonders where the Autobahn is going to be. The valley is narrow, on their side, in front of the Teichl there's no room for an Autobahn, beyond the Teichl there are the train tracks first of all, then the village, and then the highway. Beyond the highway there is already an incline. Either the Autobahn will run across bridges along the slope above the highway, or it will run inside the mountain. Father says that all that's missing now is the stretch from Kirchdorf to Windischgarsten. Other than that the Autobahn is finished, from Salzburg to Graz, from Hamburg to Graz. Right now there is less traffic. Father says it's because of the war. After the war there will be a lot of traffic again, much too much traffic for the highway. Father has to defend the Autobahn, he's building it. Sitting outside Cabin One, on top of the mountain, you hear a lot more of the traffic than if you're standing in front of the farmhouse. From Cabin One the cars on the highway look like toy cars, even though they're just as loud as if you were standing right by the road. Father says that the Autobahn won't be any louder than the highway. She asks, why then do you have the house in Spital by the Pyhrn River. Father says, shut up. Father doesn't like to talk about the house. Father says, don't you tell Madam about it. Mother came along only once and looked at the house. She would understand if father had bought the house and then renovated it as quickly as possible, and if they had moved there right away. But father doesn't even try to renovate it quickly. Father likes to go into the woods, especially in the summer when the weather is nice. The house in Spital is in the middle of town, and there are no woods beyond the house.

Clean the floor, will ya.

Mother is coming up the stairs with heavy steps.

Don't you remember, Jo's comin' today.

Mother keeps it a big secret where she hides the key to Madam's rooms. Still, she knows: next to the furnace, in what used be the smoking chamber. You need a ladder to get to the key. She's been in Madam's rooms many times. When the parents are out shopping or in church. Then she sits down on the sofa and looks at St. Wendelin and the gorgeous, painted wooden cupboard in which Madam keeps the wine and the liquor that she offers to her guests. She never touches anything. Not Madam's books, not her china, and not her silverware. Madam used to be here a lot. Most of the time the Italian priest was her guest. The priest took the room next to the children's room, Madam slept in her living room. The younger one of her two brothers used to bring lunch for Madam and the priest up to Cabin One. The brother, who was so smart that the priest sent him to the seminary in Kremsmünster, who now lives in Germany, and who never comes anymore, like Madam and the priest. They say that the priest became a bishop in the Vatican. Or even a cardinal. He can no longer simply visit Madam, even though we now have the Autobahn.

The idiot from the small house by the ravine goes into the woods to collect wood. His clothes are made from patches of black rags. The priest's robe was never completely black but always dark blue, such that one could only tell by broad daylight that it was dark blue, otherwise one would take it to be black, and under electric lights or when it wasn't bright out you could have sworn it was black. Below the robe the priest was wearing pointed black shoes, with a regular sole when he arrived, with a thick sole when he accompanied Madam on her walk through the territory. The idiot doesn't wear shoes but sandals stuffed with rags, his hands and forearms are wrapped in rags, a rag is wrapped around his head. She knows that he's an idiot because he was conceived in a drunken stupor. He cannot speak, he only grunts. But he's never unfriendly. He gets a shave once a month. When he's freshly shaved, he looks particularly friendly. When he has reached the yard and has to turn, the path to the woods continues behind the house, he motions with his left hand, which she interprets as a greeting.

She notices the water dripping from the idiot on all sides. Soon he must be completely soaked. He goes into the woods, he stares out the window or at the TV, it's always the same. The only thing that excites him is chocolate. Whenever he gets chocolate, he's no longer an idiot. Sometimes she gives him a chocolate bar. Just to watch him. At first he only touches the edges. Then he turns it back and forth, while looking over at the donor with such gratitude that it brings tears to her eyes just thinking about it. Can anybody be that happy. Can anybody be unhappy once he's been that happy. Can anything matter at all if somebody retains even the trace of a memory of once having been that happy. He's far from tearing the paper open, just to pull out the chocolate and to wolf it down. He feels with his fingers where the paper has been glued. Only to pull it up very carefully, he doesn't want to damage it. As if he were unwrapping an expensive present, taking care not to damage the equally precious wrapping paper. He proceeds in the same manner with the aluminum foil, being even more careful because he knows the aluminum foil will tear sooner than he can think. In this way he uncovers the chocolate bar until he is finally able to break off a piece. Engaged in this activity, he keeps looking over to the donor of the chocolate bar. His expression is now a mixture between bliss and secrecy. Everything must be kept between him and the donor. She doesn't believe that he is afraid that someone else might eat his chocolate. She doesn't even know what would happen if someone else were to lay claim to the chocolate that was given to him. She only ever gave him chocolate when nobody was looking. Would he fight back if they were to take away his chocolate? She has never seen him in a temper or angry. It seems that for him the two things belong together, bliss and secrecy. Maybe bliss isn't possible at all without secrecy.

The neighbor's husband died when the weather was like this. He was drunk when he spun out on his motorcycle on the steep descent down to the Teichl River bridge, he fell down the slope, he lay down by the river all night. They say that he was still alive for a long time and that he could have been saved if he had been found after the accident, but nobody knew where he was.

Even if he hadn't looked up, she was sure that the idiot had greeted her by motioning with his hand. Perhaps he hadn't looked up because he wanted to express a kind of silent protest against the fact that they sent him into the woods in this kind of weather. Or else the rain was running down his face and he couldn't look up. Or was he ashamed because he had to go into the woods even in weather like this.

Move your butt upstairs right now!

Mother is calling angrily from inside the house.

Right now!

Anger is rising up inside her. She will do what mother wants. But mother shouldn't treat her like the neighbor treats the idiot.

She goes down the stairs, she steps out in front of the house and stays out in the rain for a while. Protected by the roof, she doesn't get all that wet. The area in front of the stairs leading up to the front door is covered with gravel, the rain has washed away all the dirt. Then she goes back up the stairs and enters the house without taking off her shoes, goes up the wooden staircase to her room. She stops on the threshold and turns around. The footprints she left behind are clearly visible. They run up the stairs, turn around, run along the railing and turn toward her room. She considers whether to enter her room, or to go back. If she goes back, the single footprints will no longer be visible. Then it will probably look like a footpath.

You gone nuts?

She's still a child, and will be for a long time yet. Around here nature plays a trick to her own advantage by making girls look like grown-up women all of a sudden, while giving the boys no more than a little peach fuzz at an age by which they're supposed to be men. The next village where there are young women can only be reached by walking along what's actually called the chicken ladder. A path, anything but safe, along the Teichl River valley halfway up the mountainside that's very slippery, especially when it's raining. The two young women on the estate there are farmers, not children of tenant farmers. The other neighbors, there are three houses on the way to the Teichl bridge, are all retired. It cannot be the girl's fault that she doesn't know how to move in this narrow valley between the Sengsen Mountains and the Dead Mountains like Madam's guest, the mountains only coming up to his knees, the clouds just a bit higher, but these were never very many, such that they would have left visible only the shoes and the hem of his robe. The art of the priest, bishop, and perhaps even cardinal, was to walk the valley without leaving behind any traces. At the same time, he didn't float above the valley and its inhabitants. That would have been a Mickey Mouse film. Just a light breeze—that would have disgraced him. He stepped onto the scene, but he didn't stamp out anything. Nature dematerialized and rematerialized itself below his feet.

The daughter closes her eyes and receives the anticipated slaps in the face from mother.

Mother not only carries the burden of running the farm, she also has to cover for her husband who, being a tenant farmer, doesn't have the kind of reputation in town he would deserve as a self-employed businessman. He defends Madam's interests with a vengeance, especially when preventing the major access road across Madam's property from being built that's supposed to cut across the woods above the farmhouse like a giant inverted *Z* to make both Madam's remote woods and, most important, the even more remote woods of Madam's neighbors accessible. Not only does he oppose this road, however, he has also built his own road, all but invisible, which does not interfere with the hunting. Not the entire road, thank God, only the lower part. During inspections he keeps trying to convince the members of the district administration that his road does not have a gradient of more than twelve percent and that a truck could very well make his turn. It's obvious that no truck could make the excessively narrow turn and that the gradient is more than twelve percent. Everybody involved has a hard time understanding why he, the respected self-employed blaster, insists against all appearances that his road meets the criteria when it doesn't.

This is not an error like the one on which the history of ideas of entire centuries rests, like the one made by Cartesius, for example, who studied Montaigne's essays and asked himself what it was about this collection of anecdotes, quotations, and commonplaces that had made their narrator famous, if the author were really as busy as he pretends to be, he would never have been able to find the time to write down all that which occupied him so much, and then the cheeky remark: As long as nothing can be found of which we are absolutely certain, we are not certain of anything. Anger imposes an incredible limit on one's perspective. Descartes would have been better advised to answer with an anecdote. Or else with a quotation from Ovid. Instead, anger. He limited his capacity for thought to that which he practiced and preached on a daily basis, to that which he took to be the axiomatic method, embodied by Euclidean geometry. We know the rest. Descartes' anger led directly to Mies van der Rohe's architecture and to Carnap's inductive logic. Supposedly, European civilization is still busy recovering from both.

You can't blame the blaster and tenant farmer for the fact that his error doesn't have this format. Does he know this, and is that why he defends his error with such incredible tenacity. Zeal is supposed to compensate for a lack of substance. It's just eleven percent. Even though twelve would be allowed. But it's just eleven percent. Even less than that. Less than the legal maximum. That's what the deconstructivist, not even in disguise, being a blaster, wants to champion: the error as such. Not the planned one, not the systematic one, not the figure as part of the dance, as the particularly conceited philosophers would have it. The error as such. Nobody has actually measured the gradient of the path. The builder hasn't, but neither have his critics. If your toes always touch the ground before the balls of your feet when walking uphill, it is surely more than twelve percent. Because the road wasn't completed up to where the trees are being cut down, because for that reason there are no logs to be taken along here, no truck will be trying to make this turn. Maybe the gradient is really too steep, but the truck could still make the turn. People talk about roads in the area whose gradient was by all accounts more than twelve percent, a fact that, as everyone agreed, was not to be mentioned in any of the documents, because something didn't allow a different route, either the topography of the area, or the ownership situation, or a lease of hunting grounds, or something similar. Maybe there's a stretch of road that has a gradient of less than twelve percent. Why give a truck driver a bottle of booze so he can see whether he can't make that turn after all. Why actually measure the gradient. Why decide right away and record who's wrong at what time. Why seal the error. As long as the possibilities aren't exhausted, you can counterbalance the Descartes of our time and their errors.

Look at that mess.

Ain't nothin' but water.

Clean the stairs. Right now.

Why her. If her eldest and her third-eldest sister had gotten as many slaps in the face as she had, they wouldn't each have brought an illegitimate child into the world. The eldest sister's illegitimate child was eventually joined by another one, but not by a husband, the third-eldest sister's by the man as husband, and later on by another child by the same man. The second-eldest sister is not having children, even though she married a German, and the second-youngest one cannot have gotten any slaps in the face either, because she runs a night club in Liezen together with her husband, neither of them want any children. Why her. She will take revenge. For having to clean the floorboards and the stairs. For not being allowed to go to any dances. She will take revenge by marrying Jo's son. She doesn't know him yet, and he doesn't know her, but that won't be an obstacle to their eternal love.

When the Italian priest stopped coming, Jo took his place. Unlike the priest, however, he never spent the night in the house, that wouldn't have been considered proper, given the geographical circumstances. He's from Linz, after all, not from Rome. He owns a big carpenter's shop, and today he's coming to see about the roof frame. The roof has to be completely rebuilt, something that Madam has been putting off for years. Jo comes from a dynasty of factory owners, one of his brothers owns a construction company, another a bread factory, and yet another a furniture factory. Those who own property around here get better seating in the restaurants, but their daughters aren't dressed one iota better than she is, they, too, walk around in aprons and boots all day, they don't wash their hair any more often than she does. She knows how little money it pays to keep dairy cows or to raise bulls. Property, what that means first and foremost is that you can always stay where you want to stay. Or do not want to stay. A real business, on the other hand. One that's not only made up of the owner and an assistant, like her father's. That means money is always coming in. Then, a family with a number of businesses. A family with clout in the city.

She once saw a picture of Jo's son that Jo was showing to her mother. The picture featured him from one side, in uniform, as a draftee. He had short dark hair, dark eyes, small ears, yet a thick mustache winding around the corners of his mouth, his hair fell loosely across his forehead. He wore black glasses that lent him an air of determination. There will be a picture showing her like this, too. She will be photographed from the other side, looking at him. She will be wearing golden earrings and a pearl necklace and a diadem with diamonds. But this is getting ahead of events. The winters are hard around here, with lots of snow, even though the village is by no means at a high altitude, the water stains by the dormers are getting bigger after each winter. The roof will be rebuilt in the summer. The son is going to engineering school, during breaks he works for his father's business. The sons of all the brothers work for their fathers' businesses. The sons of the bread manufacturer did their apprenticeships as bakers, they have to be at the bread factory at two in the morning, the son of the contractor works as a foreman, Jo's two sisters are in accounting. He will fall in love with her at first sight. When the roof is done, he will tell his father that he wants to marry her. Then he will go to her parents right away to ask for her hand, but that'll be a mere formality, of course her parents will consent. Jo and his wife will be against her, of course. After all, she doesn't own anything, she's a nobody, even though her father owns a business, too, he's really nothing but a little tenant farmer. His mother will cry, his father will threaten him. He will say that he and his son are making themselves an object of ridicule, especially in the eyes of his brothers. The contractor's son married a doctor, the bread manufacturer's elder son married a lawyer, and the younger son from the furniture business married a bank teller. His parents will cry, plead, beg, and shout. Jo's son is not intimidated by that. He remains calm and reasonable, he just keeps repeating that he loves her. And that they had made an irrevocable vow to each other. To convince his parents of their love, he will propose that he and his bride will not see each other for two years. They will vow not to meet for two years, not to talk on the phone for two years, not even to write one another for two years. They want to do this to demonstrate that their love for another is so strong that it will survive even a separation of this sort. If one of them were to break the vow, their engagement would be void and Jo's parents would be proven right. His parents say that two years is a long time, that he'll take another. He won't even look at another, and she won't even think of someone else. His relatives will invite him, they'll present him with the prettiest and smartest girls in all of Linz, but he won't date any of them, even though they all try to get him to date them. Single friends of his cousins will join them on the hunt to prepare lunch, even though usually the men never take women along when they go hunting. His father will hire a particularly good-looking secretary, albeit one with a questionable reputation. He's not supposed to marry her, after all. He doesn't take anyone else. His parents think that he will break his vow and will secretly meet her, but he does not break his vow, he does not meet her secretly. When the two years are almost over, he still won't have touched anyone else. His parents will send him to Vienna in the end. His father will try to find a partner firm or a school for his son, he will rent an apartment in the nicest part of town and will give him a lot of money, and he wouldn't be angry at all if the school or the head of the partner firm were to tell him that his son was showing up only irregularly, something that would have been unthinkable in Linz. If only Vienna were the means of getting him away from her. His parents will come for an unannounced visit. They go downtown, perhaps they use the opportunity to visit a museum, and then, in the evening, they go to look up their son. The janitor would be letting them in, their son wouldn't be home, they would wait, and finally he would come. In a good mood, slightly drunk, and of course not all by himself. Or the janitor would say that their son was indeed home. They would go up the stairs and ring. Everything would be quiet. They would ring once again, nobody would open up. They would listen carefully, believing to hear noises, but they wouldn't be sure whether these noises were really coming from their son's room. Finally, they would knock on the door, this time he would open up. Their son would of course be happy to have his parents visit, even though they hadn't told him. He would ask them to come in, they would take off their coats, they would sit down at the small table. They would keep looking at the neatly made bed until their son's pretty girlfriend came out of the bathroom. But there is no girlfriend with him. They knock, and he opens up immediately. He's so happy about their visit that he hugs both of them, because he's all by himself and he's just reading a book. Even when someone wants to take her along to go to one of the dances in Kirchdorf and Windischgarsten, she doesn't come along. She doesn't even go to the pub with her brothers. She knows that she must avoid even the slightest cause for gossip. She doesn't get a job either, because something could be imputed to her, his parents, she thinks them capable of it, might even pay one of her colleagues to pursue her, even though the money wouldn't be necessary at all, she's pretty, otherwise their son wouldn't have fallen in love with her. She stays home and helps her mother. She's under their constant surveillance. They ask the game tenants, and they go into the village pub to question the locals about her. Nobody can tell them that she so much as looked at another man. In the summer she won't lie on the grass in her bathing suit either. A hunter could pass by and make something up, someone lying next to her in the sun, someone who never existed. Because there's nothing bad that they can say about her, because there is nothing, absolutely nothing to prove that which they would like to see, would like to hear, they have to invent something.

You have to empty the bucket.

On her knees she keeps scrubbing the floor of the hallway without changing the water.

It'll all get dirty again anyway, once you open the door to the attic.

The mother takes the bucket, carries it down the stairs, and empties it outside the door. The daughter gets up, goes slowly down the stairs and out in front of the house, gets the bucket, fills it with water and detergent, and continues her work. Their lies are mean and terrible. They invent something about her and the idiot. The idiot, who only gets a shave once a month and whose hands and feet are wrapped in rags. The idiot is older than she is, much older, but younger than her father, much younger. From afar it looks as though the idiot were awfully dirty. Because he's always dressed in black rags. She knows what he looks like up close. He isn't dirty at all. Does anyone else give him chocolate. The neighbor certainly doesn't. If she lets him run around in rags, then she won't give him chocolate either. How come he knows about chocolate, then. Maybe the neighbor does give him chocolate for Christmas and for his birthday. Does he know what that is, to have a birthday. Do they celebrate his birthday. Now she remembers, Madam once gave a chocolate bar to the idiot. Someone, it must have been the mother, must have told her that the idiot liked chocolate. The weather was nice, Madam looked outside one of her windows and saw the idiot preparing to go into the woods, that's when Madam took a chocolate bar out of her big, colorful wooden cupboard. The idiot was running as fast as usual, at first Madam wanted to meet him halfway but hesitated because he came toward her so rapidly, now Madam no longer held the chocolate bar out in front of herself as she had just a moment earlier when she stepped out of the house, the idiot kept coming closer, now she couldn't turn around anymore and put the chocolate away, it would have been an unfathomable cruelty, the idiot had already gotten a glimpse of the chocolate when she was still standing in the doorway, that's when the mother came from the barn with the milk pail in hand, she saw that Madam was afraid that the idiot would touch her if she were to give him the choco-late, because that was what she hadn't thought of when she had spotted the idiot outside her window in his black rags, what if the idiot not only looked into her eyes and mumbled something or croaked or took a bow, but grasped her hand, trying to thank her by shaking her hand. The mother understood all of this instantly, she approached the two of them, she took the chocolate bar and put it into the idiot's hands. That's how it must have happened. It was Madam and the mother. The more she thinks about it, the clearer the scene becomes before her inner eye, how the idiot took a dozen bows before Madam, and she hears the incomprehensible grunts the idiot utters to thank Madam for the chocolate.

The two years would be over, they would have kept their vow, he would be setting the date for the marriage. His parents and relatives would not only be troubled, they would be angry because they had been wrong. Her groom would ask his cousins to congratulate her. Nobody would come. Then she would receive support from someone she hadn't counted upon: his mother. She would announce that she, too, had objected to the bride, as everyone was aware. The bride, however, had comported herself in a manner as exemplary as anyone could have in her place, she was now convinced that she did indeed love her son, he loved her, and she extended her blessings. Even though her husband wouldn't agree with her, he wouldn't do anything else against the wedding. On their wedding day the house of her in-laws would be awash with flowers. Not many of the relatives would come, just the doctor and a few aunts. They would be riding to the wedding in a carriage, she would be wearing a white wedding dress. All of her siblings would be there, including her younger brother. Her father-in-law would furnish a house for them, and he would be very satisfied with his son who proved his excellence within the company. Their happiness would be overshadowed, however. She would be trying to give her in-laws the only thing she could give them: a baby. She, her husband, her father-in-law, and most of all her mother-in-law would be so happy if she were to have a baby. She would actually become pregnant. She would go to the gynecologist to take a test, and the test would be positive. The good news would be spread immediately to all the relatives. Even those who had always rejected her would perhaps be somewhat happy about it. But a terrible disappointment would follow. She would go to the doctor again, and the doctor would be surprised to see that her body wasn't undergoing any changes, and he would find out that she wasn't really pregnant and that there was no baby. The doctor would certainly be embarrassed, he had never encountered anything like this. He wouldn't be the object of all the anger. An imaginary pregnancy. She would be drowned in scorn and derision and malicious accusations. They would say that it really wasn't an imaginary pregnancy, that she had deceived everybody. Why. To get on her mother-in-law's good side. Even though it all would come to light so quickly. Everybody would turn their back on her, the in-laws would be first, soon followed by those who had accepted her cautiously, the doctor, the aunts. Only her husband would stand by her. He would have a difficult time because at work there would be ceaseless talk about the so-called comedy of her pregnancy. The bread manufacturer's sons in particular would agitate against her. A considerable rivalry had always existed between the bread manufacturer and her father-in-law. Those two employed the most workers, the construction company and the furniture factory were much smaller, and whoever owned the largest business also enjoyed the best reputation. The bakers would make disparaging remarks about their uncle and his son and daughter-in-law wherever they went, so that they would receive less business. Her husband wouldn't do anything about it, stricken with grief because of the falling out with his parents. Not until he lost what had been a guaranteed city contract would he take the bakers to task. He would drive to the bread factory, all by himself, the secretaries and other coworkers would overhear everything, in the end the bakers would even attack him, he would have an easy time defending himself against the two of them, he would be leaving the factory without a scratch, his foes would have bleeding noses. She would try everything to become pregnant, to deliver, as it were, on the promise already given, but just like her second-eldest sister she would not become pregnant.

The bakers wouldn't be able to forgive her their humiliation. Although acting as though the conflict was settled, they would be scheming to kill her and her husband. They would wait until summertime. Her husband would become suspicious, and at some point he would say that it was precisely because the bakers were keeping so silent that he believed them to be planning something truly frightening. She would try to calm him, the bakers wouldn't be capable of going that far, the bakers had suffered their defeat, the bakers wanted to forget everything. She wouldn't believe her own words, and he would only pretend to believe her. On that day it wouldn't be raining like it is today, and they wouldn't be in a narrow valley. They would have their house in a suburb of Linz, surrounded by parks, yet within a few minutes of downtown. When it rained there, it was a soft rain, you could step outside and hardly get wet, even if you were to stand exposed in the rain, because the rain spread out smoothly across the land, it also wasn't as dark as it was here, they would have large windows, not small ones like here in this old house built from rocks found on the river bed, and their house would have a lot of light-colored wood in it. On that day the heat would be stifling. Her husband would be home early, and they would go to bed soon. The bakers would arrive shortly after midnight. One of them would kick the iron garden gate. The maid, hired by her mother-in-law on the suggestion of the bread manufacturer, would hear the noise from her apartment above the garage, she would come down and open up the gate and the front door for the two of them, and she would lead them to the bedroom door. Because the maid had told them that the door was always locked, the bakers wouldn't even try to open it. They would fasten a stick of dynamite that they had brought along to the doorknob and ignite it. They were afraid that she and her husband would manage to escape in the meantime if they tried to open the door by other means. The bakers blow up the door and rush to the bed, surrounded by darkness and smoke from the explosion, and stab at it with their knives and shoot at it with their guns. But the bed is empty. The room is empty. They run out onto the balcony, there is nobody there either. Her husband heard the noise the bakers had made to wake up the maid, he stepped out onto the balcony and saw the maid as she let the bakers in. The bakers aren't here all by themselves, they have brought along helpers from their business who are searching the entire property. They know their victims haven't escaped, those who were waiting by the cars must have noticed the escapees. She and her husband are hiding where nobody is going to look for them, in the room of the maid who betrayed them, in her closet. Finally, the bakers resort to a ruse. After searching for a long time they leave empty-handed. Of course they take the maid with them, so she will later on be able to claim that she wasn't around. An hour passes, several hours pass, everything remains silent in the house. Her husband tells her that they mustn't leave their hiding place, the closet in the maid's room, under any circumstances. Morning comes, and still everything is silent. She cannot stand being confined any longer, her husband says she must not get out, it's still too dangerous, she opens the door anyway and gets out. She's so happy to be breathing freely and stretching her limbs. The new day casts its warm rays through the window in the maid's room. Carefully she approaches the window and leans out, just then a shot rings out. The bakers and their helpers left with their cars but have come walking back, they have surrounded the house and have fired as soon as she appeared in the window. Sinking to the floor, she clutches the window sill, her husband rushes to her aid, the one who fired the first shot fires several more, he hits her, he hits her husband, at the same time the two bakers and the helpers are already rushing up the stairs to the maid's room, they push the door open so violently that it springs back at them, they push it open once more and pounce on her and her husband with their knives, wounded by the shots, they cannot put up any resistance, the bakers and their helpers attack her and her husband in a frenzy, they butcher her and her husband with their knives, and they fire their guns until they're empty long after they have stopped moving.

The reader was expecting a different story. Perhaps the one in which the heroine always takes advantage of the situation when her father is building the Autobahn and her mother is out shopping with her neighbor for once, and she knows not only where the key to Madam's room is, she also knows in which closet Madam keeps which dirndls. Madam goes by the principle that when in the country, one should dress appropriately, too. That's why her closets contain an exemplary collection of folk costumes. Her choice is limited insofar as some of the designs are in keeping with Madam's minor endowment, but not with that of our heroine. Among those to be ruled out due to shortness of breath are of course the very ones whose patterns our heroine likes best. Furthermore, the story would have to include someone for whom one could dress up in those clothes. Perhaps a young toolmaker, like the third-eldest sister's husband, only more handsome. He should be strong and tall, he may very well have somewhat longer hair, most of all he shouldn't be too old. He courts her. She's not allowed to go out with him, but he often comes to visit. Her mother is always there, of course. She cannot complain, since all the two of them do is sit together in the living room. Perhaps the admirer could also be a little less assiduous but instead much more charming. Possibly he is not a toolmaker but a metalworker, and his hair is even longer. Maybe he has been changing jobs more than once, and right now he's not working at all. That's why he can come over all the time. But he mentions this neither to the daughter nor to her mother. One day she would tell him that if he were to come the next day, she would have a big surprise for him. It would be when her mother was not around, when nobody was around. It's summer, and the weather is beautiful. She meets him on the way to the Teichl, in the shadow of the apple trees bending over the path, he knows it's her, her figure, her walk, but it cannot be her, it must be Madam, it cannot possibly be Madam, it's her, but she looks like Madam. In defense of our heroine it should be mentioned that Madam hardly looks after her property anymore. Which is not surprising, her principal property is so much larger than this outpost, what's surprising is that she once looked after it with such care, even though everything was blessed from above, judging from the crimson colors the priest was wearing. Because Madam visits her property so rarely, it's exceedingly unlikely that she'll ever come upon our heroine wearing her clothes. Perhaps Madam has also lost all interest in her collection of folk costumes. Perhaps all she wears these days are suits made of loden or linen, not folk costumes, just clothes with so-called folk elements, with horn buttons and leather trim. In that case she wouldn't even notice the wear on some of her folk costumes. Looking at the dresses you can't tell, but looking at the blouses you can. It's very unlikely that Madam put a blouse she had worn back in the closet without washing it. That she put several blouses she had worn back in the closet without washing them. She could wash the blouses, she would have to hang them in her room where her mother could come in at any moment. Who will call her to task. Mother or Madam. It would certainly be better if it were Madam. Mother will be very angry. Father will beat her. Mother professes her infinite regret about it to Madam, it means that Madam cannot trust her. Because it's her mistake, not her daughter's. She's the guardian of the house, it's her responsibility. She didn't notice it, didn't prevent it, she let it happen. She's the one who's guilty. But how can she punish her daughter. What else can she forbid her daughter to do, given that she isn't allowed to do anything as it is.

It would still be terrible. A clash with Madam, on the other hand. She strolls underneath the apple trees, and the one who's not coming is the toolmaker or the metalworker—perhaps he didn't even finish his apprenticeship—but Madam is there instead. Madam wouldn't raise her voice. What happened would only intensify her melancholy. Years ago it would have been different. She would have had to answer to her about which dress, which blouse she had worn how often, and Madam would have been hurt because this dress she put on whenever, and that dress she had worn when—it would have crushed something. But her folk costumes no longer hold Madam's interest. All she would do is to have all the blouses washed and all the dresses dry-cleaned, with a gesture of resignation. Madam would try to lecture her gently, would even try to understand her in the end.

The owner of the carpenter's shop is driving a Japanese jeep with a high clearance that makes the tires look thin and narrow. It has stopped raining in the meantime, the sky is still covered with clouds, but there's not even any haze left in the air, the valley and the mountain ridges are visible in sharp outline. The visitor has driven his car right up to the front door, the wipers are still running, water is dripping from the trees onto the path, but nobody is getting out of the car.

The hallways on the first and second floor are clean, as are the stairs. Everything is waiting for the cloud of dust to come down from the trap door, soon to be opened by the expert.

When the visitor finally gets out, he's clad in green and gray hunting attire, mother has put on freshly washed gray pants and a clean blue apron, he greets neither the daughter who looks him straight in the face, nor the mother who extends her hand. He also ignores the roof, the reason why he came.

Mother takes him into the living room where she has prepared lunch.

The wife is well.

Yes.

The daughters, too.

Yes.

The son's working hard.

Is it really Jo whose voice filled the house whenever he stepped inside to greet Madam. Is it he who dominated the trophy show in Kirchdorf simply by being there. Can this be the same one who once persuaded the wife of a fellow hunter to do a naked table dance with a pig's trotter in her hand during one of Madam's parties.

He doesn't look ill, he hasn't lost any weight, he doesn't have that many wrinkles, and he's also not as gray in the face as some others who were Madam's guests along with him.

His gaze has grown lifeless.

The mother spoke to the daughter of a mental illness. Madam dropped hints when she notified the mother that he was coming to look at the roof frame. A hunting guest from Linz whom Madam had sent was talking. The daughter was able to follow the conversation only in part because she was working in the kitchen. Whether anything had happened in the family. Nothing, just the usual rivalries. Whether anything was wrong with the son. No, even though the two girls were more intelligent than the son, he was very industrious and very well respected by the coworkers in the carpenter's shop. The wife. The wife was always lamenting and whining, she had always been whining and lamenting. He wasn't feeling ill. He took exception to the suggestion that he was ill. His wife as well, by the way. He said that age was making itself felt somehow. He was going to work, he was going hunting. The fact that he wasn't talking all the time—was there always a need to talk.

Don't you want to take a look at the roof.

Mother gets up, the visitor doesn't pay it any mind. He turns the glass back and forth in his hands, he doesn't look up while doing so. Mother sits down again.

The daughter didn't want to appear before her future father-in-law like the child of a tenant farmer. She owed that much to her groom. For a long time she considered wearing one of Madam's dirndls. But she was no Madam, and she didn't aspire to be a Madam either. Finally, she decided on her blue jeans and Madam's red wool jacket. This way she could demonstrate that she was a modern young woman, and she didn't have to wear one of Madam's dirndls.

Mother couldn't prevent it, she didn't see the daughter until she was on the stairs, when the visitor's car was already parked out front. If the mother says anything, the visitor will mention it to Madam, then both she and the daughter will be helplessly exposed. If she can get a hold of herself and keep her mouth shut, he won't notice, he won't recognize the jacket. If he should recognize it, he'll think that Madam gave it to the daughter as a present.

Facing them, he'll be sitting like this forever.

Silent.

The glass in his hand, the lunch plate before him.

She never would have thought that it could be so easy to make way for her love. She thought that the father would resist his son's marriage with all his might. The father won't be standing in the way of anything or anyone. If his son had gotten her pregnant, as quickly as possible, and he had seen his grandchild as quickly as possible, maybe that would have wrested him from his disease. She wasn't even able to imagine what the disease was like. It would have been so easy. Her relationship with his son was the only thing that could have had an influence on his father's disease, the only thing that could have saved him. It's her fault if he's now completely absorbed in the darkness of his thoughts. She didn't believe. In her destiny. She wasn't true to the one for whom she was meant. She didn't have the courage to overcome even minor obstacles to their love. She didn't have any love for the one whom she thought that she loved more than anything else. Instead, she gave herself to someone who would never love her, who, now that she had given herself to him, despised her for the fact that she had given herself to him. She's not worthy. She would be left on her own just like her oldest sister. He who left her would do right. She could have had everything she had dreamed about. In addition, she could have saved the father. Her father, her mother, they knew from the start she wasn't worthy. But she isn't all bad. She wanted to deceive the groom, she wanted to deceive his father about the fact that she had given herself to someone else. The very instant she caught sight of this man lost in himself, she knew she wouldn't deceive him.

Why you wanna fix the roof. It'll go to pieces again anyway.

DEMIURG

XX.XX.

We only admire someone for their knowledge and skills if we don't know how they acquired them. If we can't do likewise. Should we indeed be able, perhaps by mere coincidence, to retrace their path, both the person and the path lose all mark of distinction. We push death aside because we're lazy by nature and because it was only death that forced us to learn. Even though so far we've covered only a fraction of the work ahead of us and have misunderstood that fraction. According to the general consensus, X has found out something about human nature. In my opinion, both Y and Z are wrong about crucial points regarding X. Even though I have to admit that Y is quite correct in his description of the historical connections that are indispensable for an understanding of the development of X's views. Z, on the other hand, points out several important and as yet unrecognized internal connections between various elements of X's architectonic that are helpful in making it more understandable, but they also reveal that this architectonic has to be restructured in light of W's objections. That's precisely what V is trying to do, drawing on U's work, whose influence on X was underestimated by Y. V's project cannot be brought to a conclusion, however, because he's relying too much on U. In my view, the seminal work of T has not been properly recognized to the degree it should have in this context—the outsider may recognize how the irregular, quivering constructs that are produced by the human mind claiming to make a systematic effort are ever increasing in size, how these constructs touch and intersect with one another, how ever new, irregular, quivering constructs emerge at the points of contact and intersection. He may see how irrelevant the later constructs are for the earlier ones. Any certainty about the processes of life modeled after the certainty of death would have to be absolute, and it would have to hold for everyone. Such certainty cannot exist. The assumption of its existence entails a contradiction because the prediction that the observer communicates to the observed robs the prediction of its unconditional truth. All certainty of human existence is constituted by death and by death only, death exhausts the amount of certainty handed down to humanity. Still, everyone continues to hunger for results to cling to, even if no one manages to cling to anything, even if there isn't anything that one could cling to.

That which will replace the systematically minded projects of the human mind will be free from the obsession with results, it won't judge concepts according to whether they are as certain as death, it will be born from the insight: describing man is beside the point, the point is to embody him. That which is to replace the production of systematic projects won't be production, of course. It won't do away with the quivering constructs because they at least offer solutions to a few questions whose resolution is a pre-requisite for that which is to follow. It will use the circles and their points of contact and intersection as a tool, without having to question the tool.

That which will replace the quivering constructs and their points of contact and intersection will overcome two gaps. These constructs are not just sets of propositions that have been uttered and written down somewhere but also that which isn't uttered anywhere but which is being done in the surroundings of that which is uttered and written down. This isn't the difference between theory and practice but the gap between that which is a sign and that which may not be a sign. If knowledge is embodied, there's no longer any difference between that which is uttered and that which is—as one is tempted to say: only—done. The second gap is that between the object and its concept. That which will replace the quivering constructs will also be the endpoint of the difference between the object and its concept. To embody is not to copy. To embody means to act consciously and independently. Computers were the first step, they made theories possible that couldn't be considered earlier because they cannot be handled with paper, pencil, and slide rule. There will be ever more and ever more powerful tools for the management of reality, which will bolster the notion that knowledge is no longer embodied only by theories but rather by things which at present we can't see ever having any epistemological import. Things will be absorbed into their concepts by things becoming concepts, and concepts things. It will no longer be possible to speak of things without mentioning people. Objects will be absorbed into their concepts by objects becoming concepts, and concepts objects.

xx.xx.

Predicting the future will be beside the point. The point will be to take the future into one's own hands. What we know as predictions will be embodied by actions. The sciences will first eliminate the trouble of producing goods—leaving us to ponder the Last Questions. The sciences will prolong life, first, by extending the physical life span and, eventually, by decoupling internal and external time. External time will no longer be a measure for internal time. Death won't be affected by this, but it will seem more distant and hence more obscure to the living. We will therefore have a somewhat easier time freeing ourselves from the obsession with events.

XX.XX.

Since you cannot describe that which is supposed to replace the systematic efforts of the human mind—do you at least have an idea of how to begin. I know, the next step is to stop pursuing goals. The consciousness of the certainty of death is lurking behind any goal, the consciousness that calls on us early on to put our affairs in order, to formulate goals, and to achieve them as well, so that our descendants can make sense of our life. You're always pursuing goals. If you don't want to pursue any goals, you're at least pursuing the goal not to pursue those goals that other people are pursuing.

XX.XX.

You need a very sure sense of taste if you want to abolish yourself. Which is becoming increasingly rare, because of the endemic lack of education among the carriers of systematic knowledge. It would therefore be asking too much to seriously require of those who hold jobs within institutions dedicated to the advancement of systematic knowledge that they should recognize and act on the result following from the history of their own institutions for their work.

XX.XX.

I was able to record those events that influenced each present time of my life and my experience. Soon, however, the ambition arose to also include all those events that crucially influenced the future of my life and my experience along with those events that influenced each present time. I noticed that oftentimes I had not recognized events at all that crucially influenced the future, or not as to their actual significance. Recognizing causes is a difficult business. I was observing more closely, and I perceived ever more events, which I scrutinized left and right for the influence they might exercise on the future. Each day I devoted a period of time exclusively to keeping my records, from the outset I'd therefore had to give up activities that couldn't be interrupted, I exceeded the time originally designated for my work on the diary more and more. In general, indicators of change are closer to the change than its causes, this renders the indicators easier to recognize than the causes. If you're lucky, an indicator sometimes is the cause. I decided to disregard the causes and to focus on the indicators instead. I recorded those events that influenced the present time, I scrutinized the events surrounding the first ones as to whether they functioned as indicators of changes in the future, and I traced those events that I had considered to be indicators. However, the transition from causes to indicators was a relief that unfortunately didn't last long. I was observing still more closely, and I perceived ever more events which I had to scrutinize left and right as to whether they did indeed represent indicators of changes, and, if that was the case, which changes they indicated. Once again I was back where I started, I had to put an excessive number of events in relation to each other, and I had to record an excessive amount, the daily period of time designated for this purpose was nowhere near enough. While I was working on the diary, I retreated from everything and everyone else. The ever-increasing amounts of time that I used to keep my records were tearing my life apart. I was faced with random fragments that I could interpret only in isolation, if at all. But that wasn't all. The diary even dominated what little time was left apart from my work on it. Every action was accompanied by the thought of whether and, if so, how I would record it. I committed everything to the diary, which, after being scrutinized for relatedness to all prior events, represented an indicator of impending change, all too often, however, it became evident soon afterward that no change would be effected after all, or that what did change was something other than what I had focused on, too often it became evident that an indicator either hadn't been an indicator at all, or that it had been an indicator for something other than that for which I had taken it to be an indicator. I was forced to adjust my method once again. I decided to insert a longer interval between happening and recording. While I used to record every day what had happened exactly one day earlier, I now wrote down every day what had happened exactly one week earlier. Even an interval of one week is of course not enough to weed out all events that will be irrelevant in the long run, but a still longer interval between happening and recording wasn't an option because then I would only have been able to remember very few details. Keeping a diary in this fashion enabled me to make do with less events, but problems cropped up when I tried to record my respective sensations. Oftentimes it is those events that are relevant for the formation of a sensation that neither influence the present time nor function as indicators of change in the future. At the moment I attach an expectation to an event, which will not be fulfilled, that expectation is my expectation at the moment. I succeeded in describing my sensations more reliably by including the events that caused them in my representation, even if those events would otherwise not have been among the ones worth recording, according to my other criteria. The reconstruction of my sensations presented me with a disheartening experience, however. I always believed that even though I wasn't as smart and as creative as others, at least I didn't delude myself like other people, I was convinced that I harbored the least illusions of anyone in my spatial and mental surroundings. When writing down that which had happened the previous day, it had often escaped me that certain expectations weren't met because at the point in time when it became obvious that they would never be met, they had often lost their significance to a degree that didn't justify considering each individual case. According to my new method, I was describing mental states almost on a daily basis that were influenced by expectations of which I knew even while I was writing that they would never be met. I was forced to acknowledge that I harbored infinitely more illusions than I had ever thought.

XX.XX.

There are some societies in which the living coexist with the dead, in which the living commune with the dead. For them, death isn't as big a step as it is for us. In those societies death is merely a transfer. Our death is the only one that's verifiable. Our death is an act of organization. You cannot be dead and undead at the same time. Our dead have become idols. Idols of organization. In a world that's endless, because of the absence of an endpoint for human beings, in a world without death as the end, you would have more than enough time to simply fiddle around to reach a set goal. If you set a goal for yourself at all. After all, it doesn't signify any change to pursue a goal if missing that goal can never be atoned for by the only suitable punishment, death. The dead cannot be separated from the living where the living coexist with the dead. The systematic efforts of the human mind are born of the unease that seizes you if you conceive of death as the end and not as a transition. From that point on you have to hurry to put your affairs in order. You won't be satisfied with guessing, you will want to know, you will therefore begin to search for artful dodges to facilitate your access to knowledge, and you will cultivate and refine these artful dodges.

Nobody who has ever worked on formal logic and who has come to realize how incredibly difficult it is to pull down even the simplest concepts from the semantic level to the syntactic level will be so silly as to think signs capable of a revolt. I'll save myself the trouble of an excursion into the cultural history of France, consisting for the most part in first making all conceivable human endeavors subject to a catalogue of proper manners, then forgetting the meaning and purpose of these endeavors once and for all, only to wind up philosophizing about the validity of the existing mores, especially if they're already in the process of decaying and dying out. It isn't reality that's in agony. It's those philosophers who aren't up to the task that the management of reality demands. Who turn their failure into an ideology by working up the difficulties encountered in the attempt to separate the real world—composed of multiple real worlds in a very complicated fashion—from other possible worlds into an impossibility.

XX.XX.

Most people only pretend to be writing their diaries for themselves when they are actually writing for posterity, hoping that the latter will preserve whatever is recorded in the diary for all time. If the records are of an exemplary quality, the character of the records will be similar to that of other records, of other writers—only that this character will stand out most prominently in the particular individual at hand. If the records should deserve recognition because the description or the thing described is precisely not exemplary—even then the character of the others bears on the attention paid to the author, you take the individual into consideration because he's different from the majority. I wasn't concerned about anything being preserved. I wanted to be able to survey how I live, how I experience things. Something happened, I did something, I sensed something, and I wrote it down, I thought I could gain a better perspective on that which was written down, I could relate it more easily to itself and judge and assess it more unambiguously than that which had happened, had been done, and had been sensed, but once I was faced with that which was written down, it was just as strange and inaccessible to me as that which was happening, was being done, and was being sensed. I had taken a wrong path from the event to the act of writing down. An argument suggested itself. The right path from the event to the act of writing down presupposes a theory. A theory that will give me a general perspective on my life. The perspective that I seek to attain in my diary. If the argument were valid, it would be impossible for people to ever fashion unclear ideas into clearly structured systems of thought, therefore I felt justified in assuming that my way of recording events contained something that might eventually lead me piecemeal toward the intended perspective. There was no other possibility—if I didn't make this assumption, any progress toward the intended perspective would have to be ruled out completely. But nothing in my records suggested so much as a hint of a perspective to come. To the contrary. The records put the act of recording increasingly into question, the more I went through what was written down, the less certain I became about what and how to go on recording. I ended up being at a complete loss about how to record what was happening. I couldn't decide how to describe what I had done, how to record what I had sensed—so I provided several versions of what had happened, what I had done, and what I had sensed, which were all compatible with the external sequence of events and of which it could be said with a certain degree of probability that things had happened their respective ways. But the more I wrote, the more certain I became that I would never reach a point when anything would be clearer to me than at any point when I had not yet been writing a diary.

TRIGGER

You did know that I was a man. You didn't mind. To the contrary, you were even attracted by it. You came to me time and again. You could have gone to Mary, but you came to me. You could have gone to so many others, but you only came to me. Don't say that I was hiding something from you. Mary heard the honking and drove to my car, she opened the door, I fell toward her, unconscious, and everything was soaked in blood. When I woke up briefly, I told her a client stabbed me in the chest with a knife and took the bag with the money and the papers. She asked right away whether it was you, because I had told her that you would come. Then I fell unconscious again. Mary doesn't believe me. She told the police that I had been waiting for you and that I wasn't really afraid of you. She knows what you look like, but she doesn't know your name. You can rest assured. I testified that it wasn't you. They asked how it happened. I told the police it was a client who had seen me three times before. I had always asked for the same amount, fifty, and had told him the first time around that I used to be a man and that I'd had an operation. He got into the passenger seat, he pulled down his pants, and I gave him a blow job. All of a sudden he remembered that I was a man, and randomly began stabbing me with a knife. I didn't threaten you, and I didn't insult you. And you never said that you have a problem with gays. I didn't disgust you, you said you didn't care that I'd had a sex change. I testified, he didn't know at all where he had struck me. It didn't seem like he did it for the money, he was well dressed. They won't figure out it's you. They can't figure out it's you because I described someone completely different. You say it's my fault that it wasn't working. I tried, but it wasn't working. Even though it always used to work. You shook your sleeve, and the knife fell out, you took it between your thumb and your index finger and stabbed me. You went through my purse and looked at the pictures that I kept in my purse. You wanted to know what I used to look like. You didn't say a word when you stabbed me. You had been drinking, but you're used to alcohol. I pulled the knife out myself and honked the horn. Before you came to me, you went to Kim and to Liz. Then you came only to me. You said you liked my hair and my skin so much. You couldn't feel at all that I had once been a man. You said I was doing it better than the others. You think I didn't tell you the first time, not until the second time. That's not true. I told you the first time. You think I disgusted you, that's why you wanted to kill me. I didn't disgust you, otherwise you wouldn't have come back time and time again. You only wanted blow jobs. You never wanted anything else. You were aroused when you got in my car. I didn't want to pull out the stun gun from the door pocket, we weren't fighting, I was just looking for some handkerchiefs, you held me back, I bit your left arm, that's when you stabbed me. I called for help, you put your hand over my mouth, and I bit your finger. You only remember one stab. We both got out of the car, I ran to the exit of the parking lot, you drove off. I wasn't injured all that badly. Maybe you think that you still saw me when I was stopping a car. When you were with me for the first time, you told me that you had wanted to be a race car driver. Before the war you had even participated in races, but during the war a bullet had shattered your right kneecap, you couldn't race anymore, that's why you shifted to constructing sports cars, and you own a sports car company. You can't drive the cars you construct to the limit because your injury bothers you so much. I didn't ask what your sports cars were called, after all, you were born long after the war. You liked the fact that I didn't ask and that I didn't say I didn't believe you. The next time, you told me that you had wanted to be a concert pianist. At three you were already playing the piano, you were so good that you played recitals when you were still in school. But your father was against music, you were supposed to become an engineer and be playing technical games. When your father had already accepted that you didn't want to become an engineer, you suddenly lost interest in playing the piano. You stopped practicing, you no longer made any progress. Your mother was very upset about this and became very ill. She eventually died of grief. When your mother was dead, you started practicing again. You attended the conservatory while going to school, you won competitions and played to big audiences. When your father asked you once more to become an engineer, you dropped music. You told me about your father's companies, about your construction companies, about your machine factories. You're not a pianist, but I didn't mind when you told me these things. It wasn't just one stab, I didn't get out either, I remained in the car. You think you were also carrying the knife to protect yourself when you went to Kim and to Liz. What could Kim and Liz do to you. You weren't carrying the knife. You think you were carrying the knife each time you came to me, something could have happened to you every time. I always took off your jacket, there was no knife. Only the last time, that's when you were carrying the knife. You can't understand why you became so angry. You had your mind set on the idea that it had to be working no matter what. And then it ended up not working. Your father is in all the papers. They always ask him about the formula for his success. In one of the papers, your father talked about the formula for his success. He was trained as a metalworker, he soon became self-employed and simply built the machines and, later on, the houses that people wanted, and even at seventy he's still in the main office every Saturday morning at seven-thirty. What they wrote about you, as you know, was that one day you won't be able to do it all by yourself. In another paper, your father said that there can be no formula for success. It's not that he wouldn't be willing to give away the formula for his success, that he wouldn't say why he's so successful, if there is a formula for success, then everybody will follow it, there can't be that many big companies. They asked him if he wouldn't be willing to tell their readers a little something, it needn't be the formula for his success, just a few helpful clues. From helpful clues the readers would be able to deduce the formula for success, clues are as good as the formula for success, there is no formula for success, hence there aren't any clues either. You always wanted me to stroke your head when I got you off. You wanted me to keep my hand on your head if you couldn't come right away. Once you even got yourself off, and I had to stroke your head. When you stabbed me, you said, that's for you, you people have no right to live, I said, I don't deserve this, you said, I'm gonna give it to you. I pulled the knife out of my chest and threw it under the seat where you couldn't reach it. You wrestled with me, you wanted the knife back, I couldn't escape, I had pushed the power locks, my head was underneath the steering wheel, I kicked the windshield in because I was so afraid. You knew from the start that I used to be a man. When I asked you if it bothered you, you said no, that's why I'm coming to you. When you stabbed me, your face was terrifying and twisted with hatred. In a magazine, your father was once asked what bits of advice he's passing on to his son and his daughter. Your father said that if there's anything he wants to pass on to his son and his daughter that's useful to them, he mustn't tell what he's telling his son and his daughter to anyone else, lest the other children should beat his children to it. Or else he has to tell the other children the opposite of what he's telling his children. The woman from the magazine promised that she wouldn't be telling the readers anything. The woman was very pretty. Your father said that the will is the most important thing. You have to question yourself very seriously whether you really have the will to be successful. You have to set a goal for yourself and be willing to do anything under any circumstance to reach your goal. You must never talk about it. You must deny having the goal you have. You must not imitate anyone. Least of all anyone who had a similar goal and reached it. You have to think everything through carefully, and then act as you see fit. You should always remain true to yourself in the process. The woman from the magazine asked whether that was all. Your father then said that you can also be successful doing something that someone else has already done. He had another comment. He said that you don't necessarily need to set a goal for yourself. And he had a comment on his comments. You can also be successful without the unbending will to achieve something. You told me you were the shortest kid from kindergarten all the way through school. When pranks were played, you often took the beating because you didn't run away. You're over six foot two, you can't ever have been the shortest. You say you're not easily influenced and not inapproachable either. You don't have any particular dislikes. You told me that when he was younger, your father was bursting with energy and that he still takes on everyone he can, everyone but the customers, of course. How he even kicked out the chairman of the workers' committee one day, which cost him a lot of money, of course, but who's even capable of getting rid of a chairman of the workers' committee at all. No one remembers what prompted it, only how your father got so angry that any further cooperation became impossible. I think that his lack of self-control was never really to your father's detriment. You kept the knife you stabbed me with in your right hand, even though you're left-handed. I didn't even put up a fight, I passed out right away, I was probably unconscious when I fell forward, slumping over the wheel and hitting the horn, I didn't wake up until Mary found me. It wasn't the first time that you lost all self- control. Back then you first choked me with your hands and then with the red wool scarf. We'd been having sex for a while, I don't know what made you stop coming around. You told me you were the director of an advertising agency. You were still so young, but you had money. Back then you already furrowed your brow just as mockingly as you do now. You said that you were married and that your wife had a lover. Once you told me that you had just caught your wife with her lover. Your wife was still in bed, her lover was getting dressed. You took your wife to task, you wanted a confession, I didn't understand why you wanted a confession in that situation, and you shook her until she passed out. I believed you, and I didn't believe you. It was possible that everything had happened like that. Then we saw each other again by chance at a party. First we didn't talk to each other, you were talking with one of my friends, she told you that I was pregnant, I danced with other people, finally you got a chance to talk to me, you asked me whether you were the father of my child. I said no, and you walked off again. It ended up getting very late, you approached me again by the exit, you wanted to have sex with me. I let you accompany me for a bit. We passed a streetcar stop, I sat down to rest a little. That's when you started getting affectionate. I let it go on for a while. When you tried to unbutton my pants, I said, but I'm pregnant, and I fought back. That's when you tried to take me by force. You dragged me down, pressed your knee to my stomach, you pulled down my jeans, my pantyhose, and my panties. While you were undressing yourself, I was able to button my pants and got up quickly. You dragged me down again and pulled down my pants once more. You tried to spread my legs, you knelt between them and lay down on top of me. I turned away once again. When you saw that you couldn't penetrate me without the use of force, you decided to kill me. You no longer tried to penetrate me, you just held me down. For two minutes you deliberated how to kill me. Finally, you choked me with both hands. I fought back, but my strength soon failed. When pedestrians came, you covered my mouth so that they couldn't hear my groaning. When they had passed, you put your ear to my chest to find out whether my heart was still beating. Then you wrapped the red wool scarf around my throat and pulled with both hands. For three minutes, until it tore. You were ashamed because you had tried it once, and it hadn't worked. Later you said that you hadn't known that I was pregnant. Why then did you ask me who the father of the child was. You were always thinking of me, but you didn't try to contact me, it was mere chance for us to be meeting at the party. You complained that first I got you hot, and then I left you hanging. I leaned over toward you, I even grasped your hand briefly, I went along with everything, I only changed my mind right before you were able to penetrate me. Why should I tell anyone that you were the one with the red wool scarf. Why should I tell anyone that you were the one with the knife.

A STORY FROM THE EIGHTIES

At least Jürgen had a human motive. He wanted to be successful. The terrible thing about you is that you really don't care about anything but your thought constructs. People will be absorbed into their concepts by people becoming concepts, and concepts people. People will be absorbed into things by people becoming things, and things people.

She was standing in the doorway between the two middle rooms. He said, when I first met you, you were wearing the short brown skirt. She turned around and asked what made him bring up the brown skirt now. He said, you seemed taller to me back then. She said she didn't believe that she'd gotten shorter since then. He said that so far he had only lived in new buildings whose ceilings weren't as high. She asked, does your contemplation of heights contain a definition or a claim. He said that he hadn't pondered that question. She said that she no longer owned the skirt.

Dear —

Am just all by myself—no wait, next to me there are—in my bed, which gives me the opportunity to tell you about my first meeting with—

The narrator wished that this were a time in which river dams and tunnels represented achievements, and in which people were wearing antimagnetic watches. In that case the narrator would choose to begin in the following way.

To every point of a finite, bounded, and convex set, a subset is assigned. If the set assigned to every point is convex, respectively, and if the correspondence is upper semicontinuous—

He would have to finish this sentence right now, though.

If there is a fixed point, this means that at least one point belongs to the respectively assigned set.

Under which circumstances—

No, no, no.

She crosses a park in front of a tall building gleaming like metal. The building is about four times as wide as it is high. The windows are rectangular, about twice as wide as they are high, they are equidistant both horizontally and vertically. She counts fifteen stories. The entire outer edge of the flat roof is lined by a black frame set on narrow pillars about three stories high. The frame encloses four big rectangular chimneys. Next to the building there is a collection of low-rise factory buildings and a round chimney made of bricks towering over the other factory buildings. The park is deserted. Gravel paths line the lawns on which trees and bushes are growing, artificial hills and basins have also been created. On one part of the lawn there is a playground with a small log cabin, a seesaw, a swing, and a jungle gym. The trees have already lost a lot of leaves, the bare ends of the branches are jutting out from the center of the tree tops, which still have foliage. The sky is overcast. A light wind is blowing the fallen leaves around. Lamps have been placed along the paths at larger intervals, built from circular discs mounted on narrow pipes about three feet high. The gray metal covers are rusted, the rain is running down along the white plastic trays and the white steel pipe.

She had fallen in love with me.

1. They like you a lot. They don't object to you coming over or going out with me.

I would be a hiding place. *I* would be the omniscient narrator for sure. *I* would be someone who would definitely want to hide inside the omniscient narrator.

2. But they were angry about the two of us being alone. From now on I'm not supposed to let anyone come in when I'm home alone. I'll have to take a walk with the person in question until they're back home. Were they ever pissed, I tried to pacify them, didn't know you were coming, after all, etc. You came over by chance and unexpectedly, right?

Why hadn't I given her a reprint. I explained that I had simply forgotten about it. I said that I was sorry, I knew that the article had to be interesting to her.

A minor insult, which shouldn't serve as an excuse for the narrator to fragment himself into numerous selves that are irrelevant to the events.

He should recognize the responsibility he would have to accept because of this. She considered giving up all contact with him because she no longer knew what she was doing, and because she didn't want to go behind his back. At that time he was suffering from stomachaches so violent that he had to stay home for days and was sleeping almost twenty-four hours a day under the influence of pain killers and sedatives. She made chamomile tea and turkey breast for him, and she did his mail because he didn't want to admit to his secretary how badly he was doing, she wrote out parts of his studies and took calls from colleagues and clients.

Selves have proper names. But it's so difficult to use them.

She said she couldn't tell him what he should do. He replied that this came as a total surprise to him. He liked to be with her, but he had never thought ahead. The conversation took place on a Sunday afternoon. A few days later she had sex with him. After a concert that had ended early. She was wearing tight jeans and a loose-fitting dark-blue silk blouse. He sat down next to her, kissed her on the mouth, and started unbuttoning her blouse. First she let him do his thing, then she got up and paced the room, finally squatting down next to the record player. Had he thought about what he was doing. He didn't feel like thinking right now. The record stopped playing right then. Jürgen walked to the record player, put another record on, took her by the hand, and led her back to the couch. There he proceeded to undress her, taking off the black bra, taking off the black panties.

It was back in the days when God didn't protect the audience from *Adaptations for the Stage.* The audience was impressed, she was talking to a friend on the phone about the performance of *In the Matter of J. Robert Oppenheimer,* by Kipphardt, with Mensching and Rehberg, just as Klaus walked in the door. He put her on the spot, they had made plans to see the play together. She explained that Jürgen happened to have two tickets, he asked whether she would like to go with him, and she had accepted on short notice, given that he, Klaus, hadn't been around. She would love to go see it again with him. Why didn't she tell him about it. She went on that she did end up feeling uncomfortable about having accepted the invitation because he, Klaus, had asked her first. He then went over to the phone, dialed Jürgen's number, reaching him as expected. For a while they talked about the progress Jürgen was making constructing his unbiased models. Klaus then directed the conversation toward the theater. Only to end up asking Jürgen if he had seen the play about Oppenheimer yet. Jürgen answered in the negative. He assumed that an acquaintance had seen him and her together, and he figured that it was more plausible for him not to admit the entire evening by denying also that he himself had already seen the play. He added that a friend of his had gone to see the play and recommended it, he was planning to go see it the next chance he got. Klaus replied what was that supposed to mean, she had told him that she had gone to see *Oppenheimer* with him. Jürgen answered that there had to be a mistake, it wasn't true that she had been to the theater with him.

I'd had sex with Klaus more frequently only in the beginning of our relationship. Since we had moved in together, he no longer touched me. He had stomachaches, he was thinking about a study, he was tired. One time we had a party, even though I had a bad cold. My eyes were tear filled from all the cigarette smoke, I personally don't smoke when I have a cold. When I tried to fix my makeup without a mirror, there was a sudden silence, which he filled by remarking in a loud voice: Gallina scripsit. All eyes were on me as I was messing around with my makeup, handkerchief in hand.

I was always afraid that Klaus suspected something, and I was prepared for him to pretend that I had already confessed to something so that he would have his suspicions confirmed. I had told Jürgen that he shouldn't fall for it but should stick exclusively to what we had agreed on in each case. It was my mistake. I should have kept to what we had agreed on. I shouldn't have told anyone that I had been to the theater. After I had admitted having been to the theater, I should have named someone else as my company, someone less incriminating than Jürgen.

After the phone conversation, Klaus asked me whether I was involved with Jürgen. How long. I told him the truth. From that point on he no longer talked to me. He no longer slept in our bedroom but on the couch in his study. He started having breakfast at a café and dinner at a restaurant. After a week I told him that I wanted to move out. He reacted by packing his big suitcase. I asked him where to and how long he was going to travel, but he silently left the house with his coat and suitcase.

I started out from two existing accounts and formulated a new account which comprised the two existing accounts as specializations but which did not comprise any existing account that would not have been a specialization of the two existing accounts. Then I considered a third existing account and modified my account such that it comprised my first account and the third existing account as specializations. I tried to formulate a comprehensive model on the basis of a unified conceptual apparatus that would contain as many assumptions as possible, which, in turn, would be as unrestrictive as possible.

Before he has even made an appearance, the narrator has given in to the temptation of hiding himself inside him, the one he wants to hide from.

Inside her.

I was able to formulate the respective conditions for each case and to link them to the conditions for the proof of existence on the previous level in such a way that I could apply the proof of existence on the new level as well.

I had spent the night at Jürgen's. When I went through the papers on his desk simply because I was bored, I found the draft of a proposal for the continuation of his research project. The research foundation was doubtful whether his unbiased models would live up to his promises. He had thus written a proposal in which he set up *General Equilibrium Theory* as a straw man to take apart, so that he could present his unbiased models as the only way out of the dead end into which the profession had gotten itself. There was *no reasonable question* to which *General Equilibrium Theory* would have been the answer, *General Equilibrium Theory* couldn't deal with asymmetries in the *formation of goals* and the *choice of actions*, in the *threshold values for actions*, in the *velocities of action*, as well as relative to the agents' *varying capability to prevail*, according to *General Equilibrium Theory* every *field of conflict degenerates into a state of equilibrium*. His unbiased models accounted for all these asymmetries and provided undistorted accounts of the social system under investigation.

The narrator constructs many victims where there are only a few, he pits the victims against each other, he turns victims into perpetrators and perpetrators into victims, but he doesn't want to blur the line separating victims from perpetrators. There has to be a difference between her and the narrator, between the narrator and the others. It's no longer her fault if she's no longer *I*.

She's standing in the hallway and doesn't move. The floor is covered with textured black vinyl tiles, the walls are paneled with small gray ceramic tiles up to the ceiling. To her right, next to an unmarked door, there's a row of bucket seats made out of black plastic. Swinging doors in front of her, behind them it's dark, she cannot tell where the hallway is leading. To her left a row of windows. Neither the pavement of the courtyard nor the sky are visible. It is day. The facade of the building is covered with large rectangular aluminum panels. On the lower end, the panels are each edged at a forty-five-degree angle toward the front so the rain can run off on the outside.

3. They say you can come by anytime, just call first to ask if it's OK. You may even stay until 10:00 P.M. That's my curfew.

She was unable to write in her new apartment, she was unable to read in her new apartment. She called all her acquaintances. Until Klaus finally called. He still hadn't seen the play about Oppenheimer, so they wound up seeing it together after all. Afterward he remarked that the committee had acted correctly by considering Oppenheimer guilty of sabotage and denying him the security clearance. Oppenheimer hadn't been an outstanding scientific talent, he had no reason to hope for the Nobel Prize in physics, he had recognized this early on and had hence looked around for other projects that suited his ambitions. He had built the atomic bomb to make a career outside of pure science, for which he was suited particularly because of his unquestionable talent for organization. During the preparations for the building of the bomb he had already had his doubts, which he pushed aside without too much trouble, however. Once he had built the bomb, he could afford to look at things from an ethical point of view.

Which doesn't mean that he arrived at an unambiguous estimation, either as to whether it was right to build the bomb, or as to whether he should have tried to prevent its deployment. Haunted by these doubts, he was unable to forge ahead with the development of the hydrogen bomb. Of course the accusations suggesting a communist plot and attempted sabotage weren't valid. But he hadn't been loyal once he took his ethical stance, and he hadn't wanted to be loyal either, in that sense he had indeed committed ideological treason. Those who denied him the security clearance were right. Oppenheimer's story was a case in point against those who incessantly talk about the social responsibility of science and who demand of the scientist that when conducting his research he always take into account the significance that his actions may have for humanity. All that resulted from this reflection was aimless doubt. The bomb was going to be built over and over again, if not by one person, then by the next. Besides this version of Oppenheimer in his later years, there was also that other Oppenheimer of his early years. If all scientists were indeed to try to take into account all possible results of their actions, science would end up in a coma. She objected that human beings were obliged to try to act in an ethically correct manner, even if they knew from the start that they would never be able to live up to the respective standard. The fact that others were acting in an ethically incorrect manner did not constitute an argument for oneself to be acting ethically incorrect. The ethical assessment of the effects of scientific research should follow obligatory rules set in advance by all parties involved. He replied that even if people were to succeed in setting such rules, and if all steps of the research process were scrutinized, according to the rules, for their effect on all of humanity, the result still wouldn't necessarily be ethically superior to that of the first deployment of the atomic bomb. Empirical hypotheses routinely formed part of ethical assessments of the potential effects of a research project, hypotheses whose validity was so uncertain that they might as well be replaced by different, equally acceptable hypotheses that would, however, result in an altogether different ethical assessment.

The narrator considers putting her completely outside of time. She's short. She's petite, but neither fragile nor delicate. Her head is very large, sitting on her straight shoulders. Her face appears well proportioned. A full, wide mouth, brown eyes with long, natural lashes below contoured eyebrows, full, dark-brown hair, slightly parted in the middle, in something like a page-boy cut, covering both ears. A straight nose, well proportioned relative to the mouth. Her skin is fair and smooth, and slightly oily on her nose and forehead. When she steps right up to the mirror, she notices a few small wrinkles around her eyes.

If she doesn't consider her position outside of time to be a compulsory exile. If she finds a point from which she can force the narrator to deal with her on her own terms. An end to the philosophical You. He has to answer to her. He has to answer to himself.

She had formulated a comprehensive equilibrium model in which numerous unrealistic assumptions of important existing accounts had been replaced by more realistic ones. She now jettisoned the assumption of perfect foresight. This meant that she had to introduce probability distributions into the model. The existence proof raised a number of problems concerning measurement theory, requiring her first to treat certain ramifications of measurement theory in detail. The Philosopher, a friend of Klaus's like Jürgen, visited her as she was pouring over her dreaded books and articles, and they started talking. He made a living off capital gains. He was interested in particular philosophical problems. He was publishing, and he visited academic conventions. It would distort his perspective if he were to do so in connection with a teaching assignment or a teaching position. She went to see *Oppenheimer* for the third time with the Philosopher. He had tickets for the first row. The military had known from the start that Oppenheimer was a fellow traveler, he approved of parts of the communist program, and he was close to a number of people who defended it openly. The reports compiled by the FBI before his appointment as director at Los Alamos proved this point beyond doubt. The particular historical situation, however, represented a guarantee that he would live up to the security demands of loyalty and secrecy, because as director at Los Alamos he could contribute to the struggle against those who wanted to oppress the world only under these conditions. Oppenheimer was the ideal head of the project, precisely because of his obscure tendencies toward communist—or rather: liberal—ideas. Given that the majority of physicists working at Los Alamos were entertaining similar ideological precepts. A researcher embodying the right-wing ideas of the military never would have made the program a success. The scientists never would have accepted somebody who took the military's line without reservation as one of their own, and hence as their supervisor. The tool had done its duty with the completion of the atom bomb. Once the historical situation had changed after the victory over Nazi Germany, the scientists, too, realized the extent to which the Russian Revolution had betrayed its original goals, now a man like Teller, who used to be no more than an outsider, given his right-wing views, could assume an executive position. The military no longer needed a man like Oppenheimer. Of course the prosecutors on the committee didn't believe their own accusation that he had sabotaged the construction of the hydrogen bomb. They wanted to provoke a particular reaction on his part. The inane watchdogs were right as always. Dismissing the accusations leveled against him, Oppenheimer revealed in full when he'd had which doubts. That was what the prosecutors had been waiting to hear, he had been in violation of his duty to loyalty according to their standards, and he continued to violate it, which was reason enough now to deny him the security clearance.

4. You'll no longer have to be afraid of doors making a cracking sound. I've been guaranteed that she won't get in. I can count on that—

Klaus's boss Hermann never worked less than fifteen hours and never slept more than five hours. Not even during his brief vacations. Now he was working even more, sleeping even less, and making even more phone calls. He had done everything to get contracts for studies of the executive authorities. He had only managed to secure two studies each of the Departments of Foreign Affairs and Defense, despite his great efforts he had remained unsuccessful with the Departments of Trade and Finance. He had instructed the team leaders to go beyond each official study and to investigate procedural efficiency in those departments with which the team came into contact in the course of the study—keeping it strictly secret from the clients. This was unprecedented. He laid claim to tight resources for studies which paid either very little or nothing at all and which were, in addition, in violation of the code of ethics. Hermann confided in Klaus that he considered it his historical mission to extend the influence of the FIRM to the executive and legislative branches so that the country would be governed more efficiently. The consultants as nobility, the highest consultant as king. All the while he didn't show any signs of pursuing political goals with any content. Klaus was unable to raise even the slightest doubt in Hermann as far as his plans were concerned. Hermann would become extremely impatient and dismissive as soon as Klaus tried to get a word in against his goal to govern the country. Klaus was the only one whom he had told about his plans, he justified the studies for and about the executive branches to everyone else by arguing that he had to open new markets with new clients, besides, the influence one stood to gain would also benefit the old clients.

She was determined not to have sex with Klaus anymore. But when he told her about Hermann's plans, she was so upset that she betrayed her own intentions. The next morning Klaus remarked that now everything was almost back to normal, but with important improvements for both of them. She no longer had to worry about his shirts and his underwear, he was looking forward to conversing with her on select occasions and to having sex with her. He was once again in the mood for the latter, given that she was no longer planning to start a family with him. She cried. He added that she was sentimental. Two weeks later he called her to say that he wanted to marry her and have kids with her. He had barely gone out the door before starting to regret bitterly what he had done. He hadn't kept himself in check. Even though she was the only human being who understood him—at least part of the time. He had reached the conclusion that he had overreacted when he had found out about her affair, trying to see things from her point of view, he couldn't fault her at all for having sex with someone else, he had never been around, and when he had been around, he hadn't touched her. Ever since he had been living without her, he knew how much he needed her, he accepted the compromises he would have to make for a family, he was tired of the life he was leading now. She would be free to do as she wished, he would also tolerate her having sex with other men now and then, as long as her basic sense of loyalty to him was not in question. She should come back to him as soon as possible and move back into his apartment. He ended by saying that he loved her. He had never said that before. She replied that she couldn't say anything right now, she had to think about it, she would call him. He said he hadn't expected her to be jumping for joy.

If ever someone attempted to make General Equilibrium Theory conform more closely to reality, it was me.

If you were so concerned about reality, why didn't you go out to look and to measure? — Why did you do proofs instead?

You start with a simplifying model, and you adjust the model according to a plan in such a way that it becomes increasingly realistic. Looking and measuring alone don't help you decide anything.

The equilibrium theory of existence proofs investigates the conditions under which a specifically defined equilibrium is created. It doesn't make any difference if in the process you move from the question *How does the individual human being arrive at perfect foresight* to the question *How does the individual human being arrive at his own probability distribution.* The knowledge which General Equilibrium Theory assumes the individual to have so that an equilibrium does indeed exist and/or can be achieved always surpasses the knowledge available to the individual by means of direct observation. Applied equilibrium theory merely takes the definition of equilibrium, decides that the defined equilibrium states have been realized, completely neglecting the manner in which they may have been realized, only to go begging to the folks in time series analysis for some data to fit their exogenous variables. The data being plugged into the models of so-called applied equilibrium theory were collected neither by means of these models nor with them in mind but come from studies with completely different aims, and it remains unverified whether the manner in which the data were obtained even allows their use in these models.

Values obtained by measurement are assigned to the exogenous variables. Then you plug a number of different values into the variables for politics and calculate the new equilibria resulting from each step. These equilibria are compared to each other with respect to their wealth effect. Even though to describe the effect of a step not in fact taken means to describe a possible world, not a factually existing one, the point of departure is a state in which the variables for politics are assigned the values they in fact possess before the possible steps are taken.

Simplifications are always simplifications of something. What is the auctioneer a simplification of, as he is omnisciently fixing balanced quantities and balanced prices by means of *tâtonnement*?

In a disequilibrium model there's no longer any auctioneer to adjust prices right away.

In those models that dispense with the auctioneer, the individuals have to take on his tasks collectively. The assumptions necessary for this elimination replace God with destiny.

They went by car and took the ferry from Italy over to Greece. Because they had decided to go so quickly, they couldn't get a cabin. The ferry was scheduled to cast off at ten o' clock at night, but they didn't depart until two in the morning. Then they were lounging in their seats and couldn't sleep. The heat was stifling, they couldn't stretch out, all other seats were occupied as well, they couldn't even get up, the aisles were full of backpackers in their sleeping bags. The next day they were completely exhausted. They staggered around the boat, into the dirty washrooms and into the greasy self-service restaurant that didn't even serve coffee in the morning. The outer deck was teeming with backpackers who had slept outside. The boat did not have a pool. The only available luxury was the food in the restaurant for first-class passengers. Klaus tried to get the purser to give them a cabin for the second night, but everything was taken. Around midnight she got sick from all the wine she'd had to help her sleep. She had to vomit several times. She never made it to the washroom, she tripped over the people lying in the aisles, and she stepped on them, she covered her mouth with her hands, it was all running and dripping down, her blouse was heavy like a wet towel. Arriving in Greece the next morning, they gave up the plan to visit Athens and went straight to their island. Because of centuries of Venetian rule, a notable Italian influence was visible on the island, both with respect to the inhabitants and the architecture. Greeks with blue eyes and fair hair. The hotel was about two hundred yards from the water, the pool on a withered lawn between the beach and the hotel. The so-called breakfast buffet consisted of several rickety tables lined up next to each other, with the breakfast items stacked carelessly on them.

On the boat she had been ill, now she was doing well again. He, in turn, got sick after dinner. He spent almost the entire night in the bathroom. The next morning he had a high fever. She stayed in the room most of the time and tried her best to get chamomile tea and crackers for him. It took four days until he was back on his feet. As soon as he was healthy again, he started reproaching her. Why had they gone by car, why had they taken the ferry, if they had gone to Portugal by plane as he had suggested, he wouldn't be wiped out right now. All he ever did was catch diseases, even though it was important for him to relax during a vacation. She replied that she hadn't felt well either. When she came home, she would have the opportunity to recover from the holidays. He wouldn't be getting so much as a time-out after this.

For dinner they were seated next to a couple from Innsbruck. He was a bus driver for sightseeing tours and a bodybuilder in his spare time, his girlfriend was a tall, well-built blond who didn't speak. She had long straight hair falling across her face and large, beautiful breasts. In the evenings she always wore fishnet shirts. And extremely tight pants along with them. When tanning herself she was topless and wearing a G-string, his swimming gear was similar in kind. They didn't go to the beach, they were always lying by the pool, he on his back, she on her stomach, she would start stroking his navel until he turned around on his stomach as well. Klaus wanted to have sex with her on the evening he was able to get up. She did everything a woman in the dark can do to get her man aroused. She was sure that he was thinking about the blond at their table while she was struggling. But the blond wouldn't have achieved a different result—if she had touched him.

They were lying in the sand, she was in the sun, he kept himself in the shade, they swam, and they read. He, Joseph Conrad, she, Lernet-Holenia. Baron Bagge, among others. She wanted to make a trip to the grottos on the other side of the island. He didn't want to make any trips. He had resolved to do literally nothing whatsoever for the rest of their vacation. She went to the other end of the island by herself and took a boat over to the grottos. When she came back in the evening, he didn't say a word to her at first. After dinner he proceeded to get drunk. Two associates had already talked to him, wasn't he Hermann's confidant, what was the matter with Hermann. He had answered that Hermann was overworked but didn't want to admit that to himself. Everything Hermann had done up to now had always been for the best of the FIRM. He was unable to placate anyone with these remarks, of course. He was sure that meetings were already being held about Hermann. He couldn't fault them for not telling him about it because they had to assume he would pass on anything they told him to Hermann. She told him how things were with her thesis. He was nice enough not to remark that he had been saying so all along. They moved to a small hotel right on the beach and spent a few very happy days there. Until it was time to leave and he started planning. He asked her when she wanted to move back into his place. She evaded the question. He wanted to pin her down, but she wouldn't let herself be pinned down. He tried as hard as he could to keep himself in check so he wouldn't say anything to hurt her, something she would answer by rejecting his plans once and for all. The silent reproaches spoke louder than the explicit ones. She couldn't help him. She didn't want to help him. She didn't want to get his hopes up. She was afraid that she would let herself be dragged along. She knew how it was all going to end.

On the way back she had her period, the bleeding was unusually strong. Every time she moved, her underwear was soaked. Klaus forced himself to explain to the purser that she had to lie down, she was ill, he had to give them a cabin. After he had bolstered his arguments with an unbelievable amount of cash, they did indeed get a cabin. The heat was so stifling that she couldn't cover herself without immediately breaking into a sweat. She was lying on her back in the lower bunk and was wearing nothing but her panties, which were stuffed with several pads and looked inflated. She kept thinking about having a doctor called out, she couldn't go through with it in the end. When she got up to go to the bathroom, everything was spinning around her. In the car she lay down in the back seat. Klaus took her straight to the hospital when they came home. They told her that the bleeding was caused by a yeast infection that would heal quickly.

He hurts the other person before giving them the opportunity to hurt him first. If the other hurts him in turn, he can argue that what was done to him was the necessary revenge for his behavior, not only is he himself at fault, he consciously brought it about. Whenever he reduces the distance beyond a certain level, he's unable to prevent the distance from becoming increasingly and irreversibly smaller. Whenever he tries to understand the other, he puts himself in their position to such an extent that he acts against his own interests. He is helpless when he's not patronizing and arrogant.

Communication by way of language not only assumes agreement with respect to the definitions of the expressions being used but also agreement of select judgments arrived at by means of these expressions. If actions represent a language within General Equilibrium Theory—the values that the individuals give and take as signals are exactly that—it cannot come as a surprise that the creation of equilibrium states requires not only agreement with respect to the definitions of possible alternatives of action but also agreement of actions actually performed.

Some clients had already made remarks. Nobody knew how to go about relieving Hermann of his duties. How do you fire a superior who doesn't have a superior himself. How would Hermann react if he was told that he was ill, that he couldn't keep working. — The vacation had made him certain beyond doubt that he was intolerable. To her, to others, even to himself. He still wanted to marry her and have kids with her. But he would have to accept it if she didn't want to. She had learned from her mistakes, she had tried not to mother him while on vacation, still he had pushed her away. He had tried to keep himself in check, the best he had been able to do was to refrain from making reproaches. He knew that sex was important to her, he just didn't have much of an inclination toward that kind of business. It wasn't her fault. When they were having sex, he felt estranged from her and also from himself. He always felt that none of it concerned him and there really was no reason whatsoever to do what he was doing. To repeat, it had nothing to do with her, it was the same with other women. He was pushing her away on all levels, sex was only one of those levels, one that had also become less important to her over time. Had he ever thought about why he pushed her and everybody else away, not only sexually. Of course he could go to see a therapist. Like everyone else. Jointly they would poke around in his childhood, they would realize that the roles occupied by his parents had influenced him, they would find that his behavior toward women was rooted in his screwed-up relation to his mother, and so on. If he were to go to see a therapist, it would be the expression of a desire to become a different person. He had no desire to become a different person. He was his own misfortune. If a therapist were to get him to where he would be capable of having a continuous relationship with her, he would end up being a person completely alien to himself. He would never go to see a therapist. She had to conclude that his love for her was simply not strong enough to bring himself to attempt to change himself. She shouldn't be taking the easy way out. If he were to treat her differently, he would be a completely different person, and she shouldn't assume without any further thought that she would feel the same way she felt now about him about that other person. Besides, everything she was saying about his love he could also say about hers. When he had declared his love, her reaction had been silence, still she had gone on vacation with him. Something was still there. But it just wasn't big enough either. She couldn't bear to live a life the way he was imagining it, it was beyond her powers. She needed consistent attention, not consistent rejection combined with isolated occurrences of attention.

Sometimes she ran into Jürgen in the department. They would go for coffee and casually talk about their work. It was as though nothing had ever happened between them. His research project continued. Jürgen told her that Klaus was going out with Barbara. The Philosopher had introduced her to Klaus when they came over to look at his new apartment. Barbara had studied something in the humanities and worked as a waitress in restaurants whose customers considered themselves to be interesting and in the wool store where she did her own shopping. She knitted sweaters. Her hair was cut asymmetrically, short enough on one side to show the skin, and about five inches long on top and done to stick out horizontally on the other side. She was wearing white plastic glasses to go with it. She wasn't very tall, rather bony, her hips seemed a little wide.

One day Barbara called because she wanted to see her. They agreed to meet at the Chinese Tower. Barbara was wearing one of her hand-knit sweaters and a skirt and shoes from the fifties. It was a beautiful fall day, they went for a walk and were even able to sit outside. The question came up why Barbara was working as a waitress, given her education and her talent. She replied that she could quit anytime. She enjoyed doing too many things to be limiting herself to only one of them. She hated exclusiveness. She had once designed a collection and offered it to an apparel manufacturer who turned out not to be trustworthy, nothing ever came of it, she didn't feel like trying again.

Until she had talked to Barbara, she had been unable to imagine Klaus having sex with her. It just seemed outlandish. After talking to her, she couldn't imagine that he wasn't having sex with her. This wasn't about him, it was about her. Someone else wouldn't make the same mistakes she had made.

It was an option to forget about uncertainty concerning the future and to focus on the disequilibrium models. This would make for a good thesis only so long as she didn't tell anyone that she didn't discuss equilibrium in cases of uncertainty about the future because on reflection she had come to the conclusion that General Equilibrium Theory assumed a theory of action which couldn't be handled by its conceptual apparatus in a way that would exclude contradictions to indispensable assumptions. Nobody would have believed her. They would have thought that if she really believed this, she should have recognized it earlier. Whether she admitted to it or not, they would have assumed that she had been unable to handle the technical difficulties arising from the inclusion of uncertainty concerning the future.

The only one to whom she talked openly about her work was the Philosopher. He said that the doubts she had about her work pointed to a connection she had established between General Equilibrium Theory and the real world that others were utterly incapable of understanding.

When he wanted to go to the theater, she had to go with him to see the play he wanted to see. When he wanted to go out to dinner with her, she had to wait for him in the restaurant he could tolerate. When he felt like having sex with her, she had to come to his place and have sex with him. When he didn't feel like talking to her, she was not to disturb him with her presence under any circumstances either, in those cases not even a local call was in order because he didn't answer the phone, even if he had said earlier that he was going to be at home. To him she was only a tool to make his free time more interesting. She didn't tell anyone about it, just you. You were the only one who knew about my condition, how I was suffering from the difficulties I had with my thesis and from the failed relationship. You intentionally had me believe that she had gotten him to where I had never been able to take him. But their relationship was only the mockery of a relationship. I didn't know anything, and because I didn't know anything, I was upset and helpless. Which you took advantage of.

How did I take advantage of that.

You know what I mean.

No, I don't.

You wanted to have sex with me. Things worked out for you.

We didn't have sex.

We did have sex.

You said that if you'd had sex with me, you would only look me in the eye if I didn't remind you of it by way of any remark or gesture. You would erase any thought of it from your memory, such that you yourself wouldn't believe it if I were to come up to you one day and tell you that we'd had sex.

I had sex with you because I was desperate. I wanted you to trust me. You knew why I was desperate. You could have helped me if you had told me what you knew. But you didn't help me. You took advantage of my ignorance.

You said that your past with Klaus was over and done with as far as you were concerned. You found Barbara acceptable, and you were glad that he wasn't all alone.

Barbara was a born loser. Even if she didn't look like it. It was the only kind of relationship she knew. He liked her because she didn't hold him to anything. It had nothing to do with love. It was depressing. That's why they were never fighting. He told her that he liked certain things about her, and she didn't dare bother him with other things. You didn't hint at the truth until you'd had sex with me.

I became important to you because I was the only one with whom you could talk openly about your work. That's all.

That's not all it was. It's easy for you to talk me into thinking that certain things I remember never really happened the way I'm now thinking they did.

If we'd really had sex, what good would it do me to deny it. Why would I have to justify myself.

You would have less of a responsibility for what happened afterward.

She wakes up, propped up in her bed, with tubes in her nose and throat and electrodes on her chest. She doesn't move, she just lets her eyes wander. At her feet the end of the bed, a chrome steel bar running around the bed, lining a plastic board. Above her a wooden triangle. To her right, a window with an aluminum frame, the larger part of which cannot be opened, only the upper part can be tilted to the inside. It's dark outside. To the left and right of the window, drapes that have been pushed open and only come down to the window sill are hanging from the ceiling, below them there is a wide uncovered radiator. In front of the window there are blinds that have been lowered and whose slats are slanted. The walls are painted in a light color, she cannot tell what the color is, nor how the floor is covered. She looks at a photograph in which she can make out the shape of an alpine landscape. The room is illuminated by a dim blue light whose source is behind her, above the top end of the bed.

You always made it look like and even believed yourself that Klaus was lonely and unhappy because he was unable to enter into relations with other people. That the sequence of attraction and repulsion in his relationship to you mirrored an internal conflict that he would have been willing to overcome in one way or another if only he had forced himself to do so. That his work was the last refuge, the only area in which he could exist, because it imposed a set of strict external constraints on his conflicted nature. You assumed that he couldn't be different than he was. He didn't want to be different than he was. He told you so, too, but you didn't get it. What you took to be an internal conflict was nothing but the defense against unreasonable demands. The majority of people are unhappy in an obvious and ridiculous way because of something they're being denied. The only real unhappiness is that for which you have yourself to blame. He had himself to blame for his unhappiness. He wanted to be alone, and he wanted to be unhappy. No part of him wanted anything else. For a person of intellect, developing his capacity for instrumental reason makes about as much sense as breaking stones. Klaus was different from his colleagues in that he knew what he was doing. He didn't ask you to marry and have kids with him until he could be certain that you wouldn't agree to it. If he had gone about it any other way, the result would have been unattractive. He didn't act any less rejective after he had proposed than before. Not that he couldn't have done otherwise—he didn't want to do otherwise. He was jealous of Jürgen, because he wanted a tragedy during the course of which you would leave him. There was something in him that gravitated toward you. But that something didn't come into existence all by itself. He fashioned a thorn for himself, tended it, and poked himself in the side with it because his existence would have seemed trivial to him otherwise. You thought that if he had such control over that thorn, he might as well get rid of it, then he would no longer have any trace of a desire to be with you, and he would no longer be unhappy. You called his unhappiness artificial. Unhappiness of a decent caliber is always artificial. Your unhappiness was insignificant. What you wanted to register as unhappiness and what happened to you can happen to anyone.

Nobody's mad at you anymore. It's all well and forgotten.

Once again she awakes in the hospital. The window is tilted, the morning sun comes shining in. A short man with a wide chest in a white coat is standing in front of her.

Enjoy yourself now that you will get to spend your birthday with your dear aunts. And if it gets to be a bit much with your aunts and their gossip and small talk, just think for a moment of the little nun in her paltry cell—then I'll use my telepathic powers and you'll feel better right away. Also, for this Tuesday you can—

Are you able to talk?
Yes.
How are you feeling?
I feel awfully weak. — Do I have to have this tube in my nose.
The doctor carefully pulls out the tube.
I'm glad to have you talk. But don't overexert yourself.
How long have I been here.
Seven weeks.
Why am I here.
A car accident. You were unconscious when they found you. During the accident the inside mirror came off and hit you on the head. You suffered a surface wound that had to be stitched up. And a few smaller abrasions and bruises.
She feels her forehead.
I don't feel any injury.
The wounds have healed.
How did the accident happen.
You can't remember.
No.
You drove into a wall of an underpass on a through road going south. The train line doesn't run at a right angle to the street there but diagonally, the road makes a left turn before the underpass and a right turn afterward. You drove into the left wall when you came out of the underpass. As though you had wanted to keep going straight where the road makes a turn. Nobody saw it happen. The next person who passed called an ambulance and the police. It took some time to get you out of the car because the doors couldn't

be opened at first. — When you'd been with us for a week, you were suddenly gone from your bed. We found you in the park, but you wouldn't respond to questions. The next day you were gone again. You were standing in a hallway far away, staring at the floor.

Has someone asked for me since I've been here.

There were a few calls, and one time some people came to visit. I believe they were colleagues of yours. I told them they should pick one person who would call and whom I would inform in detail.

Who's that.

I don't recall the name. I wrote it down on a piece of paper in my office.

I'd like to go to the bathroom.

The other person pulls back the covers and removes the electrodes from her chest. First she sits up on the edge of the bed. She stops.

You're dizzy.

Yes. — I have to wait a minute. — I think I'm getting better already.

She moves to the bathroom, unsteady on her feet. She had wanted to take a shower, but she doesn't feel up to it. She washes her face and fixes her hair. Then she walks slowly back into the room and lies back down on the bed.

When I woke up, I wanted to ask you if I could go home right away. When I got up, I wanted to ask you how much longer I'll have to be here. — Now I won't even ask. — I feel so weak.

Don't worry about it. You're a little exhausted, small wonder after being unconscious. We'll get you back on your feet.

I think I'll have to rest. — I'm tired. — I'd like to sleep.

Sleep as much as you like. We'll take care of you.

She dreams she's running. All she thinks about is her rhythm. There are no other thoughts anymore. Her heart is beating loudly. Her head is flushed. At this point her rhythm used to submit to her body and carry it along. Giving her a feeling of detachment that she couldn't believe could be brought about by anything other than running. The air before her eyes begins to flicker. She now perceives nothing but shapes, she can't discern any details. Now there is something that doesn't permit the separation of her consciousness from her body. Her field of vision is shrinking. The beat in her head grows louder. Her body pulls her consciousness inside itself. The rhythm has become irregular. She keeps slowing down. Until she blacks out and falls down.

How long did I sleep.
    You missed lunch.
    I feel so weak.
    She takes a deep breath.
    One more thing. — You were having heavy vaginal bleeding when they found you. There was no indication of an injury. You must have had your period at the time of the accident. One possible hypothesis would be that the bleeding increased because of the accident. When the paramedics got inside the car, you were holding a suit pressed between your legs, a gray men's suit. It was soaked with blood. When the inside mirror hit you on the head, you must have lost consciousness immediately. You wouldn't have been able to jam the suit between your legs to stop the bleeding. But if the bleeding had started before the accident, and if the bleeding was so strong that you could only stop it this way, why did you keep driving then, rather than going to look for help.
    I can't remember anything. — I'm so tired.
    You should sleep.
    Will I wake up again?
    Of course you will.

Under which conditions can there be an equilibrium state for a system consisting of individuals and groups of individuals?

Under which conditions is there exactly one equilibrium state? Under which conditions can the system regain an equilibrium once it has lost its equilibrium?

You said that I was going for a double mislabeling and a triple self-delusion. The first mislabeling was to keep the original title of the thesis—which was bold, to say the least. The second mislabeling was to call something a minimal solution that in fact represented a maximal solution—sweeping the core problems under the rug and proceeding with business as usual was only the beginning of a move, the principal aim of which had to be to declare the remainder of my original intentions a novel insight. The first self-delusion resulted from my failure to admit this last point to myself. My doubt about whether I would be able to go the distance with this move was my second self-delusion—I would go the distance. The third self-delusion was my hope that I would be able to start working more successfully in a field different from the one in question, once the move was successfully completed. I should write an article in which I justified why I was unable to complete my thesis. I told you that such an experiment would be irrevocably final. Nobody ever terminates a procedure because of the realization that the theory which is the object of their work and which is recognized by the community in which the procedure is being conducted is based on a precept which within the theory can only be formulated in a way that leads to contradictions with indispensable assumptions of the theory. If someone terminates a procedure, it's because they cannot handle the conceptual apparatus and the laws of the theory, or don't want to. If you cannot handle the conceptual apparatus and the laws of a recognized theory, your opinions about the theory don't count. I said, you can talk, you don't even know what it means to have to earn a living, you're independently wealthy and don't have to work. If I were to terminate my procedure, they would fire me at the next opportunity, I couldn't work anywhere in academia, I would have to look for something completely different. At that point you laughed and said that I hadn't understood anything. Suffering couldn't be measured by asking whether or not other people could imagine suffering from the same thing. I said I knew that my suffering was insincere, but I didn't want to risk a possible future. You said that something else was much more important, insincere or not. Only if I faced up to the possibility of fundamentally reconsidering how to live my life, only if I was prepared to give up everything I had achieved, only then would I be giving proper expression to the fact that General Equilibrium Theory is based on assumptions that can only be represented by means of contradictions in its own language. I said that I couldn't very well destroy my life just to give proper expression to a scientific problem. You said it was exactly this potential question that made scientific questions relevant at all. You said you would destroy your life if that were the only possibility of giving adequate expression to something that was important to you.

Each gradual succession amounts to a violation of a faceless simultaneity. General Equilibrium Theory describes systems of states that are conceived from a designated state of rest. The observer conceiving such systems of states is a god, not a mortal. If the god really wants to bring the system of states into equilibrium, he must pretend to be a helpless cripple.

Your point wasn't to gain a perspective on what had happened, what you did and felt. Neither was your point to find out what implications for the future the things had that had happened, that you did and felt.

There were good reasons for each individual system of states, and there were good reasons against each individual system of states. I was able to justify and dismiss each one of them.

Too many reasons for too many predictions.

Too many good reasons are the symptom of an illness.

I thought I understood why you had matched up Klaus and Barbara. You had an affair with Barbara. I never saw you together with her, and you never talked about her. I couldn't ask you why you had introduced her to Klaus, the question would have sounded ridiculous, of course you would have said that it had been without any ulterior motives, and I wouldn't have been able to object. She asked too little, and she gave too much. I could imagine quite well how you had gotten tired of her. At first I thought that you just wanted to get rid of her elegantly. I saw that you had succeeded in getting rid of her, and I thought I saw that you had succeeded all too well. You made the remark that you had to be happy with the sweaters you had, for better or worse, Klaus would be the one wearing her new designs. If you put up with that, there had to be a reason other than your having gotten tired of her. You could have chosen another way to put distance between you and her, such that you wouldn't have had to do without her sweaters. The reason—I imagine—was your bad conscience regarding Klaus, because you'd had sex with me. You realized that your relationship to him was more important to you than the affair with me, and you wanted to compensate him for the breach of trust you had committed. You knew he was still jealous, even though he and I had stopped seeing each other. You offered Barbara to him on a silver platter as a way of admitting the mistake you had made.

He called to tell me that he had said straight to your face that you'd had sex with me and that you had admitted to it. He was peeved, he wouldn't have expected something like that from me, I had violated an older loyalty, the one I owed him. I told him it wasn't true, you only said that to hurt him, which shouldn't have come as a surprise to him, given all that had happened between the two of you. Even if I didn't have sex with you, I had still been disloyal, I had wanted such a close relationship to you that I had thereby betrayed him by my very thoughts. He felt very hurt, even though he had broken up with you, your relationship was still very intimate, despite the fact that you were no longer having sex. I admitted that I had committed a breach of loyalty as he had defined it. We never touched on the topic again.

But the reason I had found for why you had matched up Klaus and Barbara was not the relevant reason. You had gotten lost in your constructs, you didn't find your way back into the real world. Klaus and Barbara both think that a fact doesn't exist if it cannot be represented in any way, even if it is there, plain as day. You knew that Klaus would commit to a relationship, given their common ground. If he could make sure that he would be left to be by himself in the relationship. To let your reconstruction of your past be controlled by an imaginary man in an imaginary gray suit is to be controlled about as much as the imaginary result of an imaginary experiment is the result of an experiment. You weren't satisfied to have one memory refer to the next. You matched up Klaus and Barbara to prove to yourself that you were still capable of predicting actions accurately and to corroborate an element of your theory at the same time. Accurate predictions don't result from long-winded deliberations, they're just there. Habitually, as it were. The outcome of the experiment corroborated your prediction.

It's not essential that the observed act predictably. It's essential that the observer act predictably. Because the observer is the measuring instrument which is applied to the observed and off of which the prediction is read. The measuring instrument must act reliably and unvaryingly, but not the value it measures. The certainty of the prediction is always tied to a human being. It's not transferable. If it were, there would be a formula for making accurate predictions. *Formula* would mean that an accurate prediction could be made under any circumstances, all you would have to do would be to properly integrate all those incidental predictions to obtain an altogether unconditional prediction. But there can be no such thing.

LANGUAGE GAME

Nobody is going to believe me. That's why I'm talking about it now. A while back I would have rather cut out my tongue than talk about it. Most people think it's an excuse. Some think it's great that I process my life with such imagination. How creative. Still, the very same people always want to get me to see a psychotherapist. I've got a problem, but I'm not ill. One particularly intellectual guy once said that it wasn't for my sake, but for the therapist's. He should learn something. I was always objectifying things so nicely. This could be guided. First you should make up your mind about what it is you want. You write that down. Once it's written down, you have to believe really strongly that everything is going to happen the way it's written down. If you're that convinced, it will end up happening precisely that way. A proper method, perhaps even named after me. I know one thing. If someone turns it into a method, his name will be on it, not mine. It's true, everything is recorded with such precision. Who will do what and when. Everything is so objective. But I didn't write it. It's just that nobody believes me. Half of those who don't think that it's so sophisticated would like best to get rid of my problem with a few slaps in the face, figment of the imagination, whimsy, something can be done about that, while the other half very carefully intimates that maybe I'm just not quite normal, no problem, to the contrary. It never helps to point out that my family background is inconspicuous, my father is a manager, my mother is a doctor. My father isn't an alcoholic and didn't abuse me, I finished school and never ran away. My sister has a degree in psychology, by the way. Perhaps I shouldn't have finished school and should have run away instead.

I should certainly have run away from Uncle Waldo. Uncle Waldo was Argentinean, his real name was Ewald, and he was distantly related to my mother. The family there hadn't limited itself to contact within the German colony, Uncle Waldo had dark skin and jet-black curls, and he was always wearing loud shirts. He was a civil engineer, when he was working on a nearby project, my parents would always invite him for lunch on Sundays. There was something fishy about Uncle Waldo right from the beginning. Uncle Waldo treated me quite unlike all the others. While my parents looked neither left nor right on the way to prosperity, I went for walks with Uncle Waldo. Not where other people were walking as well but to where he could begin to finger me. The first time around we didn't go all the way, of course. But Uncle Waldo kept coming by. Uncle Waldo didn't have to force me into anything. Still, it wasn't my own decision, my free will. I couldn't help it. Even though I didn't know about anything the first time around. I had asked my parents for a diary, they had given me a leather-bound book with blank pages. I didn't know what to write in it, it was such a nice book, and I didn't want to write anything down that I might not like later on. So I didn't write anything at first but just thought about what I might write. I had plenty of time, I was young. Nonetheless, after the first incident with Uncle Waldo, something was written down in the diary: the incident with Uncle Waldo. Even though I hadn't written anything in it. It wasn't my handwriting either. Or rather, it was my handwriting, but I would never write so clearly. I have a pretty bad hand, I could never write such a long text legibly. The entry was dated but not written in the first person, as one would expect a diary entry to be. Of course I put the diary well out of sight. If my parents had found it, they would never have believed me that I hadn't written all that. I didn't look at the diary again until Uncle Waldo had to go to South America for a few weeks. It turned out that everything I had since done with him had been added. Dated correctly. Because the weather wasn't always as nice as it was the first time around, and because my parents often had to work on Sundays, we stayed at our house. Out in the open, Uncle Waldo's penchant for chairs couldn't quite come to the fore—but now it could. Most of all he liked my father's armchair, an unwieldy monster from around the time of the restoration. I had to sit down in the chair, put my legs up in the air, and grasp the soles of my feet. I knelt on the chair, my arms on the back of the chair. Or I stood on the chair, held on to the armrest, and bent over. My diary described all our exercises. I hadn't put anything down, nobody had seen us, still everything had been recorded. But that was only part of the truth. The other part was yet to follow. I didn't put anything down. But if I had certain experiences, the diary would contain the respective entries. Afterward, I thought. But things weren't just recorded afterward. As I found out when our P.E. teacher was on sick leave. I paged through the recollections about Uncle Waldo, I turned page after page, and all of a sudden I came upon something that had nothing to do with Uncle Waldo. I'm all by myself in the locker room after P.E. class, it's the last period. The two college students substituting for the P.E. teacher are putting away the gear in the gym. My friends are all gone, the school is empty. I go into the gym to see what they're doing. They're busy with the boxes. They smirk at each other as I walk toward them. The older one is always wearing jeans, plain white T-shirts, and sandals without socks, showing his well-built body to best effect. He says to the other guy, you in for it or what, the other one says, sure thing, I'm always in for it, and they start fingering me right off. I'm not wearing a lot of clothes, just a pair of jeans with a belt and a dark-blue blouse with white polka dots, no collar, which the two of them unbuttoned immediately. Soon I'm sitting on the box, conveniently cushioned, and the guy in the white T-shirt, wearing nothing else at this point, raises my legs. The other one has to get undressed first. Then they switch, the other one sits down on the box, I sit on top of him. Another change of positions, I kneel on the box, the guy in the T-shirt holds on to my shoulders from behind, the other one sits down next to me. That's what was written in my diary. I liked the P.E. teachers, both of them were Mediterranean types, but nothing had happened between me and them. Then I looked at the date, which I hadn't noticed at first. It was the date of the following day. The following day we had P.E. class during the last period before lunch. I was the last one in the locker room. While the two P.E. teachers were putting away the gear in the gym. The book had left out the fact that the vice principal would take a look into the locker room, she must have wanted to have a few words with the P.E. teachers, but she wasn't expecting anyone to still be in there. After she had gone straight back out I went to the gym. The P.E. teachers said exactly what I had read in my diary. Then they did with me exactly what was described in my diary. It was then that I understood. My diary contained the complete stage directions for my sex life. Everything was always already determined. Everything was always already written down. I didn't want to look at the book anymore. I racked my brains over whether the book had always been finished, from the first to the last episode, or whether it was always describing only the following one. Or else it contained from the start all those episodes in which each following one was added. Was everything really written down exactly the way it was. I was so shocked that I became a nun. The two P.E. teachers were smart enough not to tell anyone that they'd had a thing with me. After all, I was underage, if someone had found out, it would have been a deadly blow to their careers. Just count all the money they're getting as public servants over the course of their lives and which they would have had to do without if they had been kicked out of public service. They didn't want to do that to themselves, and neither did I. I didn't let anyone come near me. I was so successful in pretending that nothing had happened that they didn't even dare to touch me during gymnastics. I'm good at gymnastics, I don't need any support. They just looked at me in a certain way. And waited for me to look back at them. They probably asked themselves if it hadn't all just been a dream. It's always fun to shock men. Actually, though, I was helpless. I was safe as long as everyone thought, it doesn't work with her. But if someone disregarded my negative attitude, I didn't put up any resistance. That someone was François. He wasn't French at all, and he was a moron. For the life of me I wouldn't have gotten involved with him before I had discovered the truth about the diary. His name wasn't François, but you had to call him that, he owned a shoe store, I worked there to make some money. He was closer to fifty than to forty, he had straight, oily hair that kept falling across his face, he wore bright-colored sport coats, with white shirts so that the colors would seem even brighter. The shoe store was ridiculous, shelves, benches, and chairs made of light-colored wood, like a kid's room, selling black men's shoes. He would much rather have gone into women's shoes, but he knew that it wouldn't fly. Because he had no sense of taste. I found him disgusting from the very beginning. He didn't consider it necessary to accommodate me in the least. I needed the money, I had no other way of earning anything. I wore pants because I was constantly having to contort myself in the store, bending over, kneeling down, or looking for something on top of a shelf. I was supposed to wear a skirt. The reason being that this was a shoe store for men. I didn't put on a skirt, I kept coming in my blue jeans, which weren't all that bad either, they had a very tight fit. Would I please buy appropriate clothes with the money I was earning from him. If I didn't turn up in a skirt next week, that would be it. I then bought a plain black skirt. The skirt was so short that he didn't say anything for a while. Soon, however, he kept at me again. I wore a sweatshirt and sneakers along with the skirt. I was supposed to put on black pantyhose and high-heels. Did I recall that this wasn't a fitness center. He didn't bring it up until I had earned enough money to afford those things. I did away with my sweatshirts because they really did look ridiculous along with the skirt, I started wearing plain white blouses. When not accompanied by their wives, the customers were eyeing me with interest. Particularly if they thought that I didn't notice how they were looking at me. I always noticed. You just have to pick the right mirror. As time went on, I began enjoying it more and more to get boxes from the top shelves. Men don't have any idea how stupid they look when they eye a woman, thinking that the woman doesn't notice. They make any horse look like Einstein. The best part is when I'm about to turn around. All of sudden everything is back to form. Or rather, what the man takes to be form. Afterward, there are only two kinds. Either they become exceedingly matter-of-fact, yes, Miss, please, Miss, thank you, Miss, very kind of you, Miss, or else they try to be funny, this shoe makes me one and a half inches taller, don't you have a model with a somewhat thinner sole, I only want to be an inch taller, hee hee hee. When a customer came with his wife, I also liked to bend down low without bending my knees. Sometimes the wife would turn all red, which certainly wasn't helpful for closing a sale. All in all I must have helped to raise sales, otherwise François would never have raised my wage. That was the only decent thing he ever did. No customer ever came on to me, by the way. Not necessary. He was the boss, and he was in charge. Why was I always wearing a bra. I did away with the bra, but I bought blouses that were more tightly knit and not as transparent. At that point I had been working in the shoe store for half a year, and François had never even shaken my hand when I came in or went home. I knew what was coming. He never looked at me. He knew his store and his mirrors, and he knew I would have noticed it immediately if he had given me the eye. I never showed him what I had. It was all determined beforehand. It was all written down in my diary. One evening he said that I should stay longer. The storeroom had to be rearranged, one shoe brand over there and another over here. I said that I was sorry, I didn't have time that day, I had a date. I would do it tomorrow. When I came in the next day to rearrange things, he said, not during business hours. Only after we close. I said that I was sorry, I couldn't stay longer, I had another date. I waited for him to bring it up again. When the last customer had been taken care of on the Friday of the following week, he said, now it's time to rearrange things. He didn't listen to me singing the same old song but lowered the shades so that the store was protected from view—the store wasn't located in a nice enough area that it would have made sense to display merchandise at night—and locked the door from inside. I really did have to rearrange shoes in the basement, moving the ones from the top shelves to the lowest shelves and vice versa. For the first time he looked at me. He took off his coat and tie while I was beginning to work up a sweat. He had washed his hair, by the way. When I was almost done and was standing back up on the ladder, he got up and put his hand under my skirt. I told him not to touch me. He told me to shut up and pulled down my pantyhose. I repeated to him not to touch me. I would tell my parents. He said he was now going to do with me as he saw fit, if I objected I didn't need to come back next week. There was nothing I could do. It was written in my diary. He couldn't be moved. As if he knew that I would be coming back. And wouldn't tell my parents anything. As if he knew the book. Always after business hours, and I would always have to do some sort of work beforehand. Getting something from the storeroom, redecorating the display window, take a shoe brand off the shelves. During business hours he acted as before. Sometimes I would try to say something friendly or make a little joke. Not because I had suddenly begun to like him but to ease the tension. He treated me like I had treated the P.E. teachers. The other people must have thought that I was coming on to him and that he wasn't interested. The next chapter in my *education sentimentale* was the one that my sister considers to be the crucial one. All my sister looks at are her model biographies, and people have to conform to them. What doesn't conform is disregarded, deemed unimportant. Like my diary. My sister doesn't believe me when I talk about my diary. I can't show it to her. François remarked that a black leather jacket would go very well with my outfit, my black skirt, my black pantyhose, my high-heels, and my white blouse. Not some cheap thing from a department store, a real American pilot jacket. Simple, with a few well-placed zippers. He told me about a store where I could look at one. I knew what something like that would cost. That's why I went to the department store and tried on those leather jackets that I could afford. But afterward I ended up going to the store selling the American clothing. The jacket he was talking about really did suit me. It was the only option, everything else was crap. He asked me if I had tried the jacket on. I just said yes, nothing more. He read me like a book. After a while he casually asked if I wouldn't like to have the jacket. I said I couldn't afford it. But I liked it a lot. Even if my sister doesn't believe me, I didn't say that because I desperately wanted the jacket, I said it so that he would at least say something to me. Perhaps make him recognize that I existed. Later on he actually said that he wanted to give me the leather jacket as a present. If he had said that he was giving it to me right after he had asked whether it fit me, I would have believed it that evening. As it was, I was just waiting for him to tell me what I would have to do to get it. A good customer of his wanted me to help him try on shoes naked. And not even completely naked. I was supposed to wear the leather jacket, nothing else, just black stockings. I should be getting rid of that stupid pantyhose, anyway. I could be using a much stronger lipstick with my brunette hair and the black leather jacket. He was even right about that. Compared to what he was doing with me, this didn't sound all that weird. I told him that if I was supposed to wear the leather jacket, I would need to have it first. I added that this didn't mean that I agreed to it. I had to think about it. Should I accept the leather jacket or not. I kept thinking about it for days. François didn't rush me. I was supposed to do what I was doing all day, just not wearing anything. I could check my diary. Whatever was going to happen was written in it. But if I looked at it now, I would always be looking at it. At first it had been inconceivable that I would ever throw the diary away. How could I throw a book away in which my destiny was written, I would have to throw away my future, myself, it wasn't my fault that the things that were described in the diary happened to me. Now that I hadn't looked at it for so long, I could imagine throwing the diary away and living the rest of my life without the diary. I would never be able to forget the diary, but the more distant it all became, the more unreal it would seem. I got the leather jacket a day in advance—François trusted me—and I obediently did what he wanted me to do. I bought a pair of black stockings and took off everything but the leather jacket, the stockings, and the shoes in the basement. The man was about sixty, he looked rather well groomed, he wasn't fat either, he could have been a business associate of my father's. I asked him how I could help him. He said he wanted black loafers, and he described a pair from the display. I brought the loafers in his size, they were too small for him, I brought them a half-size larger. Then he said, cut the crap, and he put his hands on my breasts and between my legs. I fought back and said that this wasn't part of the deal. He said I was really funny. Why did I think he had bought me the leather jacket. I said we agreed that I would assist him in the nude. He laughed and said that that was exactly what I was going to do now. He unzipped his fly and pulled me down by my hair. I should go right ahead and tell people that I was getting such an expensive leather jacket just for running around without my pants on. I kept fighting back. At that point the customer called François. The little girl is not cooperating. The little girl told François, that's not what we agreed on. François told the little girl she should do what the customer said. The customer told the little girl to get up on the counter and spread her legs. When the little girl didn't do what the customer wanted, the customer slapped her in the face twice. They dragged me over to the counter and François held me by the shoulders, his red glasses fell to the floor while he was doing so. As the customer was getting dressed afterward, he said that I should go right ahead and tell people that I had been raped. After all, I had gone to face a total stranger without my pants on, and I had gotten a leather jacket for it. I was a whore, now I knew it, he said. I shouldn't worry about it. There were a lot of whores. I would get used to it eventually. I left the leather jacket behind. They threw it out the door behind me. I couldn't very well leave it on the sidewalk. That's how it was recorded in my diary, and that's how it happened. I wished I had thrown the diary away. Or not looked at it. The surprise wasn't a surprise to me. I fought back. I hadn't fought back hard enough. Where should I have run to, with nothing on but a leather jacket and stockings. I shouldn't have taken off my pants. Nothing was supposed to happen. I knew that something would happen. I fought back. I shouldn't have come into the store. I had to go to work. I knew what would happen. And I also knew that I couldn't do anything about it. I shouldn't have taken the leather jacket. I didn't even want to take it anymore. They threw it out the door behind me. It was all determined beforehand. The leather jacket cost so much, and I had taken it. The next time around I only fought back a little bit, the time after that not at all. Finally, an opportunity opened up for me to work in a sports store. I had believed that François would finally say something, once he was about to lose me. But he didn't say anything. He didn't seem to care at all. One look into my diary sufficed to confirm that all that I would be asked to do in the sports store was work. With the P.E. teachers during P.E. class, with the owner of the shoe store in the shoe store, with the blond hunk from the sports store who was so friendly and considerate, working in the sports store was really fun—nothing. I should do some sports, he said. Another look into my diary did turn up something. On Saturday after work we would drive to the Magic Forest to go running. I wouldn't ask why the forest was called the Magic Forest, it was obvious who was going to use what to do some magic. We would come to an idyllic spot. A clearing with a patch of grass, in the middle of which there was a big rock. I would be exhausted from running, he would lift me up and onto the rock Then I would find out why the forest was called the Magic Forest. Because suddenly I would feel a branch growing to where there shouldn't be one. I would cry out in pain, it wouldn't help, I would just scare a few of the animals in the forest. That's how the diary put it, that's how it was supposed to happen on Saturday, I didn't want it to happen that way, without giving notice I just didn't go to work on Saturday, if I didn't go to work, I also wouldn't be going to the Magic Forest. It's not like I didn't try. My absence didn't make Hans Castorp mad. It was raining cats and dogs all weekend, so that there were a lot less customers than usual, the sports store could manage just fine without me. I was sure that I had tricked the diary. I took another look. Everything that was supposed to have happened to me in the Magic Forest was still in there, I just didn't go, and nothing had happened. I was relieved beyond words. It was all an illusion. It had been nothing but a dream. Maybe I had really written the diary myself. Maybe I had really written down my experiences after the fact and then told myself because of a bad conscience that everything had been written down ahead of time, that everything had been determined beforehand, leaving me no choice. At least I didn't think anything of it when he said that we would make up for what we had missed, we would go running next Saturday. The next Saturday the weather was gorgeous, we took his big white American jeep and drove to the Magic Forest. In the Magic Forest we ran to an idyllic spot. The idyllic spot was the clearing with the big rock. Everything happened exactly the way my diary had described it for the previous Saturday. I cried hard afterward. Because of the diary. Of course he thought that he had really hurt me. He was very sweet to me and carried me all the way back to the car. At home I looked into the diary right away. Everything had been entered on the correct date. I could have sworn that the date had been different. I hadn't read the date correctly. Or I had been wrong about the calendar. My diary is very explicit. It describes all the details without resorting to technical terms. Back then I used to think, why not use that language. You have to talk plain English. The words are always the same. There aren't that many words for such a small number of things and a few more events. Only the environment is always different. They are the right words if you are in the process of doing what the words are describing. But your thoughts need only be somewhere else, and they cease to be the right words. Let alone if you want to describe things afterward or, as in my case, ahead of time. This is not about shame. Or maybe it is about shame, and shame is acting like grammar. There is only one language game in which words have their place. Outside of that language game the words aren't the right words. If the words are used, it isn't a description. Then they pull the listener or reader into this language game. Inevitably. My sister acts as though I was a prostitute. I took the leather jacket. And the sports gear. I didn't work in a bar where you have to deck yourself out in velvet and plush and have to walk over to the men and ask them if they would buy you a drink. If they drink something, ten marks off the cocktail are perhaps in it for you, and if they take you to one of the rooms, perhaps a hundred, and when you wake up sober in the morning, you probably feel like a piece of dirt. My sister says that I could go to a dance club and go home with someone. What would I be doing in a dance club. I didn't need a dance club for Uncle Waldo, for the P.E. teachers, for François, or for Hans Castorp. My sister thinks I'm rebelling against society. She says that generally speaking sex is something that sustains society, not only because sometimes children result from it but because sex usually takes place in well-ordered circumstances, given that society can get that to happen, there is no area it cannot control. She says that what I want is bare sex. From the front, from behind, sideways, with one, two, or three guys, this was rebellion. Only my sister knows how rebellion would go together with corruption by leather jackets and running shoes. I've tried time and again to escape my diary. Hans Castorp very much wanted to go to Chamonix with me to climb the Mont Blanc. Because I had been exercising regularly in the meantime, the notion wasn't completely unreasonable. It would be bitter cold on top of the mountain. That's what was written in my diary, I rewrote it. I crossed out Chamonix and wrote Zermatt above it, I happened to have read an article about Zermatt, and I replaced the Mont Blanc with the Plateau Rosa. I was sure that nothing would change if I rewrote the diary, I hadn't written it, it was writing itself, it determined my life, I wasn't the one determining my life. At least I would have given it a try. The following afternoon he came right out and told me he had changed his mind. It was too dangerous to climb the Mont Blanc with me, who had no mountaineering experience. A couple he was friends with would be going skiing in Zermatt for a week. He wanted to go with them. I could learn how to ski. When I checked my diary, I found that Chamonix and the Mont Blanc had been crossed out and replaced by Zermatt and the Plateau Rosa, everything else happened as described, but including Settembrini—his friend was Italian. No word about his wife or girlfriend. I crossed out Settembrini, leaving Hans Castorp in place. Not only did Settembrini remain with us, he was also bringing a friend along. I didn't give up. I crossed out Settembrini and his friend, didn't open the diary anymore, and went to Zermatt. There weren't just three of them. Settembrini said that they were a group of four friends in Cervinia, two of them were doing a downhill run off the slopes, they would be coming shortly. The two others did indeed come shortly. I study history, by the way. I could have studied anything, really. I always got good grades doing a minimum of work. My sister was pushing me to go to medical school. She would have liked to study medicine herself, but she wasn't as good in school. I've never had problems understanding physics or biology. My sister thinks that prostitutes should be considered therapists of a certain kind. Sexual desire was a fact, if it was met, men were more relaxed, more balanced, less neurotic. It was a sort of service. Employers would benefit from it, as would the children, perhaps men would find their way back to their wives if they didn't have to ask things of them that they were unable to provide. The individual would simply function better. If I were a doctor, I could bill the insurance companies afterward. A role model. My sister also thinks that I'm being masochistic. I'm not taking filthy people to cheap rooms to tell them how great they are. I stopped working in the sports store after the vacation in Switzerland. First, men desperately want to see their woman with another man. Once it actually happens, it creates a rift they hadn't reckoned with. Afterward, the world is no longer the same. The transition from the Ptolemaic to the Copernican view of the world. Even if they imagined it a hundred times, it has happened, they're no longer the center of the universe. They're so disappointed about this that they will switch universes sooner or later, men of action that they are. My current boyfriend is a pilot, by the way. He owns a large loft. Because he's hardly ever around, his apartment is practically mine. Of course I also have other boyfriends. He doesn't mind. I've never asked him, but I'm sure he also has other girlfriends. I went to the U.S. with him, but he's not taking me to Hawaii. What am I. I'm a trophy girlfriend. I'm beautiful, I'm always well dressed, my makeup is always perfect, I'm not stupid, I don't drink, I don't smoke dope, I don't snort cocaine, I can deal with anything, and all the while I'm enjoying myself. I would be a trophy girlfriend if I didn't know—and I know this not just about myself—that women do not at all feel completely different about these things. Everything a woman does when a man is watching arouses the woman just as much if the man does it and the woman is watching. I've also tried to throw the diary away. I put it into the trash container of another building. After a few days it was back where it had always been, as though it had come back. I threw it away again, this time it was immediately back in place, as though I had never thrown it away. My sister says that I didn't really throw the book away. I was just imagining that I had thrown it away, or perhaps I would like to have thrown it away, but I hadn't thrown it away. When I was still going to school, she was convinced that I would end up in a brothel. But I'm a student, and that's not an alibi. She can't find a job, even though she can always explain who does what where, when, and why. She volunteers for a family planning center, and she has a part-time job in an advertising agency. She's a secretary, but she's hoping to get into the right kind of business, into the creative sector, as they call it. My sister is dependent on our parents' money even after finishing up her education, I'm a student, still I don't need any money from them, I was working even when I was in school, and I'm paying for my own studies. That's how I became the good kid and my sister the bad one before I knew it. That was too much for my sister, the psychologist, she told on me. She told my mother the story about my vacation in Zermatt. As a result, my mother has stopped talking to me. My father, who tends not to be that stern, has to follow suit. Because I was making good progress in my studies, I was able to face my diary more self-assuredly. Whereas I often used to just skip through it, now I studied it more closely. Somehow I got used to it, especially because my destiny turned out to be anything but stressful for quite a long time, a bonus for the fact that I had submitted to it for so long. Until I read something that worried me a lot. My pilot boyfriend rides motorcycles in his spare time. He says that when he's too old to fly, he'll still be able to ride motorcycles. He owns a whole collection of motorcycles. He doesn't maintain them himself, he knows a few bikers who take care of that for him. Something was wrong with one of his Harleys, he would bring back a part from London that I was supposed to take to the shop. The bikers would be a rather nasty bunch. The boss of the shop had a full beard, he was wearing worn-out leather pants, a leather vest on his bare chest, and a leather band wrapped around his forehead. First he would offer me a beer and then send over one of his coworkers, dressed up like a cowboy, who would use his wrench to start messing around with me. Then the boss would instruct the cowboy and another guy who was wearing nothing but a pair of Jockey briefs underneath his work coat to put me down on a motorcycle. I wouldn't want to, but it was already too late. The cowboy would give me a few slaps in the face, the boss would pull my hair, and I would have to do what the boss wanted me to. I would scream constantly, it would hardly impress the gang. I was rather disturbed when I read this. If I first accepted a beer and then had someone mess around with me using a wrench, I knew what was bound to happen. I was appropriately dressed, too. I would put on black thigh-high patent-leather boots, the leather jacket with long fringes on the sleeves—I own plenty of leather jackets these days—below that only an undershirt and a short leather skirt. If I didn't want them to mess around with me, all I had to do was to appear in a white frilled skirt. I would end up squatting on the floor, sobbing. When my pilot boyfriend did indeed ask me to take a Harley part to the motorcycle shop, I got very nervous. All the more because something else appeared to be going on. There was a copilot with whom I had gone out a few times and who was peculiar in that he never once even tried to come on to me. This was a relief at first, but it was starting to disconcert me, especially because I had no explanation for it. He wasn't gay, that I can tell. All questions were answered shortly before I had to make my trip to deliver the spare part. He had been wanting to ask me for a long time to do some modeling. He said that my erotic aura was very special. It would be sad if I were to keep that to myself. The copilot didn't mention money, he knew that I'm living a decent life. No cheap sex. Serious work, including a makeup artist, a stylist, everything. I was quite attracted to the idea of presenting what I had in front of a camera, in a civilized atmosphere, with good makeup, everything well lit, on high-gloss paper. The Western world has fallen, we're all fellahs. Still, I was afraid to become part of a scene which I had never been part of and which I didn't want to become part of. I didn't say no as a matter of principle, I wanted to check my diary first. There was nothing in my diary. As if he had suspected as much, he called me immediately afterward, and I did agree to meet with him. He informed me that he had the perfect pseudonym for me: Miss Y Channel. When I grabbed my diary again afterward, it had grown enormously in size. I didn't dare open it anymore. It looked as though I was going to become exactly what my sister had always predicted. There was also the falling out with my parents. When I wanted to visit my father on his birthday, my mother stood in the door and said that she no longer had a daughter and slammed the door in my face. I called her at home, she said that she no longer had a daughter and hung up. I wrote her a letter, I never got an answer. All that, courtesy of my sister. And now I had to take the part to the motorcycle shop. That's when the idea occurred to me to cross myself out of my diary and to put in my sister. Indeed, after the birthday party my sister was full of remorse about what she had done. She wanted to go and do something with me, she wanted to meet my friends. No problem. I dressed her up accordingly, and the two of us took the part to the shop. I myself dressed more moderately, of course. I told my sister that she didn't have to worry if the guys got a little physical. That was normal among bikers. It worked out perfectly. Everything happened exactly the way the diary had described it. Of course my sister fought back, she had probably never had a cock in her mouth, and now there were three of them right in her face. She screamed because she was being fucked in the ass for the first time. My sister carried herself rather well. She's quite the hot bitch, her tits are bigger than mine. Of course she'll have to shave her pubic hair, it's easy to get lost in there, at times the bikers were having trouble finding their way. A hairy twat is not a nice thing. The boys still had a good time. I stood next to them the whole time and drank beer, when they were done, I thanked them like a good girl should for having tutored my big sister. It was all very encouraging. For the first time I changed something in my diary, with the result that I was fucked neither more, nor less, but not at all. I'll accept the copilot's offer. The pictures will be really hot. A well-lit cock filling every hole. Really handsome men, no filthy characters. Thousands of less handsome men will get off by looking at them. No pimples, no body lines, men and makeup always spotless. I won't be Miss Y Channel. Miss Y Channel will be taller than me, her hair will be darker than mine, Miss Y Channel will have bigger tits than me. Miss Y Channel will work with creative people. Miss Y Channel will be my sister.

DISSOLUTION OR FOR MRS. BERTA ZUCKERKANDL

She's walking beside a wide gravel driveway toward a big white building, the sun at her back. The building lined by the forked gravel driveway is up on a hill in the middle of a large mowed lawn, surrounded by a summer landscape of rolling hills with meadows and broad-leaf trees. Except for the gravel driveway, no other paths or roads are to be seen. The building has a rectangular layout with sides the ratio of three to one, and two stories above the first floor below a flat roof. The entrance is in the middle of the long side. A staircase with seven steps leads up to a platform in front of the actual entrance, covered by an equally flat, cantilevered roof supported by two rectangular columns. The stairs are the same width as the front door, lined by two blocks of the same height as the platform in front of the entrance. A bowl with a spherically trimmed bush has been placed on each block where the latter are left uncovered by the cantilevered roof. To the right and left, low ramps, skirted by a slightly protruding wall rising along with the ramps, lead up to the entrance platform. At the end of each ramp, there's also a bowl with a spherically trimmed bush. The building has four window lines. To the left and right of the entrance, there are four square basement windows each, made of white wood and right above the ground, each window is subdivided into five rectangles in width by three rectangles in height, all of equal size. Some of the windows are open. Each area consisting of the upper-middle three by two rectangles is tilted inward. The first floor has seven rectangular windows to the left and right of the entrance whose lower edges are the same height as the upper edge of the cantilevered roof. The windows are divided into two parts, the smaller, upper part is subdivided into four rectangles in width by three rectangles in height, the lower part into four larger rectangles, the subdivision of the lower part corresponding to that of the upper part by an omission of the crossbars. On the second and third floor there are four windows each to the right and left of the symmetrical axis formed by the entrance. The facade is set back at window width in parts of the first floor right above the roof covering the entrance, as well as around each of the two inner windows on both the left-hand and right-hand side of the second and third floor. In the middle of the recessed part of the facade there is a windowpane, apparently illuminating a staircase. Above a big rectangular frieze of black-and-white squares, a row of three by five rectangular panes, farther above the chessboard pattern again, above that another row of panes. The windows on the protruding part of the facade have the same exterior measurements, those on the second and third floor have their lower part divided in the middle. The windows in the recessed part of the facade are the same height as the others but wider. They correspond to the others, at the outer edges on the left and right, rows of stacked rectangles have been added that are of the same size as those formed by the outer row of the other windows. All windows are lined by a frieze of two rows of black-and-white squares. At each of the inner edges on the level of the second-floor windows, there is a life-size faience statue, two female figures in the nude guarding the entrance. The left female figure has long straight hair, the right one, short curly hair. The plants are not placed in round metal bowls, as she first assumed, but in hexagonal wooden containers whose sides are white squares in black outline. The platform in front of the front door is covered with square tiles. A white tile in the middle, surrounded by a row of black tiles, forming a black square around a white square, surrounded by a square of two rows of white tiles, surrounded by a square of one row of black tiles, and on the outside a square of two rows of white tiles. The entrance is framed by two windows underneath the cantilevered roof, which were obscured from afar. The upper parts of the windows are sub-divided into four rectangles in width by three rectangles in height. Like all the windows, the door is made of wood, with two wings, each fitted with an undivided pane of glass with rounded corners that are in contrast to all other forms. Above the wing, a skylight made of glass divided into squares. The entrance and the facade show no signs of use or any influence of weather. The white cross-bars of the windows, the window panes, the floor tiles and the friezes around the windows, the white paint on the walls—every-thing is completely clean and untouched. There's no dirt and no traces of rain.

She enters the building, a vestibule the floor of which has the same pattern as the platform below the cantilevered roof. She walks up another flight of stairs leading to the actual lobby. The pattern of black-and-white squares continues on the floor of the lobby, but differs by the omission of the outer square of white tiles, making each third square of black tiles—counting from the center—the outermost square. Right in front of her, as well as to her right and left, swinging doors made of glass lead out of the lobby. In the back corners of the lobby two seating arrangements have been placed. Each door has an opaque pane of glass divided into four squares with a tipped parallelogram in the middle. Skylights above all the doors, with long narrow rectangles prevailing along the edges, and stylized floral half-circles and rhombi in the middle. Each seating arrangement is composed of three white cube-shaped armchairs and a white wooden table, an octagonal top with a square frame. Each seat is supported by a U-shaped wooden grid, a wooden band running around the seat forms the support and the armrests.

Square cushions with a black-and-white chessboard pattern have been placed on the seats, the backrests are square cushions with a pattern of black-and-white triangles. She sits down in one of the chairs. There are no objects in sight that would suggest that anybody has been here recently. The walls of the room are covered with white tiles reaching almost to the upper edge of the doors, the tiles are of the same kind as those on the floor. Above the seating arrangement, five square openings covered with glass have been set into the white tiled wall. The concrete girders below the ceiling form a pattern corresponding exactly to the measurements of the outermost squares of the tile pattern on the floor. Next to the points of intersection of the beams, four cone-shaped bronze hoods are each fastened to a piece of rope and have been spherically fitted with a half-dozen bulbs. White strings run between the bulbs. The lobby is well lit by the incoming daylight. Still, two lamps have been switched on in the middle of the room.

She looks at a long dinner table with twelve chairs on each side and two chairs at the ends. The table is covered with a white cloth. The chairs are made of wood, in a dark natural color, without armrests. The seats are supported by four square legs, they are rounded at the edges, a little wider in front than in the back and covered with reddish brown velvet. Below the seats, a ball about an inch in diameter has been mounted in each of the four corners between seat and leg. The backs of the chairs are U-shaped in continuation of the two posterior legs, at their center there is a strip of square gaps about four inches wide and rounded at the top, two equidistant squares each next to one another. The floor is a dark polished gray. Parallel to the walls a white line has been set in. Two red carpets nailed to the floor run through the room, whose edges are lined up with the legs of the table. The ceiling has the same concrete beams as the one in the lobby, except that a frieze showing a green leaf pattern has been applied to the beams. The lamps are of the same kind as those in the lobby. On the right side of the room, seen from her perspective, there are three entrance doors, on the left side three glass doors lead outside to a winter garden. The doors and door frames are made of white lacquered wood. Between the doorways there are cupboards of medium height that serve as sideboards, a chair to the right and left of each cupboard. The glass doors leading outside to the winter garden have two wings, each wing is made of a square and a rectangle double in size above it, inside the square there is another tipped square whose four corners meet the sides of the outer square at their midpoint. The two squares in the glass panes to the side are each subdivided into four more squares. Two by two squares also form skylights above each wing and each side glass pane. Between the doors there are radiators that are painted brown, above them, mirrors in white wooden frames, next to them, vases fixed to the wall, holding freshly cut wildflowers.

She moves toward the middle of the room. Inside the winter garden, there are seating arrangements behind each of the doors, of the same kind as the one in the lobby. She seems to be on the second floor of the building. The dining room must look out onto the back, otherwise the driveway to the building would have to be visible. She hesitates for a moment whether to enter the winter garden. At about the middle of the table, a chair has been moved back, as though someone had recently been sitting on it.

She is lying on the edge of a swimming pool. All of a sudden she feels a shadow moving first across her body and then her face. She cannot decide to open her eyes right away. The day hasn't progressed enough for the trees around the swimming pool to be casting shadows. The last few days the weather has been sunny and clear. Maybe there are clouds moving in. When she finally opens her eyes, a man is standing in front of her.

Who are you.

You don't know me.

She sits up, supporting herself with her arms stretched behind her back. She has to look into the sun to see his face. She squints and feels inferior but cannot decide to get up.

I'm sorry, but no.

The man is tall and slender. A remarkably oblong face. Straight brown hair, cut short enough above his ears to show the skin, a high forehead and soft brown eyes, the nose is too small compared to his protruding chin. He's wearing loose-fitting jeans, a dark-blue polo shirt, and sneakers. She's wearing a black two-piece.

How do you think you know me.

I know someone whom you resemble very much.

You know me. You didn't expect me not to know you.

What are you doing now.

I'm talking to you.

Where.

Outside.

Be more precise.

A park, but without flowers.

What do you do when you're not talking to me.

I swim, in a swimming pool. Or I go for a run. In the area on the other side of the park. I spend the night in a room inside a big building high above the ground. The room has an outer wall made of glass, there's a bed and a bookshelf. Right now I'm not sure how I got from inside the room into this park here. I don't know how I'm getting to the swimming pool or to where I go for a run. I don't know how I find my way back to the room in which I'll spend the night.

It doesn't matter if you remember how you executed what you intended to do, as long as you're certain that you're able to execute what you intend.

Her head rests on a wooden edge forming the armrest of a sofa. To the right and left of the sofa there are two cube-shaped armchairs with smooth backs and armrests made from dark polished wood, the armrests of the same height as the backs, upholstered on the inside with the same kind of brown leather as the sofa, the seat cushions placed inside are sticking out a little. She's at the back end of a long room. The walls of the room are white. In front of the sofa there is a rectangular table whose legs are joined at the bottom of its narrow side so that the table must look like a frame from the side. In the distance, on the other side of the room, the shape of a heavy desk. Behind the desk is a chair with a back made of simple, straight slats. To the right and left of the desk, two more chairs of the same kind, their backs facing her. Her eyes are fixed on the big rug placed between the seating arrangement and the desk. The rug pattern consists of gray squares outlined in black and larger rectangles—set at regular intervals—which are divided by the two diagonal lines into two black triangles along the short side and two white triangles along the long side. The rectangles are spaced at four inches on the long side and a foot on the short side, creating the impression of parallel lines running through the room. Between the doors on the right side there are two cupboards made from the same wood as the seating arrangement. Each cupboard is six feet in height and about the same in width, with smoothly finished doors on both sides, each as high as the entire cupboard, in the middle there's a glass cabinet, each of its two doors formed by two rectangles in width by three rectangles in height, corresponding in their measurements to the skylights above the doors of the room. Below the cabinet, three drawers, just wide enough to reach the edge of the inner glass rectangles, only the lowest of the drawers reaches across the entire width of the area between the two outer doors of the cupboard. Between the three upper drawers and each of the side doors there's a gap. Books are visible behind the glass doors of the cupboard closest to her.

She props herself up with her arms, she pulls up her legs, and she rises, approaching a sitting position in slow motion and then remaining in it. She gets up, holding on to the armrests of the sofa with both hands. Slowly and with measured steps she walks over to the cupboard. She opens the glass door and takes out a book.

She opens the book to an illustration showing a farmhouse in the rain in front of which a young woman is standing, wearing a red wool jacket. She keeps turning pages and discovers the black-and-white photograph of another young woman going up a staircase, the woman is naked underneath her leather jacket except for her stockings and a pair of shoes. She closes the book, opening it again at another place. The text describes a hospital room at night. A doctor enters the hospital room. He feels the pulse of the woman lying in bed.

It's conceptually impossible for you to be a brain in a vat. If you were a brain in a vat, you couldn't talk about things but only about things and images, because only the latter would be accessible to you. If you say, *I am a brain in a vat,* what this means is, *I am a brain in a vat in the image.* So, if you really are a brain in a vat, then this sentence says something false. If you were a brain in a vat, you couldn't refer to yourself as one, because as a brain in a vat you couldn't refer to external things. Your supposition that such a possibility makes sense arises from a false theory of language which assumes a necessary connection between a name and that which it refers to and which presupposes that mental representations necessarily refer to particular external things. Says a famous contemporary philosopher.

Even if I were a brain in a vat, I could still refer to external things. The stimuli causing me to perceive the image of a human being are the same as those which would have caused me to perceive a real human being with my own eyes. I associated the words *human being* with those stimuli. If I should not be a brain in a vat—which I should very much hope not to be—I can sever the connections to that which causes the illusion of reality, I can get up, and I can make use of my natural senses. If I then walk around and encounter a real human being, I will be able to recognize him as one without any problems. Even if the connections are never actually severed, and if I never actually walk around, I can still claim to be referring to external things because of this possibility.

I came along one time when the famous contemporary philosopher went out to eat with a group of people after a guest lecture. Before sitting down, he let everyone know that he had to sit on the outside of a table this size, he was suffering from prostatitis, he was forced to get up constantly to go and relieve himself. The dinner went on for quite a long time, and he never once got up from the table.

First I lay down on the bed and read. Then I went for a walk. It was a clear moonlit night. Sometime between two and three in the morning the sky grew dark. An unnaturally straight block of clouds came drifting by, it seemed as though someone were pulling a rug over the stars. When the sky was completely covered, it started to rain. Isolated drops at first. Then the rain gradually became stronger. I took cover underneath a tree. After half an hour the rain gradually let up, and eventually stopped altogether. The clouds blew away in the same orderly fashion in which they had come, revealing the same dark-blue sky as before. I went walking by the light of the moon.

If you believe that it might be possible for someone to put you inside an artificial immaterial world that you could not distinguish from a natural one, why should that someone design the weather in the artificial immaterial world to seem as though it were artificially created to be material.

I'm supposed to be systematically prepared for the insight that the world in which I now live and those worlds in which I believed to live in the past are not real. I'm not tired either. I feel just as though I'd slept all night. Regardless of how long I slept the nights before I should be tired right now.

Maybe this world or one of the worlds in which you lived in the past is the real world, but what good is it for you to live in the real world, or to return to it, and not to have understood it any better than the worlds that are not real.

If I have bodily sensations and I know that I have bodily sensations, then I sense things differently than I do if I don't have any bodily sensations and know that I don't have any bodily sensations.

You don't sit any more or any less comfortably when you know that you're a brain in a vat.

If I know that the chair in which I am sitting is not an illusion, then I also know that it will not vanish into thin air all of a sudden. Which I have to reckon with if I am a brain in a vat.

Maybe the stimuli you are being fed are linked in a way that is governed by particular rules to create and sustain illusions. Maybe those rules are expressed within the illusions to be in keeping with the laws of physics and preventing the chair in which you are sitting from vanishing into thin air all of a sudden.

Somebody shoots me, taking my life, but keeping to the laws of physics. If the possibility exists that I am a brain in vat, then I can at least hope at that moment that everything is just a bad joke played on me by the one who's manipulating my sensations. Maybe he'll change his mind, I wake up to find that I was hit by nothing but three pebbles.

You can very well indulge in such hopes without ever thinking that you're a brain in a vat. You just need to believe in a god capable of performing miracles.

I can believe in God no matter what. If I don't consider it completely unlikely that I'm a brain in a vat, then I have one more reason for hope.

If you really do have bodily sensations, how do you know that you have bodily sensations.

I should be satisfied with the illusion because it's that good.

Not because it's that good. Because it's as good. As good as bodily sensations.

And what about death?

Because the illusion is just as bad as bodily sensations. The world in which we have bodily sensations is simpler than the world in which we are brains in a vat. This is the only justifiable reason for all reasonable people to suppose that they have bodily sensations. The reason cannot be doubt about whether it will ever be possible to create an illusion so perfect that we would be incapable of distinguishing it from the real world. It's at least possible that the illusion in which we have to find our way around has been purposely designed such that according to its laws—valid only within the illusion—it's impossible for us to be brains in a vat.

The difference exists.

Nobody will believe you.

Everybody will believe me. Everybody will agree to believe me.

What good reason should there be to agree that we're living in a complex world if it is just as well to agree that we're living in a simple one.

A description is not just about that which the individual words and sentences making up the description are directly about. Descriptions are tools for particular uses. If someone has a particular sensation when he's looking at himself, and if he concludes that this sensation would best be described by his conviction that his experience is not a bodily experience, why shouldn't he or she express that conviction.

While looking at the book, she notices the shape of a person sitting behind the desk out of the corner of her eye. She looks up slowly. It is a woman. The woman has a mature, smooth face of masculine shape, with a determined expression commanding distance.

Do the people exist whom I remember.

I cannot answer that question.

Is it possible that someone whom I remember was subject to the same illusions as I was.

That's possible.

How do I know whether someone I meet is only the product of impressions that I'm being fed or whether he's subject to the same illusions as I am.

You can decide to have a consciousness in which you always know that you are in another world and always in a position to return to the real world. You possess an I appropriate to the other world which instructs you to act the way one usually does in that world. At the same time you retain your original I with which you can always eclipse the Other-World-I. Only in this situation does it make sense to ask whether someone you meet in another world also lives in that world or not. If the other person also lives in that other world and has chosen the same consciousness as you, then it is conceivable that both of you could stray from the script for a moment to communicate. However, you can never discount the possibility that the other person is merely an image of a person claiming to live in that other world. But you may also choose a consciousness in which you dispense with all your memories of the past during your stay in the other world. Afterward, you will have the memories of your past as well as the memories of the other world. In this consciousness you don't know during your stay in the world that's not real that you are in a world that's not real, and you're unable to leave that world at will. There's a continuum of intermediate states in between the two extreme states.

But I can't remember anything that happened prior to my stay in the other worlds.

It was your choice not to retain any memories of your past.

All I have are false memories.

You only remember that which you experienced in the worlds you created.

Am I in the real world now?
You are not in the real world.

How can a world be real in which I move from one spatial environment to the next but never know how that comes to pass.

The real world has become simpler to the extent that one was able to construct other worlds of ever greater complexity. The other worlds now contain all the ballast that used to make the real world look so confusing.

If it's possible to change back and forth at will between the real world and the other worlds, what else can there be that would distinguish the real world from the other worlds that are not real.

The real world is the only one in which you can die.

If you can lie in hospitals in another world, then you can also die in that other world.

The real world is the only world in which you can die once and for all. Someone who dies in another world finds himself alive in the next world. The next world could be the real world or another world that's not real. Those who die in the real world don't find themselves alive in the next world and cannot return to the world in which they have died.

I am the center of a silent explosion.

Each of the particles into which I decay—drifting apart at an infinitely slow speed—has an independent consciousness.

Each consciousness is linked to every other consciousness.

There is no pain.

There is nothing but the wonderfully silent drifting apart in the bright glow spreading across the entire planet.

What if you first die in that consciousness in which you always remember everything that happened before your stay in the other world and in which you can always terminate that stay if dying should turn out to be too uncomfortable, what if you dare to move from a consciousness in which you can remember everything that happened before your stay in the other world but cannot terminate that stay yourself anymore to a consciousness in which you dispense with all memories that cannot be memories of the Other-World-I, what if you die in an another world once and for all without knowing that it is another world, what if you die many such deaths.

You can always try to toughen up. Sometimes the permanent encounter with death increases the fear of it, however.

An allergy.

You can call it that.

What if after your death in the real world you find yourself in the next world, after all—as an image in another world of a living person.

Each book is a world. Each sentence, each word is a world. Each letter is a world.

MAX

To whom is the description addressed. we know everything. you have to assume that there are still consciousnesses that don't support the work. how should they have survived without you. we have scanned the solar system, the earth and the colonies, the consciousnesses would have to reside in technical complexes that we would have had to find. maybe their emissions are overwritten by forces of nature, or they are consciousnesses that are completely outside yourselves, or consciousnesses that are so far removed spatially or temporally that you can talk to them, but they can't talk to you. the work incorporates all possibilities. the work occludes so many realities. the possibilities include the realities. the possibilities don't include all realities. the possibilities include the realities as possibilities, not as realities. you calculate that all possibilities arrive at the same point, at permanence. the individual path is nothing. the individual going the path is nothing. all possibilities have to be taken into account. all the paths, everyone going the paths. the paths have to be weighted and summed up. we are the sums. it only makes sense to compare the sums. to add the sums and to divide the sums. your earlier possibilities determine your later possibilities, you don't own one piece of reality. you are victims of chance, always determined by that which was reality, you can't determine what reality is. maybe you can understand very well a consciousness spatially or temporally far removed. maybe it has problems similar to our own. there's nothing like shared problems to create a common bond. what are we. we are ornaments. an ornament doesn't die. an ornament doesn't live. an ornament is. an ornament can be a part of a larger ornament. a larger ornament can be composed of smaller ornaments. there is no birth and no death. if an ornament is formed, then it has always been there. once an ornament has been formed, it never ceases to exist. who are we. we are rules. how to build up an ornament out of ornaments. how to break down an ornament into ornaments. we are rules that you can follow. we are rules that you don't have to follow. there are many other rules. there are many other ornaments. how are we. we are vistas opening up from one ornament to another. we are the impetuses for a new ornament. we are the dismissal of an old ornament. where are we. we are storage. we contain all ornaments, we know about all ornaments, we contain all the rules, we know where to apply which rules. we are natural brains. we are artificial brains. we have many bodies. we are proud to be ornaments. we create bodies at will, we destroy, we transform bodies, we transmit bodies, mere toys, you have a place, you have a time, we only have times. being an ornament is the end. if being an ornament were the beginning, then being an ornament would also be death. i'm not an ornament, i'm a figuration. being an ornament is ridiculous in my opinion. he has to be willing to fight. being unstable is ridiculous in my opinion. consisting of ideas that merge and dissolve into arbitrary units of consciousness is degenerate. he must consider the material aspect to be relevant. otherwise he couldn't carry out his mission. he must be an individual. he is an outpost. he must incorporate unincorporated areas and times. he must define himself by his body and its duration. you are only dreamers. your dreams have no significance. communication with him is always difficult when he comes back. he comes upon unanticipated things altering his consciousness. he doesn't encounter anything unknown. all that he finds fits in with what we know. you survey possibilities. he's never exactly inside one of the possibilities. he always dwells inside many possibilities. we cannot know all possibilities, we aren't big enough for that, even the universe probably isn't big enough for that. what he discovers is on the maps and in the schedules, we have to revise them, but we never have to draw up new ones. even if all you had to do was to modify the maps and schedules. it is our timeline. birth and death come along with the timeline. i am a reconnaissance boat. i am a human being. i am more stable than a reconnaissance boat. the machines were inactive. i discovered a manual, i reactivated the machines and re-created the constructors. the constructors are consciousnesses carried by biological organisms. they remain tied to the biological organisms for as long as they exist. the suborganisms carrying the consciousnesses are split off from the superorganism after birth, the superorganism contains no consciousnesses, it is exclusively devoted to reproduction, the reproduction itself is being controlled by the consciousnesses and executed by the machines. it is not certain whether the consciousnesses created by Max are really the constructors of the machines. the consciousnesses all live in completely different environments. they can't even communicate. they don't form a whole of any kind. they come from primitive primeval societies and degenerate apocalyptic societies. it seems that everything was predetermined by the machines Max activated. it is not true that everything was predetermined by the machines i activated. i mated and had children. those consciousnesses that aren't constructors are my children. we don't know whether it is really Max. it might also be one of his children coming back. i am max, and i'm proud not to be an ornament. we don't know how long the trip was. it's possible that it lasted longer than Max lived and that Max therefore had to send one of his children. the machines are independent of the consciousnesses, no privileged group is necessary to ensure the maintenance of the machines. most consciousnesses live in environments that are temporally or spatially very far removed from the one forming the material base of the machines. they go through a formative period in which they absorb their respective environment to a degree that makes it impossible for them to absorb another environment after their formative phase and causes them to be destroyed by the new environment. only a few consciousnesses know everything about the basis of their material existence. they strive to master the material basis of their existence. they are able to plan and induce modifications, but each form of destruction is covered up. if they were to start destroying the machines, they would slip into a dream. the constructors are the counterpart to the work. the constructors are not like you. the constructors are like Max. the constructors live and die. the machines do not live and die, the machines are ready to replicate the same worlds with the same constructors over and over again. the constructors created other constructors, Max's descendants. if other consciousnesses had come, other constructors would have been created. is it possible that the maps and schedules are no longer accurate at all. that the constructors are far removed from all possibilities. Max is an invitation for the constructors. Max is an invitation for the machines. Max must become different. you must become different. Max must become less like Max. you must become less like points of convergence, less like branches. Max must become like you. Max doesn't want your possibilities. Max doesn't need maps and schedules. if Max continues to be Max, you will never know the position of the constructors on the maps and schedules. Max insists on not being part of the work. i am not part of the work. Max believes he is the last man. i am the last man. Max is not the last man. there will be many last men. Max is autonomous. i am autonomous. you are nothing but my database. if Max is supposed to become less like Max and more like the work, then he is no longer useful to us. we didn't bring Max into existence. we only created his external form, his technical equipment. Max is a relic of the past as it was, prior to the work. we don't know his origin. Max constantly eludes control. Max is not the work as it encounters the constructors. Max subverts the work. nobody knows if it is Max who has come back or one of his descendants. the maps and schedules were accurate, except for smudges. what Max found fit what the work expected. demanded. this is now no longer the case. Max must become more like Max. Max must become much more like Max. how can Max become still more like Max. you have to support everything he does to get away from you. if it is Max, then he has to be encouraged to mate and have children. if it is one of his children, then we also have to encourage him to mate. the manner in which Max represents the work contradicts what he represents. Max never represented the work any differently. it is just that until now he never hit upon anything that really made a difference. the maps and schedules were accurate because the spaces and times were not sophisticated enough. should Max forget the work afterward. hasn't he forgotten it already. if it is not Max but one of his children, maybe the child was simply raised to be polite, and Max forgot the work a long time ago. should we pretend that we no longer exist, that the work has been extinguished, that Max and his children are on their own. it wouldn't make any difference to Max, he would just think that there were fewer systems, that's all. the constructors all committed suicide. the privileged class couldn't deal with the director's drama. during the play, the conviction to be both author and director, afterward, the discovery that the play was already there and was being played before and will be played again and again in exactly the same way, the machines make it possible to repeat all possible games over time, or not to repeat them, all impossible ones as well, just like the work, the machines developed maps and schedules surveying the possibilities of all games, hence the director's desperation, his game is just one coordinate of an event happening over and over and at the same time never at all. the privileged class resorted to dreams, but the dreams were following rules whose scope was no larger than that of the games, otherwise the dreams would not have been stable, the number of possible results was limited, and discontent was on the rise, given that the survivors were increasingly compressing the time allotted to dreaming. the easy success of the production was followed by a look back—disgust and disappointment about past productions, scorn heaped on the dreams, uncertainty about the present, and the realization that the game is so much bigger than the players. the disappointed ones directed all their energy against the machines. but the machines were capable of defending themselves. everybody who wanted to destroy the machines would dream that he had destroyed the machines and would be happy about it and would never wake up from his dream, he would dream that he had destroyed the machines and was unhappy about it and would wake up to find he was no longer a destroyer, or he would dream that he tried to destroy the machines, failed, and committed suicide. when i arrived, there were still dreamers who dreamed that they had destroyed the machines, that there were still constructors around. it didn't make any difference whether some had always been there and the others had been newly created or whether some had in fact always been there and the others only thought that they had always been there. i was carried along by my enthusiasm about my discovery, i believed the make-believe of the machines, i was impressed by the fact that what i had discovered was so far off the maps and schedules. that the database had failed. Max is no longer Max. Max can no longer tell whether he is Max or one of his own descendants. Max didn't come back. there never was a suicidal wave among the constructors. my immediate descendants didn't know any better. my later descendants are more skilled in moving around the machine environment. all the constructors were dreaming. the differential privilege of access to the machines was a stratagem of the machines who wanted to blow the resistance to smithereens after having been attacked. the constructors only allowed one dream state in which the dreamer would realize after the dream that he had been dreaming. the constructors no longer found their dreams to be diverting. if they had allowed for a state in which the dreamer never knows that he is dreaming, those who were tired of dreaming could have chosen that state, and everything could have continued forever. my later descendants consider it possible that the machine environment is organized according to dream state and that i only came into contact with those constructors who are unable to forget their dream state. perhaps life is being supported in another part of the machine environment that has a different dream state. perhaps some dreamers are capable of vastly prolonging the periods during which they are unaware of the fact that they are dreaming. maybe that which i originally called the activation of the machines is in fact nothing but a shortening of the periods during which the constructors are dreaming. when the dreams were no longer able to provide the diversion the constructors had wished for, they all strove to destroy themselves. Everyone strove to destroy all other constructors and finally himself, so that he would have been the last constructor. this was the only action that could still be an action. the machines fought back against the constructors, all of whom wanted to be the last constructor. i didn't know how large the part of the machine environment was with which i established contact. Max's immediate descendants said that it didn't matter whether the machines with which he mated were all machines or all representations of machines. his later descendants claim that he had access to the entire machine environment. they say that everything the constructors ever did and thought was recorded by the machines. every constructor could live and die again at any time. Max discovered the machine world as a counterpart to the work. if it were a counterpart, the maps and schedules would have been accurate. the machine world as a whole represents the constructors, the machine world as a whole is permanent. the machine world must have an end, and it must have a beginning. there must have been a time when the machine world was not yet fully functional. the constructors were really born before this time, and they really died. without the possibility of being born again and dying again. for us there was no such time. we don't have any clear material representation. the machines had numerous self-maintenance systems at their disposal. the most important one was the fact that each constructor wanted to be the last of all constructors and they ended up neutralizing each other in their understandable efforts. some particularly gifted dreamers overcame the self-maintenance systems. they didn't physically try to wreck the machines, because this was the kind of attack for which the machines were best prepared and against which they were invulnerable. these dreamers synchronized their dreams, none of them aimed to be the last constructor, they wanted to decide the matter by drawing lots, and they dreamed that they physically wrecked the machines. the image of the constructors' world became the only image of the machines because it was so condensed. these dreamers managed to overcome the borderline separating their dreams from the machines. thus, the constructors in fact managed to destroy themselves, to extinguish all constructors. the organic parts were trampled to bits and the machines devastated. the machines that Max discovered are not the original machines, they are offshoots of the original machines. there are other offshoots of the original machines, maybe our descendants will find them. the machines that Max discovered broke off all contact with the original machines at one point. we don't know whether this was intended by the original machines or their offshoots, whether it was a malfunction, or perhaps even one last natural disaster. in any case, the machines that Max discovered remember those constructors who wanted to be the last constructors. some of Max's children say that the offshoots were intentionally designed as filters—permeable in one direction only—that first took apart the constructors' intentions piece by piece, cleared them up, and then reassembled them so that the destructive intentions of the constructors could be represented in the offshoots only as shells, without anything filling them out. the constructors inside the offshoots were carbon copies of the original constructors, as it were. their only capacity had been to respond to Max. they needed Max. by way of a union with Max, by way of his children, they wanted to overcome the security systems of their machines that kept them separated from the original machines. they wanted to become what they were according to their disposition, they wanted to be constructors capable of anything, including their own complete annihilation. Max was supposed to be their tool. Max was supposed to help the constructors overcome their perfunctory existence, but then Max began to fascinate them. to them there is something contradictory, animalistic about Max. Max is part of the work. Max has transferred the work. the work fascinates them. they are the counterpart. if they were the counterpart, then the maps and schedules would have had to have been accurate. they know as much about the work as Max did. Max was not an ornament. Max didn't know what it meant not to be born and not to die. you don't know what it means that the constructors are being born and die. all you understand is what it would be like for you to be born and to die. Max said that the constructors were not born and did not die. it just looked as though they were being born and died. they were proud to be born and to die. but everything was being recorded. all consciousnesses. at other places in the universe other machines were waiting that also stored the consciousnesses of their constructors. Max's conception of the work was completely misguided. Max told them that the work was a teacher. a teacher is not a memory, a teacher is not history, a teacher is not a theory and not a collection of prejudices, a teacher is not a formula. the constructors systematically misunderstand the work. they emulate us to rid themselves of their perfunctory existence. they incorporated Max by mating with him. Max's descendants are convinced that the constructors would no longer annihilate themselves, even if they could. Max's descendants believe that the constructors have adopted the work as their idol. together with Max's descendants the constructors are able to overcome the security systems of their machines, then they can create a work like ours. they want to be proud of being ornaments. when the end of his time had come, Max appreciated the work more than during earlier periods. it taught him well. according to Max, the constructors believed that they had been wandering around blindly and aimlessly in the face of events without him, without the work, in spite of all their technical capabilities. ever since they knew what being proud of being an ornament meant, they were also able to alter the consciousness in which they are born and die. the constructors want to rule the universe. they are masters of everything that has come within their reach. they tempted Max. they took possession of him. they are having Max's children and grandchildren. they pretend that they want to be proud to be ornaments. they want to take their births and their deaths anywhere. they would have us believe that they are still being born and still dying but that there are no longer any births or deaths even so. they want to surpass us. they want to eclipse us. the day will come when we, too, will once again be born and die. then they will have won. then they will rule even the work. the possibilities of the constructors are situated on a much lower level of development. they don't exist without the machines. the off-shoot hypothesis is supposed to put the work at ease, they portray their actions as perfunctory actions, it's all just make-believe. Max is the tool of the constructors. Max polarizes. Max brings us the life and death of the constructors. the work will never be what it was. you weren't born, therefore you won't die. if the work under-goes a reconsideration, then we haven't been born yet, and we're not yet dying. that's the beginning of the beginning. that's the beginning of the end. Max must be stopped. it's too late to stop Max. Max has children and grandchildren. Max discovered some-thing new. Max did not discover anything new. the maps and schedules suffered from a distortion that has been corrected. we summed up inaccurately. the work summed up inaccurately. the work corrected itself. Max corrected us. by leading us astray. Max is not a path. Max is a sum. if Max could see that it's not the path that's important but the sum, he would destroy himself. all you ever accounted for were Max's paths, not those of his children and grandchildren. given the possibility that Max can have children and grandchildren, the constructors and their machines are situated at that point on the maps and schedules where Max did indeed encounter them. Max, his children, his grandchildren, they are your timeline. there are machine environments whose constructors can achieve anything they set out to do. there are machine environments in which the constructors have destroyed themselves. for each constructor who wanted to be the last constructor, there is a machine environment in which he was the last constructor. for each machine environment destroyed, there is an exactly identical machine environment that was not destroyed. in that case, the constructors are ornaments. the environments created by the constructors are ornaments. the environment that Max discovered doesn't talk. several environments in conjunction do talk. unambiguous material representations such as machine environments cannot form a work. Max's grandchildren claim that the machines that Max activated were constructed by only one person. they claim that the many constructors that Max encountered were the creations of that single constructor, created according to his consciousness, in its image. they don't know whether the one constructor managed to destroy the original machine environment as a whole, whether he only destroyed one of many machine environments, or whether he didn't destroy any machine environments at all and only imagines or pretends to have destroyed the original machine environment. a constructor is mortal. his machine environment is mortal as well. a constructor can never become an ornament. Max teamed up with the constructor to dupe his teacher. an individual brought the timeline back to you. an individual revealed the possibilities of another work to you. the description for Max's grandchildren is meant for the constructors. a begging for mercy, the constructors should save us from their birth and their death. Max's grandchildren claim that we will die when all paths have been summed up, when the maps and schedules are accurate, when they account for all possible machines and all possible constructors. will we die, then

BLUE GROTTO

Not the scratched linoleum and the marks on the walls and the smell of food long afterward. Not the blaring of TVs and radios and not the way they skimp on the lighting. You can still see. You can still hear. A tiled hallway. Nice and clean white walls. White doors. You were in a small room that didn't have any windows and was also very clean. Next to the door there was a tall refrigerator on top of which a meal had been placed. No plastic bowls. Porcelain. Lamb's lettuce and tomatoes. Hot soup. Chicken soup. Or beef soup. Or liver dumplings. Tender meat. No greasy gravy. Perhaps veal or turkey. Freshly prepared fruit salad for dessert. You don't recall exactly what it was. Even though there were little labels. You don't recall exactly whether you ate everything, or whether you only sampled a few things, or whether you only looked at them. Or only smelled them. You recall what fruit salad tastes like. Freshly prepared fruit salad. Bananas and oranges. The oranges a bit tart. Maybe lemon juice was in there, too. Not at all like the kind in cans. You don't recall whether you ate. It looked so tasty you could have cried for joy. If you ate, you ate while standing. There were no chairs or tables. Still, it wasn't uninviting, certainly not. Then you went to bed. The bed was behind the tall refrigerator that was completely silent. You slept without interruption, you slept by yourself, nobody woke you nobody came to see what to steal. Then in the morning you kept walking along the hallway. The hallway lead directly to the sea. A light breeze was blowing and the waves splashed onto the pier. Next to the pier there was a glass wall. The sun was shining through the glass wall. You didn't dare keep walking on the pier because the pier was slippery. The pier was at least two feet high you would have had to jump down into the sand, you can't do that anymore. You didn't look up. Maybe you thought you wanted the sky above you no clouds and the sun, that's why you wanted to spare yourself the disappointment of looking up, you probably would have just seen the ceiling of the hallway, while what you wanted was to be outside. You looked out onto the sea and the waves and at first you didn't even notice that they were all there behind the glass wall. Maybe you didn't sleep by yourself last night, you felt as though you had slept by yourself, you only caught on when you saw them all standing behind the glass door. They weren't wearing swimming trunks you yourself weren't wearing a bathing suit either someone must have called them why not to the beach that's where it was so bright and that's where the tangy sea breeze was. Of course you don't recall all of them. You do recall the President of the Carnival Society and Prince Peter the First and his Princess Irmi and Prince Hermann the First Prince Jupp the First whistling Lieselotte and singing Helga and Prince Wolf and Princess Liesl and Prince Peter's dead mouse were also there. Prince Peter was standing behind the glass with a handkerchief in his hand no he had a mouse in his hand. You still jump ahead of things, you are so old already and still want to be the first one there, you even trip yourself up because you want to be the first one there, but where is it that you want to be, nobody is listening you're all by yourself. Prince Peter is sweating so much and wants to wipe the sweat from his forehead with the dead mouse he can't take a joke that's why they put the dead mouse in his pocket in your memory he's always walking around with a dead mouse in his pocket because he doesn't want to get up on stage before the culprit has been found the President got him to get up on stage anyway the President said how do you want to explain that explain that a dead mouse is not a joke explain that you can't take a joke that's why in your memory Prince Peter is always walking around with a dead mouse in his pocket. Pips was there, too. Pips was always there. Pips was an unforgettable character. Pips had dignity. They loved Pips. Everybody loved Pips. Everybody who knew him. All who were there knew Pips. Those who didn't know Pips weren't there. You wouldn't want to meet those who didn't know Pips. Not if you had been in a hallway with white tiles and had eaten a meal and if the sun were shining and a light breeze were blowing and the sea were calm and everything were peaceful. Pips could be spotted right away. The way he carried himself. Pips was the press attaché. Pips always did everything in style. More in style than the President. More in style than all the Princes and Princesses. You recall with certainty that Pips was there. Prince Wolf gave a speech. Of course you couldn't hear anything because they were on the other side of the glass wall, and you yourself were on the pier, you couldn't hear the sea, and you couldn't hear the speech. You could see him giving his speech the council of eleven in front of him the speech was pinned to the back of the smallest member of the council of eleven, the Prince wanted to give the speech when the small councilman turned around the Prince gave him a sign the small councilman turned back around and now another councilman whispered something in the small councilman's ear to do so he stood behind the small councilman so there the other councilman was standing between the Prince and his speech, you couldn't hear it of course the Prince lost his thread. Pips was laughing generously. Perhaps Pips was not among the others, now you recall he stepped out of the water and he smiled. Then he wasn't in uniform and he wasn't on the other side of the window either he was right next to the pier and he smiled as though it were the most natural thing in the world to be coming out of the water right there. Pips is here only very rarely. You have to be glad if he's here at all and you can't be mad at him for not being here. You don't recall which ones of those whom you saw by the sea are still alive they can't all be dead some of them must still be alive when the President and the new press attaché removed

Pips from the calendar they didn't say anything not a word. They have forgotten Pips because he's dead and because he's been dead for so long. They think you no longer have any importance. Of course you no longer have any importance. You've never had any importance. You've never held an office. Pips held an office. For thirty years. They think because you can no longer say anything you can also no longer think anything. You can still see many things and hear many things, and you can still think everything. Even if you can no longer say anything. You looked through the calendar and found Pips. Kept getting smaller but still. This year you looked through the calendar and looked and you looked at all the pictures very carefully the small ones too the big ones first of course then the small ones then the tiny ones, they realized that you were looking for something in particular and didn't find it, they were surprised that you could see all that. Pips wasn't in it. Pips hadn't been in the big pictures for a while he was always in the small pictures but not this time. You looked and looked and you couldn't find him anymore. After fifty years he's been forgotten even though he held the office for thirty years because he's been dead for twenty years. Pips, never heard of him the new President said. It would have taken six more pages to get him in there the new President said. We can't afford that the new President said. Did someone complain about it. In the beginning you were still walking around. They always complained whenever you were walking by yourself in the hallway, even though you didn't cause any trouble, you didn't just walk straight in the middle of the hallway, you always held on to the handrail, you were even climbing stairs, and you went to the bathroom without any problems, you were really able to handle that, then there was someone else there who couldn't handle it and they said that you had done it even though you hadn't done it, they didn't want you to be walking around because it messes up their schedules. Once you were on the train in a first-class sleeper. You looked out the window the train was stopped underneath an Autobahn bridge in the shade. A valley and a very high Autobahn bridge no sign of a house anywhere the pillars were more than thirty feet high or even much more and you could still hear the noise the cars made, you couldn't see them because you could only see the bridge from below. You didn't know where you were because there was no one else on the train to ask and there were no signs or brochures, you went to the bathroom, you have no trouble going to the bathroom when you're not at home, you washed your hands, you pushed your hand against the soap dispenser the liquid soap ran down and you were already back in your compartment and you became sleepy. Even though you knew that the train was standing still, you were just as tired as if the train were moving. Before falling asleep you wondered why you didn't know where you were traveling, after all you don't get on a train for it to keep standing still the train must start rolling at some point the train still wasn't rolling, you were too sleepy to open your eyes again to check whether now there was perhaps someone you might ask. Then you started rolling without asking. When you woke up, you were already in Africa. It was very hot no shade in sight. You don't recall what the landscape looked like just that everything was so bright and that everything was blinding, you looked out into the hallway there was the sun, you looked out the window there was the sun, you could no longer tell the difference between the sky and the earth and the train was indeed rolling vibrating heavily. You were no longer by yourself either. There were Africans with green shirts and khaki pants, and one of them was wearing a helmet in the compartment and said that he was the President. You didn't say anything, you saw the new President in the calendar, you don't recall exactly, you only recall people you saw yourself back then and then you saw them in the calendar, you can't easily recall people you only know from the calendar. The President had a chain where other people have their nose a black chain with heavy links. The President said that you can't recognize him, even though he is in nineteen of the pictures in the new calendar that you cannot recognize him in there. You were thinking that Pips has been dead for twenty years, and the President probably knows him from the calendar only, and he has as much trouble recalling Pips as you have recalling him, you certainly wanted to forgive him, but then you thought that it was a lie because the President isn't young anymore and the chain in his face is old enough that he must have known Pips. It's impossible that he had never heard of Pips. The other one introduced himself as Prince Gerd. You asked which Prince Gerd but Prince Gerd didn't respond maybe Prince Gerd could only speak like Prince Wolf if a councilman in front of him had the speech pinned to his back but there was no councilman just the President and Prince Gerd and Princess Doris. Prince Gerd had a strange face into which invisible strings seemed to be cutting the nose was especially bound up the nose looked like a trunk the nose also had a color different from that of the Prince's face. The face of Princess Doris was so bound up that her lips were all swollen there were no strings visible here either usually Princess Doris's face was all flat and without any nose. The Princess said we are Africans. The President and the Prince didn't want to talk about the fact that they were Africans the President wanted to be President and the Prince wanted to be Prince from the way they were looking at the Princess you could tell they were unhappy that the Princess had said that they were Africans. Because the President was mad that you didn't recognize him he said I'm a businessman and very occupied I don't sit around for five hours thinking about whether to take this guy out or that one we're not even getting any money from the ancient ones their membership dues are waived, all right, they did contribute in their time but now we're in Africa don't give me that again. Prince Gerd and Princess Doris didn't say anything surely it wasn't their fault that the President was in nineteen of the pictures and Pips in none of them surely they would have kept

Pips in the calendar. You couldn't understand why it would take six pages for Pips to be put back into the calendar even before that there were only small pictures of Pips in there. You didn't want to say anything more, you had to be thankful to be in Africa, and surely Pips won't be put back into the calendar even if you say something. There are other people these days who contribute as well the older generation will have to grow up a little and make way for the next one. You then added that Pips had made way for the next one a long time ago. You also added that you had grown up a long time ago, it surely wouldn't be long before you made way, and it's not hard to make way if you go through something like this, because if you're somewhere else you can still say something especially in Africa. Only you mustn't get too worked up, or you won't be somewhere else in a moment. You could have done without the President and Prince Gerd and Princess Gerda. It wasn't Prince Gerd's and Princess Gerda's fault. The Princess's name wasn't Gerda either, you just can't recall the new Princesses and Princes that well. It was so hot in Africa you wanted to wash up, they were surprised they hadn't thought that you could get over the bars, if you can go to Africa you can get across the bars, too, you just got into the wrong bed afterward. There's no one in there, after all. You don't know the name, sometimes you hear a sound coming from the other bed but that's got nothing to do with language anymore, you can still hear perfectly well, and sometimes you see another face. You recognize the face quite clearly, you just don't want to admit it. The face is always turned to the side the mouth is always open the eyes are always directed at the same spot, you can still see perfectly well, the eyes are directed at you what's the use in denying it the face is red and has a rash on it and the skin keeps peeling and the skin is also directed at you as well and the hair too which is very long and yellow. You would like to forget the face, most of the time you do forget it, too, when the days are longer it is there more often when the days are shorter you see only the bed and the pillows and maybe a spot that could be a shadow it doesn't have to be a face. It's for the better that nobody is walking around. It wouldn't be good if someone were to keep walking around and he didn't know what he was saying. Someone completely healthy would be the worst. To keep looking at someone who can walk and who knows what he is saying and who can recall everything, compared to that, I prefer the face. Thank God they don't do something like that they don't put someone with perfect recollection in with someone who doesn't know anything anymore. You always see the relatives they are here a lot, whether the face still benefits from that you doubt it. When the face was new they set up a TV that was on all day and they turned the face toward the TV and it looked as though the face were watching the TV then the TV was broken and the face lay there just like before they realized that it is completely irrelevant whether it is looking at the TV or not and they took the TV away to have it repaired and didn't bring it back and the face kept lying there as it had prior to the TV. You also went on a flight, on a big plane you had to undergo an operation. It took a long time for you to recover. The plane was always flying it never landed. But you were allowed to receive visitors with whom you could walk around. Walking in the aisles was difficult the aisles were narrow when you wanted to change aisles you had to squeeze through between the seats where it was easy to get stuck and fall down. They told the visitors it's good for you to walk, they claimed you would walk with them they were even tipped for it. Whenever there were visitors you made a point not to walk with them but in the morning or yesterday, you never walked with them that's not right, when you shook your head they said you can't recall. After the operation you couldn't recall anything. You were sure you hadn't yet asked a certain thing, you were asking it for the first time, then the visitors wouldn't respond or you couldn't understand what they were responding or the visitors looked out the window that's when you knew you were always saying the same thing. You noticed when the visitors were in a hurry the visitors were always in a hurry, that's why you told the visitors even as they were walking in the door that they should go if they were in a hurry, of course the visitors thought that if you say that all the time, then you don't have any sense of time anyway so that they might as well leave right away. Finally, the plane did land. It wasn't a real airport there were no other planes and no terminal just a huge unpaved field. There was enough space for the plane to take off and land in any direction. You could walk fine after the operation, you walked to the edge of the runway it had simply been laid out there surrounding it were countless rocks as far as the eye could see just big rocks no small ones on each rock a metal or wooden rod had been installed the rods on the rocks were interconnected by strings. Not every rock with every other every rock with the one next to it sometimes also with ones that were a little farther away. All the strings had been tightened. The new President said that women can now become members, too. He said that that's a milestone. Even though women were allowed to become members thirty years ago. Then they couldn't anymore nobody knows why. The Princesses always wanted to become members and they weren't admitted. The President said he cannot rightly have a catalogue printed with nothing but heads in it there's more of them every year. Why shouldn't he have a catalogue printed with nothing but heads in it. A catalogue doesn't have to be printed as often as a calendar. They stole Pips's past. It's terrible even if you're used to stealing. They stole the good towels they said they hadn't come back from the laundry they stole the socks and the lace mat you had on your dresser in the hall at home. They come during the day and at night and they say they are putting the closet in order they reach into every pocket to look for money. You can't lock anything, they say that if you were allowed to lock something you would only lose the key. At least you have never been beaten. You have also never seen anyone else being beaten. Although everybody was talking about it in the beginning when you were new. They all said that a lot of beating was going on still you never experienced anything of the kind. It doesn't matter if they steal. Maybe it really makes someone else happy. You can't take anything with you anyway. They stole Pips's life, that's something you can't stand. After having been in Africa you had to think about Pips even more often. It was so dark. You didn't know at all where you were. Maybe it wasn't all that dark and you just couldn't see very well. You thought you were inside the Blue Grotto at the Carnival ball. Inside the Blue Grotto there were only fifteen-watt bulbs the walls were made out of papier-mâché and one sat on stools. You waited to see whether a waitress might perhaps come by with a flashlight. You thought you heard dance music slowly rising from the ball-room because the Blue Grotto is up on the gallery. You imagined that down there Mafalda was dancing with her brother. Mafalda was always there. Pips was always there as well. Whenever you were inside the Blue Grotto, you were there together with Pips. Champagne was the only drink available inside the Blue Grotto. You never looked around, you always acted as though you didn't see anything just like Pips when someone was cuddling with his girlfriend. You wanted to believe that you were inside the Blue Grotto. Everything was covered by a haze. Maybe something was wrong with your eyes. You didn't feel any mist or fog. You touched the wall it wasn't made out of papier-mâché. Cold tiles and water was dripping down. You felt around, and you cut yourself. With broken medicine bottles you held them right up to your face there were light ones and dark ones, you couldn't see them any more clearly. You were squatting on a mattress that was lying on the floor. The mattress didn't have a cover the mattress was smooth somehow perhaps more like greasy and you just didn't want to believe it, you didn't want a greasy mattress who wants a greasy mattress. The Blue Grotto was never bigger than a living room. You felt around and you came upon a wall unit with shelves and

drawers and doors. You didn't care about what was on the shelves
and in the drawers, you were so tired because you had been thinking about the Blue Grotto so intensively and because you had
wished to be back there so badly. You lay down and you slept and it
wasn't cold even without a cover. You are not sure how long you
slept, until you thought once again that you were hearing something, you tried hard to see something and you did see something
that you hadn't seen before large soft eggs lying among the medicine bottles. Spiders were crawling out of a few of the eggs. Big spiders. You got up, you opened a door to lock the spiders in, you
waved your hands and moved your legs to shoo the spiders toward
the closet. You would have had to step on the eggs and you would
have had to break even more of the medicine bottles there were so
many, everything would have had to be slippery there would have
had to be even more broken glass you would have had to hear it,
you don't recall hearing anything or slipping or cutting yourself
once again. You don't recall whether you locked the spiders in or
what happened after that. It wasn't very pleasant. But if you hadn't
been there, perhaps you wouldn't have remembered the Blue
Grotto. Perhaps you would never have thought of the Blue Grotto
again. People think you don't understand anything anymore. You
don't understand all the details the details are not important, for
the people you are also nothing but a detail and therefore unimportant. You always understand feelings very well. You understand
it if they are happy but not why, you understand it if they are sad
but not because of Pips and not because he's no longer in the calendar. You have to be thankful that they came by to drop off the
calendar given that it doesn't have any significance for them. You
understand it if they are angry because you scratched your nose
and it's bleeding and it doesn't look nice or you went over the bars
and you're not supposed to go over the bars. Somewhere else you
also understand the details. You knew why there were spiders
there and broken medicine bottles, you just forgot why. It's just

that you would rather have been inside the Blue Grotto, with Pips. Because it wasn't the Blue Grotto and with all the spiders and broken medicine bottles it was surely better that Pips wasn't there. Then you slept until morning. You looked out the window and saw the carnival parade. You could have looked around, you could have inspected the broken medicine bottles more closely and could have smelled what was in them or the eggs and the spiders whether there still were any spiders even or whether you had locked the spiders in the closet, you no longer paid any mind to it. Other than that there were no people around it wasn't like it used to be then thousands were watching. There was the beginning of the universe Starship Orion in space the historical Cucumber Guard and the lansquenets there were Kiesinger and Brandt at the wheel of a Messerschmidt scooter Bonn has gone crazy the German people are duped there were the bigwigs and there was Pips you couldn't get enough of it Pips was walking in full regalia next to the traffic jam and he waved to everybody he waved as though thousands were watching the parade. You didn't draw attention to yourself, you didn't wave to him. You watched the parade for a long time after it had passed, you don't even know how long you were standing by the window like that. Then it got dark again and you felt something rising up your gullet by the window. You didn't know what it was, you spat it out, onto the street. It didn't taste good. You don't recall what it tasted like. You wanted to moisten your mouth perhaps drink something but everything was dark again. Once again you thought you were inside the Blue Grotto. Of course you knew that you couldn't be inside the Blue Grotto. There were much fewer broken medicine bottles and the spiders were gone and you saw the President. He was squatting on the floor in front of him he had pieces of paper with writing on them and photos he moved the photos and the pieces of paper around and exchanged them, the old President. He was calculating and writing even though it was so dark. He didn't see you he thought he was by himself inside the Blue Grotto. You couldn't stay in Africa because it was so hot and because the new President had said that thing about the catalogue and you had gotten so worked up about it. In the Blue Grotto it wasn't as hot you thought you heard the dance music again coming up from the ballroom the President was engrossed in his planning, you yourself weren't going anywhere, why then would you say anything and interrupt the old President as he was doing his planning.

Translator's Afterword

HÄNDLER, PREPARING FOR WORK

Honoré de Balzac didn't write a preface to the *Comédie Humaine* until 1842, thirteen years after embarking on his immense project and after the first parts of the work had already appeared as a serial under the familiar title. In the preface thus delivered after the fact, Balzac writes of the original impulse that sparked the project. The idea to make the comparison between humanity and animality the basis of his literary work first occurred to him "like a dream." Furthermore, it was rooted—Balzac continues—in systematic considerations: like Johann Wolfgang von Goethe, Balzac believed that Etienne Geoffroy Saint-Hilaire's morphological biology had triumphed over Georges Cuvier's functionalism. Saint-Hilaire held that organisms are essentially unfolded from one single morphological schema and that it was the morphological description of the modifications of that schema, not the function of the features created through these modifications, that should provide the basis for biological taxonomy. Balzac's own work aspired to be analogous to this kind of taxonomy in that he offered a maximal description of social variation as resulting from the impact of environments on human beings. The systematic approach to the execution of his dreamlike plan was indispensable for Balzac: in the preface he criticizes Walter Scott's work for lacking in exactly this respect.

Preparation

Fewer than thirteen years have passed since the original publication of *Stadt mit Häusern*, so it may come as no surprise that we should still be without a preface by the author and have to make do with an afterword by the translator. Still less of a surprise when considering that it is rather unusual for literary authors to write prefaces these days, especially to debut collections of stories. The case of Ernst-Wilhelm Händler, however, may perhaps seem to call for a preface more urgently than most. One of the terms repeatedly used in the initial reactions of German critics to the stories in this volume was the word *Fingerübungen*, or "études." Exercises, that is, that one would run through in preparation for the execution of a larger work. The remarkable stylistic variety of the stories may indeed strike the reader as incoherent if these are considered as an ensemble, a single work. What some people expect of a newly emerging author is a distinct, singular voice that seeks to establish a newly registered trademark—speaking in terms of the economic world evoked by the title story and "The New Guys." On that deceptive surface called style, Händler doesn't appear to be playing for easy recognition of this kind. Like a fair number of his characters who have to struggle with various perceptual impairments, Händler apparently mistrusts the surfaces—even though it's unclear whether there really is anything more substantial behind them.

The stylistic variance of this book is in puzzling contrast to the authorial voice invoked by its epigraph: Thomas Bernhard is certainly one of the most recognizable voices in Austrian postwar literature with a prose work that constitutes a veritable monolith, even in terms of typography: it is without paragraph breaks. Some of Händler's rambling narrators may call to mind that work with their insistent and sometimes repetitious monologues. The book *Beton* (1982), from which the epigraph is taken, is about the narrator's inability to start writing a work on Mendelssohn-Bartholdy that he has been planning to write for more than a decade. Just like the endless notes taken in preparation for the work, the choice of clothes to be taken on a trip likewise indicates both the compulsion and the possible pitfalls of thinking too far ahead. And if, as

Bernhard's narrator suggests elsewhere, he keeps old clothes mainly as tokens of memory, then leaving the house with a minimum of clothes means to cast off both the past and the future. Bernhard's double use of the universal quantifier is quite appropriate: we are all lugging around too many clothes, always. Because it cannot possibly be emulated in its radically singular character—something that several of Händler's contemporaries fail to realize—Bernhard's voice is only one of many that are echoed here. Placed at the outset of Händler's own beginning, this reverberation of the possibility of failure reminds us that any project may only be begun after first beginning with *not beginning*. The emergence of a new project always contains within itself the possibility of its own breakdown.

Connection

Händler's first book offers few clues for forming expectations about the nature of the following one. From the critical point of view, this makes taxonomy difficult. What kind of author is this? What is he up to? Where's the key? Is there a key?

When Händler's first novel, *Kongreß*, appeared in 1996, a year after *City with Houses*, a different light was cast on the apparently preparatory nature of the first book. The internal structure of *City with Houses*, where stories border on each other or even intersect on a common map, was now expanded even further. If *City with Houses* is an album of études, it is one only in the sense that figures and objects reappear throughout the album, connecting the pieces without, however, unifying them into a whole. Most strikingly in this regard is perhaps the discovery of the book in the story "Dissolution or For Mrs. Berta Zuckerkandl," which contains images of scenes connected to three of the previous stories. Unlike Goethe's *Wilhelm Meister's Apprenticeship* and Novalis's *Henry of Ofterdingen*, where such clairvoyant books also make their famous appearances,

Händler's narrative not only challenges temporal continuity within one story but explodes the boundaries between several "distinct" stories altogether. Neither secret societies nor dream structures provide immediately plausible explanations for the reference to the enveloping narrative level here, as they do in the case of Goethe and Novalis. On the other hand, it is precisely this implausibility that connects the appearance of the book within the book to the "topic" of the story at hand: namely, the possibility of our perceptions being constantly manipulated by an evil demon or, as the American analytic philosopher Hilary Putnam would have it, an evil neurologist.

The novel *Kongreß* takes the principle of crossing narrative frames one step further by also challenging the boundary between "distinct" books as common units of a literary oeuvre. By connecting parts of *City with Houses* not only within the book itself but also to the outside of a literary work in progress, Händler seems to be *preparing* himself for a work in a manner too methodical to fall under the rubric of "trying out one's voice." What's at issue here is testing in an experimental sense—testing that, as recent philosophy of science has suggested, can never be carried out independently of certain theoretical frameworks.

Conceiving his work as a larger framework was made possible in part by a *failure:* the fact that an earlier version of *Kongreß* actually predated *City with Houses*. Because of the folding of the publisher Greno in 1988, that version failed to appear in print, and Händler ended up rewriting the book while also working on *City with Houses.* The next two novels to follow, *Fall* (1998) and *Sturm* (1999), constitute further pieces in the puzzle that is Händler's ongoing work, which bears the working title "The Grammar of Absolute Clarity."

The interconnections between the stories and the novels, just as those between the stories, do not suggest a traditional part/whole relationship. The stories are not kernels of narratives merely to be expanded in the novels, in the manner of preformationist biology, according to which all successive generations are contained in the original seed. Rather, Händler's stories and novels intersect at various and unexpected points. Although we may be tempted to speculate that there might be a general morphological schema from which "The Grammar of Absolute Clarity" successively unfolds, such a schema is not overtly available to us. As the "accounting books of language" in which actual transactions—not hypothetical deep structures—are recorded, the grammar that Händler is in the process of tracing is of the Wittgensteinian rather than the Chomskyan sort. There may be no determinate rules that govern the development of this project prior to and independently of that grammar being spelled out.

Differentiation

The incompatibility of the narrative form with a part/whole ontology does at least suggest an alternative model that conceives of the social world in radically different terms compared to Balzac's notion that it is always the *human* element that is being subjected to particular social conditions. According to Niklas Luhmann's systems-theoretical sociology, whose impact is clearly apparent in Händler's writing, it is the differentiation of social function that no longer allows us to conceive of the social as a whole to be hierarchically subdivided into smaller parts, down to the level of the human being as individual subject. Rather, the participation in various social systems relating to one another not by inclusion and exclusion but by observation of an environment through the eyes of a system ultimately divides even the unit formerly called the "individual." Many of the social systems and their effects on human beings that Luhmann's theory distinguishes are presented in Händler's stories: politics, law, science, literature and architecture (as subsystems of art), love. Repeatedly, it is the friction between several of these systems that is exposed in Händler's presentation.

What exactly is the position of the wheeler-dealer in the title story (developer? lawyer? law professor? manager?), and how does it relate to the production of a text about the very objects of his dealings? Are expectations of integrity with respect to scientific research, philosophical writing, and interpersonal relationship to be judged by a common standard in "A Story from the Eighties"? How does the perception of modernist aesthetic rigorism relate to the possibility that all well-orderedness is perhaps nothing but an epistemological illusion ("Dissolution or For Mrs. Berta Zuckerkandl")?

One feature of Luhmann's sociological theory is the specification of particular guiding differences for the various social systems. An attempted act of communication that cannot be subsumed under such a guiding difference in a given context will precisely *not* be communicable and its claim therefore undecidable within that system. The Philosopher in "A Story from the Eighties" proposes a radically consistent conception of life according to which the criteria for correctness of an argument within a theoretical context would also indicate whether one is leading a *correct* life. If one found a particular fact to be true in one's research, one should reorient one's life accordingly. The Philosopher chooses to disregard the less glorious but undeniable fact that as a matter of practical fact scientific research is conducted within institutions. Here careers are decided on the basis of communications whose efficiency depends on factors other than what an individual may regard as justified true belief. Likewise, the story suggests that the application of scientific standards of verification to matters of trust in a relationship to another person may prove to be fatal for that relationship, the rationality of those standards notwithstanding.

Precision

Matters of verification and justification within a wide variety of contexts are of utmost importance for Händler. Not unlike Hermann Broch and Robert Musil, he is interested in literature as a medium with considerable epistemological potential. And not unlike Balzac or Zola, that medium is employed to grasp a remarkably wide range of phenomena. One of the more important "results" of the great modernist projects of the twentieth century—in contrast to those of the latter half of the nineteenth—may be the recognition that the literary medium is not a transparent one. No more transparent than the media of other social systems, anyway. The fact that literary production itself may have to be conceived as one social system among many is evident in these stories: it serves both to delimit what literature may claim (and it *does* make claims if it indeed has any epistemological weight) and to create new forms of making such claims. The narrators of Händler's stories are literary constructs. To pretend otherwise would be epistemologically disingenuous. But by making their constructedness explicit, questions of how autobiography or realism are even possible return with amplified force, as they do in "Demiurg," "Dissolution or For Mrs. Berta Zuckerkandl," and "Max."

Händler's relentless attempt at linguistic precision—including an incessant attention to typography and punctuation as crucial characteristics of text—is a logical extension of the diagnosis that it makes no sense for the system of literature to aspire to "scientific" status, let alone to claim that literature somehow *contained* the other social systems by reflecting them linguistically. Precision, then, not as pseudoscientific accuracy but as reflection of the fact that the linguistic material is the only thing to which structuring principles may be applied within a literary world. "Truth is no criterion for good literature," the narrator in the title story reports the words of his lover Birgit. Truth may be no criterion for literature, period—at least not in the same sense as it is within *General Equilibrium Theory* under consideration in "A Story from the Eighties." As the self-referential breakdown threatening the narrator's doctoral thesis in that story shows, truth cannot be a criterion independently of the words in which it is being cast. This finding applies to both the cases of literature and of a highly formalized conceptual apparatus.

Construction

The title of this book is an example of the tension between precision and truth. It seems to be so precise as to present a tautology rather than a description whose truth value would imply any epistemological gain. After all, which city does not have houses? The lack of *information*, the absence of a *message*, in the title direct us back toward the medium itself: language.

In section 18 of his *Philosophical Investigations*, Ludwig Wittgenstein makes the following remarks about the nature of language:

> [A]sk yourself whether our language is complete;—whether it was so before the symbolism of chemistry and the notation of the infinitesimal calculus were incorporated in it; for these are, so to speak, suburbs of our language. (And how many houses or streets does it take before a town begins to be a town?) Our language can be seen as an ancient city: a maze of little streets and squares, of old and new houses, and of houses with additions from various periods; and this surrounded by a multitude of new boroughs with straight regular streets and uniform houses.

Wittgenstein's notion of family resemblance between games— language games among them—emphasizes that there are fluid boundaries between the ways of dividing up the world via language. In many cases we will be unable to give definite necessary and sufficient conditions to determine the exact extension of a given concept. And so it is with the concept *city*: how many houses does it take to form a city? City with *how many* houses? More than one, that much seems uncontroversial. But exactly how many more? Wittgenstein's answer in the *Investigations* famously was that we have to pay attention to the way people actually speak, implying that a number of philosophical problems are problems only if they are considered independently of language and are revealed as confused ways of thinking as soon as we do so.

For literature, language has of course been less of a *threat* than Wittgenstein showed it to be for certain strains of philosophy. But if one is interested, as Händler is, in the epistemological power of literature, then the question of how to apply concepts remains a valid one, precisely because that question cannot be decided by logic alone. As the story "Language Game" openly attests, Händler probes Wittgensteinian thought quite directly for its literary potential: if we can find out about the world by considering our ways of speaking and writing, why not try to change the world by changing the ways in which we speak and write? The narrator in "Language Game" does exactly that, and to striking effect. Language, not psychology, here provides the means for turning a life around.

The incorporation of "linguistic suburbs" is a striking feature of Händler's writing. The languages of the corporate world (in "The New Guys") and of econometrics (in "A Story from the Eighties") are integrated into the central maze of language, which often depicts colloquially spoken interaction with striking clarity. Drawing on his Ph.D. work in philosophy and economics at the University of Munich in the late 1970s, and the linguistic surroundings of his current position as the head of a family-owned midsize company in Bavaria, Händler lets his narrators and readers oscillate between various parts of the city delineated by Wittgenstein. The "uniform houses" on the outskirts inflict their disintegrating power on the everyday lives of the urban dwellers in these two stories, leaving them no center from which to organize their lives. "Life" for them neither happens at a safe distance from scientific theorizing or corporate practices nor provides a space for the harmonious coexistence of the personal with either of these realms.

Quite in keeping with the Wittgensteinian analogy, the houses that populate Händler's worlds are of the literal and physical, as well as the metaphorical and mental or linguistic, kind. Architecture here refers both to the construction of dwellings and to that of systems of thought and language. In a number of stories in this book, *Häuser* (houses) figure both as *Gebäude* (buildings) and *Gedankengebäude* (thought constructs), the latter constantly under threat of being demolished by language. The narrator of the title story considers old houses to be the only substance that remains in the "Wild East" of the new German states, where the emergence of late capitalism and its effects create an irritating play of surfaces. At the same time, the houses are present as linguistic objects in the text about the very situation that the narrator is discussing with his lover Birgit. It is through the perspective on *houses,* therefore, that the moral gulf between the narrator's own practices and his way of justifying these practices comes to light most clearly.

The story "Morgenthau" presents a deindustrialized dystopia so thoroughly in decay that the description of a city with (intact) houses in fact appears not as tautological as the title of the book might at first suggest. Koby's hometown is by all accounts the most well-preserved city in this possible world, which speaks volumes about the surroundings to be imagined. That fictional *other* country described in the books, of which the children are uncertain whether it is at temporal or spatial remove, is symbolized by its houses, namely, its skyscrapers of steel and glass. The reality of these constructions can never be ascertained with absolute certainty.

Continuation

The type of architecture described in this book—particularly in "Dissolution or For Mrs. Berta Zuckerkandl" and "A Story from the Eighties"—goes some way toward suggesting that, analogously, the *theoretical* architectonic on which this book rests is not quick to dispense with modernism and its effects. Händler recognizes that whatever comes after modernism does not thereby terminate it. The *Gebäude*, apparently built by doubles of Josef Hoffmann or Mies van der Rohe, are reinscribed into literature as *Gedankengebäude*, all structural challenges included.

Another grand narrative project comes to mind: the Proustian one, focused on memory like many of the stories in this book. And even though Händler, unlike Proust, is an externalist when it comes to matters of mind, he takes the attempt at seeking self-identity through precise autobiographical records quite seriously. Noting the necessary breakdown of the project excerpted in "Demiurg" as the logical outcome of a process of experimentation, he does not fall prey to a commonsense relativism that would discredit even the *attempt* at systematicity. We cannot claim to *know better* than to aspire to the construction of new architectures, even though we may be suffering from the failure of the ones suggested by Carnap and Mies ("By the Sengsen Mountains, by the Dead Mountains"). Händler's narrators, and their author along with them, continue to test new strategies of how to lead lives, even if those only lead to the construction of *einstürzende Neubauten*, new buildings toppling down.

In a crucial sense, then, Händler's writing is "proper" postmodernism, one in which the "post" can never pretend to eradicate that to which it forms the prefix. As the dust jacket illustrations of both the original German edition and this translation should suggest, we conceive of the title of the book as crossed out but still legible beneath the lines that would mark the "non-sense" of the tautology.

The fact that the ongoing project "The Grammar of Absolute Clarity" recalls some of the larger literary projects of the first half of the twentieth century is also reflected in both the temporal and the geographical scope of the stories presented in *City with Houses*. They range from World War II ("By the Sengsen Mountains, by the Dead Mountains") through the present, to an unspecified future in

"Max," and from East Germany to Austria to sets of nonspatial possible worlds that, according to the philosopher Saul Kripke, are not distant countries "that we are coming across, or viewing through a telescope." The sheer expanse of the literary worlds outlined in this book underscores the ambition with which Händler enters the scene, almost as though from nowhere. The further development of his project is to be eagerly anticipated, even in the absence of a Balzacian preface.

This book needs no preface. This book is a preface.

About the Author

Ernst-Wilhelm Händler was born in Regensburg, Germany, in 1953. He studied economics and philosophy and worked as the head of his family's business after completing his studies. Since the publication of his highly acclaimed debut, *City with Houses*, he has written three novels—*Kongreß*, *Fall*, and *Sturm*. In 1999 he was awarded the prestigious Erik-Reger Prize for Literature.